DAVID TALLERMAN

THE BAD NEIGHBOUR

This is a **FLAME TREE PRESS** book

Text copyright © 2018 David Tallerman

FLAME TREE PRESS
6 Melbray Mews, London, SW6 3NS, UK
flametreepress.com

Distribution and warehouse:
Marston Book Services Ltd
160 Eastern Avenue, Milton Park, Abingdon, Oxon, OX14 4SB
www.marston.co.uk

Thanks to the Flame Tree Press team, including:
Taylor Bentley, Frances Bodiam, Federica Ciaravella, Don D'Auria,
Chris Herbert, Matteo Middlemiss, Josie Mitchell, Mike Spender,
Cat Taylor, Maria Tissot, Nick Wells, Gillian Whitaker.

The cover is created by Flame Tree Studio with
thanks to Nik Keevil and Shutterstock.com.
The font families in this book are Avenir and Bembo.

Flame Tree Press is an imprint of Flame Tree Publishing Ltd
flametreepublishing.com

A copy of the CIP data for this book is available from the British Library.

HB ISBN: 978-1-78758-028-2
PB ISBN: 978-1-78758-027-5
ebook ISBN: 978-1-78758-030-5
Also available in FLAME TREE AUDIO

Printed in the UK at Clays, Suffolk

DAVID TALLERMAN

THE BAD NEIGHBOUR

FLAME TREE PRESS
London & New York

For Loz, who's overdue one of these.
Thanks for your friendship, man.

CHAPTER ONE

As I heard the body's impact against the wall and the raucous cry of "Fucker!" that accompanied it — both clear despite the intervening layers of brick, plaster, and faded paper — I knew the mistake I'd made. I'd got it all wrong, yet again.

Only, I didn't know quite how badly. Not then.

The signs had been there to see. Aren't they always? The glorious benefit of hindsight is a highway stretching into memory, and there on the roadside twenty metres high are the words of warning you could have heeded and didn't. That you *chose* to ignore, because doing so was easier, and just maybe so that one day the cynical part of you, the part that doesn't like you all that much, could turn around and say *I told you so*.

I had. I'd told me so. I'd chosen not to listen.

The problem wasn't that the choices hadn't looked like mistakes while I was making them, either, because they certainly had. No, the problem was that they hadn't looked like *choices*. A case in point: fifty-five thousand pounds (or, let's get the specifics right, fifty-four thousand, three hundred pounds) coming unexpectedly into my possession. The death of a well-off relative I never knew I had, a cousin that when — still breathless, still wondering if this was all someone's weird idea of a joke — I asked my mother who she'd been, turned out to be so distant and unmemorable that she needed three minutes to place the name, another two to calculate the precise relationship.

At which juncture, we both realised, or at least began to suspect, that my mother should have been the beneficiary and not me. We're not a big family, but we're a profoundly disjointed one. I quickly understood that there had been some spite involved, and that the bad blood likely related to my dad, bless his heart, who gets more sympathy – from certain quarters, anyway – for being in prison than my mother ever did for dealing with his bullshit all those years.

Probably I should have offered to give her the money. I definitely should have volunteered to split it. I think I sort of tried to, though the recollection is fuzzy. I'd like to believe that I did and she said no; that she told me how much more I needed it than she did. I'd like to think that's how the conversation went, and if it did then she was right. Her: nice house in the countryside, happily remarried, close to retirement. Me: a shitty flat on the outskirts of Leeds, supply teaching work I'd taken as a stopgap until something permanent came along, the steadily growing comprehension that maybe it wasn't coming after all. Penny-pinching. Disillusionment. Mild depression.

Nearly fifty-five thousand pounds.

A wealth of possibilities. Pay off the student loan first, of course, and the credit card. Settle the car, actually own the damn thing before it gave up the ghost once and for all. Then – what, a holiday? I could take Yasmina away for a long weekend. We'd not even been dating a month, but the notion of spending a few days alone with her already seemed an attractive prospect. All of that together would still leave a sizeable chunk to bank for the inevitable rainy day.

Almost too many options. And by the time I was off the phone with my mother, I was starting to recognise the flaws in each of them. My student loan hardly needed repaying; it might be years before I was earning enough for the debt to become an issue. The car wasn't a necessity; I'd been thinking about scrapping it anyhow. If I asked Yasmina to go away with me, the result was less likely to be the weekend of passion I'd imagined, more me frightening her off. I could save the money, but how quickly would it devalue? With the economy in free fall, what was fifty-five grand really worth?

It was worth a house, that was what.

I knew it was possible. Real estate was dirt cheap around Leeds. A guy at work had bought a two-bedroom semi in the suburbs with his girlfriend only last month; that had cost them a little under eighty thousand. Obviously they'd paid most of that with a mortgage, something my unsteady work situation would doubtless rule me out of. But what did that matter? Even if the place was a slum, it would be home, and even if I was hanging off the bottom rung of the property ladder, I would still be on it. Compared with where I was at present, that was a hell of an improvement.

I wasn't working that day, so I spent the rest of the afternoon on the internet, searching property sites. It didn't take long for my heart to begin to sink. My budget stretched to grotty repossessions and rundown terraced houses – and then barely. After an hour I had to stop because my hand was shaking, panic setting in at the thought of actually living in one of these miserable hovels. I got up, made a cup of tea, and drank it leaning out the window of my third-floor flat, gulping the fume-soaked air.

I just had to lower my expectations. I was going to have to do some renovating; that was okay. So what if the money I was currently paying out as rent was going on paint and curtains instead? Perhaps I'd need to be flexible on location and hang onto the car. The compromises wouldn't be ideal, but what about my life was?

I made a shortlist of the least awful places. I made a few

phone calls. A lot of them had already gone – and mostly I found myself feeling secretly grateful. My shortened shortlist comprised five properties, which I made appointments to view on Friday, the next day I had off. I spent the intervening days with a gnawing tension in my gut, and half a dozen times came close to phoning Yasmina to tell her what I was intending, before thinking better of it at the last minute.

The first place I looked at, one-bedroom flat that had seemed pleasant enough in the photos, stank of mould. I could only assume a pipe had burst somewhere in the foundations, and I couldn't imagine that any amount of air freshener or incense would erase that biting odour. The estate agent pretended not to notice, and I pretended not to notice them pretending.

The second was opposite the crummiest cemetery I'd ever seen. Most of the gravestones had been kicked over or smashed, and the paths were liberally strewn with dogshit. As I was driving away, I realised that the large building behind high walls on the next street was in fact a prison.

The third, another flat, this time a two-bedroom, was dark and dingy and made me feel uncomfortable the moment I entered. The door to the smaller bedroom was gouged deeply, and I spotted similar marks in the bare floorboards. When I asked the estate agent about it, she said absentmindedly, "Oh yes, I think this is the room they kept the python in." I almost laughed, until I grasped that she wasn't joking.

I can't remember what was so dreadful about the fourth place. I was starting to tune out by that point. Maybe it was nothing specific, merely a background sense of grime, inexplicable smells, frayed carpet, chipped work surfaces, and peeling wallpaper. At any rate, I had to interrupt the estate agent's dispirited efforts at a sales pitch when my mobile rang. The call turned out to be from the agent for my next appointment, ringing to tell me that the couple he'd just shown round had put in an offer, and the owner was taking the property off the market.

Good luck to them, I thought.

I went outside and assured the estate agent I'd think it over, both of us knowing I was lying. I hurried back to my car, grateful to discover that it hadn't been broken into while I was away. Given the state of the neighbourhood, I'd half expected to find a burned-out wreck propped up on breeze blocks.

I felt a little better by the time I got home. Wasn't this stupid, really? Nearly fifty-five thousand pounds had dropped into my lap, and all the money had brought me so far was misery. Perhaps I'd been right the first time; perhaps settling my debts, a few days in the sun, and having a solid chunk of capital in the bank was an infinitely more practical option for a windfall that, after all, I hadn't done a thing to earn or deserve. By the end of the weekend, I'd convinced myself that my failed efforts at house-hunting were probably for the best.

Then, on the Monday morning, just after I'd finished with my first class, I got another phone call.

"Mr. Clay?" A woman's voice, chirpily enthusiastic. I wondered immediately what she was about to try and sell me.

"Yes?"

"Oliver Clay?"

"It's Ollie, but yes."

"Oh. This is Katy from Relocale Leeds. You made an enquiry about a property last week? Number twenty-eight West Mount Road?"

Had I? "Okay," I said.

"There'd been an offer, but it's now been withdrawn. Would you still be interested in having a look round?"

I could hardly remember the house in question; they had all merged into one disappointing blur by then. I was so disheartened with the entire enterprise that I almost told her no – almost. "Why not?" I said. "Sure."

We set a date for the next evening, and by the time I'd hung up I found myself feeling oddly excited. Ten minutes before, I'd been prepared to give up on any hope of home ownership, and here I was reading what must be a perfectly normal circumstance as some kind of a sign. Maybe all those other places had needed to be lousy so that I'd set my standards to a realistic level. Maybe this could be the one.

Of course, I never thought to ask why anyone would make an offer and then change their mind.

What did occur to me was a sudden impulse to involve Yasmina. I didn't know what had kept me from telling her about the inheritance – perhaps only that doing so might seem as if I was bragging – but now I felt ready. I rang her up and, after a minute's small talk, said, "Look, I'm actually calling with some big news. Like, really big."

I told her about the money and, while she was digesting that, mentioned that I was considering putting it into a house.

"That sounds sensible," she agreed.

She had a way of pondering for a moment before she made statements like this, and then pronouncing them solemnly, that I found immensely charming. "Actually, I've just arranged a viewing for tomorrow evening," I said. "Why don't you come with me?"

As soon as the words were out, I saw what an odd suggestion it was. We'd been on three or four dates at that point, and though we'd got on well – and though I was secretly hoping that the next time she might invite me to stay over – we weren't quite at the stage where I'd have dared describe us as a couple. What if she took this as some madly presumptuous proposal that we move in together?

But Yasmina wasn't the type, even if I didn't know her

enough to realise it then; not one for jumping to conclusions or for deliberate misreadings. "I'd like that," she said.

*   *   *

From the outside, the house resembled half the properties I'd seen the week before and two thirds of those I'd viewed online. Most of the housing in and around Leeds is terraces, and plenty of that consists of back-to-backs, which are exactly what they sound like: parallel rows of boxy dwellings with adjoining rear walls. But this one, I recalled, was a plain old terrace, and even had a yard. The idea of owning a yard was appealing. A yard would mean barbeques on summer afternoons, and maybe a few potted plants to brighten up the place.

The house also had bars on the downstairs windows, as did most of those on the street. Again, that was a common feature, in certain areas at least. At first their presence had shocked me, but I'd quickly rationalised that, if the alternative was making life easy for burglars, there were worse things to put up with. The property to the left, in fact, had a broken pane patched with cardboard and gaffer tape, despite the protective cage. Yet noticing the damage was all the attention I paid; I didn't pause to wonder how or why it might have happened.

Perhaps that was because the estate agent chose that moment to pull up, in a new-looking, metallic-blue Audi that seemed almost exotic on such a street. The driver wasn't the woman I'd spoken to on the phone but a young Asian guy, impeccably dressed in a well-cut suit; even his tie had likely cost more than my entire wardrobe. Climbing out, he greeted us cheerfully: "Evening, folks. Ollie Clay, is it? And would you be Mrs. Clay?"

"Ms. Soroush," Yasmina corrected pleasantly. "Call me Yasmina."

"Yasmina," echoed the estate agent, as if to fix the name in his memory. "I'm Imran. You two seen a lot of properties?"

"This is the first we've been round together," I said. "But I viewed a few last week."

My tone must have betrayed me. "Not so hot?" Imran suggested.

"Not so hot," I agreed.

"Yeah, if this is the kind of price bracket you're looking at, then I'm afraid there's not much. The better places tend to go quickly. This one, though…you could do a lot worse. Might want to snap it up fast if you're interested."

He took a set of keys from a pocket, wrestled with the lock, tried a second bunch, and finally succeeded in getting the door open. Beyond was a small living room, with a staircase directly before the entrance heading up to the first floor. The carpets had been stripped, leaving exposed boards; the light bulb, too, was bare. The paper on the walls was a horrid Seventies affair in green and gold, the sort of eye-watering design you couldn't believe anyone would ever have chosen. Most of it, anyway, had begun to peel, in one spot in a great, drooping strip.

"The electrics were rewired recently," Imran announced. "There's central heating, and a combi boiler that's fairly new."

He escorted us through to a narrow kitchen, little more than a tunnel with a window. The worktops were scratched, dinted, and ingrained with dirt; the cupboards above were in a similar condition, with one panel hanging off-kilter and another missing its handle. Out the window I could see the yard, a rectangle of concrete confined by high fences, with a gate opposite the back door that looked as though one good kick would take it clean off its hinges. I couldn't imagine myself inviting friends to socialise in that desolate space; I couldn't see potted plants doing much to soften its bleakness.

As we traipsed back into the living room, I noticed a

second door, sunk in the side of the stairwell. "What's through there?" I asked.

"That's the cellar," Imran told me. "Most of the places around here have them. Want a look?"

"Why not?" I agreed.

Imran went first down steep stairs, of bare stone to my surprise. From the moment he'd opened the door, I could smell the mustiness of long-trapped air, and by the bottom step it was threatening to suffocate me. The light switch achieved nothing, so Imran made do with the torch on his phone. Its glow gave an indistinct impression of crumbling brick, a dirt floor, and cobwebs so vast and opaque that they must have housed spiders by the generation.

"Good for storage," Imran said, doing well not to choke in the stale air. "Or I've seen people convert them. TV room, maybe, something like that."

"Yeah," I agreed, and hurried back up into the living room.

There, Yasmina, who hadn't braved the cellar, caught my eye. Her expression said, *Why are we wasting our time?* I found myself wishing I'd shown her pictures of some places, to give her a little perspective. But before I could respond, Imran had appeared behind me and said, "Want to check out the upstairs?"

There was a bathroom and two bedrooms, one decently sized, the other not much more than a closet. Of the three, the bathroom was in by far the worst state. The bath panel was a sheet of chipboard and was hanging loose; the tiles, which ran halfway up the wall around the tub, were cracked and some of them were missing; on the opposite wall bloomed great smudges of mould. I took one glance in there, attempted to calculate the work that needed doing, gave up, and hurriedly withdrew.

We trooped back to the living room once more. Imran was

toying with his phone, this time with a sense of urgency. "So, got any questions?" he asked, some of his upbeat politeness vanished.

"Do you think the owner would negotiate?" I wondered.

"They've already come down once," Imran said. "It's a good buy at this price. You can try, but…." He let the sentence trail.

Nearby someone shouted, loudly and unintelligibly, and all three of us started. I couldn't tell if the cry had come from one of the neighbouring houses or from the street. *Thin walls*, I thought absently, as though such a thing was positively a virtue. And I knew then that I'd made up my mind.

Maybe Imran read that from my face, or maybe he just wanted to get out of there. "If you're interested, don't leave it too long," he told me. "Like I said, the better places get snapped up quickly." He checked his phone again, and jabbed at the screen. "Yeah, the next showing's a couple, tomorrow lunchtime. So if you're tempted, make sure you call the office before then."

"I will," I said.

"Great. Well, good meeting you guys."

He led the way into the street, locked the door behind us, and in moments was back in his car and pulling away, off to whatever important business had come up.

I felt more excited than I had any reasonable right to be. It wasn't that I hadn't noticed everything that was wrong with the place; I wasn't blind to how crummy it had been. But it was *okay*. And after what I'd seen the previous week, okay struck me as pretty damn great.

"Let's get going," Yasmina said.

Yasmina lived on the edge of Leeds, in one of the nicer suburbs. I realised to my shock that this area was making her uncomfortable. "Just a minute," I replied. "I just want to… you know…think for a moment." I gazed at the outside of the house, trying to imagine that it was my home and how that might be.

She needed a second to understand. "You're not thinking about taking it?"

"You don't like it?" I sounded more irritable than I'd intended.

Yasmina gave me a look that said plainly, *What's to like?* but she caught herself quickly. "It needs a lot of work."

"It's under my budget," I told her. "I mean, it's majorly cheap for what it is. Two bedrooms, the cellar for storage, and a lot of these places, they're so small that they have the kitchen in the living room."

Yasmina nodded, clearly not willing to argue.

That only increased my frustration. "It's probably this or nothing," I said.

I was beginning to feel really cross. Just in time, it occurred to me that Yasmina wasn't the one getting me so wound up. She was being sensible, which was more than I could say for myself. What was frustrating me was that her misgivings were agitating mine, the ones I was trying hard to quash.

"Why don't we get some dinner?" I proposed. "Come on, my treat."

Yasmina's expression was one I'd already learned to recognise: forbearance mingled with forced calm. "Just don't do anything hasty," she said.

"Of course I won't," I lied.

*   *   *

I got up early the next morning to make the phone call. I spoke to Katy again. I gave her my name and the address, and said, "I'd like to put in an offer." As I spoke the words, they had the air of some magical incantation.

My offer was barely an offer at all; I simply said that I'd pay the asking price. I had no reason to be surprised when they rang back to tell me the seller had accepted, though I still was. I felt like a kid playing at being a grown-up, and I couldn't believe anyone was taking me seriously.

I decided against a survey. The inheritance funds hadn't arrived yet, though I was told I'd get the money any day. In the meantime, my account was close to empty, and a couple of hundred pounds seemed a lot. Anyway, what could be wrong with the place? It was the same as thousands of properties around the city; it was hardly going to collapse. So what if there turned out to be a bit of damp, windows that needed resealing, or a few loose roof tiles? Plus a survey could only mean more delay, and every month that went by was another month I wasted money paying rent on my flat.

As it turned out, the sale went through quickly. I'd heard horror stories from friends and colleagues of endless delays, but it soon became apparent that the seller was every bit as eager as I was to keep things moving. The whole process was exhilarating: whenever anything happened, whenever I received a phone call, I got a brief shot of purest adrenaline. I especially liked it when people asked about my mortgage arrangements and I told them, "No, I'm paying in cash." I had the money by then, and even just reading my new bank balance gave me a buzz. If I had doubts, I repressed them quickly. I was going to own a house; I'd never imagined I would and now I was.

I didn't talk to Yasmina much about what was going on. I told her what I'd done and left the matter at that. I sensed she thought I was being unwise, and I knew that in a way she was right. But I knew my reasons too, though I couldn't entirely put them into words. I assured myself that everything would be okay once I'd moved in, and once I'd done the place up. Then she'd see how much more attractive a boyfriend with his own house was compared with one who rented a shabby flat he could scarcely afford to furnish. Anyway, we were getting on well, and I didn't want to risk doing or saying anything to disrupt that.

Two months after I put in my offer, I got a phone call to say that my keys were available for collection. Number twenty-eight West Mount Road was mine.

★   ★   ★

It was a Friday evening. Determined to save every penny I could, I'd arranged to borrow my plumber mate's van for the afternoon and roped said plumber mate into helping me move. Paul was an old school friend who'd chosen to learn a trade instead of half-heartedly blundering through higher education as I had. As such, he was pulling down a solid living and owned his own firm, whereas I was barely making ends meet. However, of everyone, Paul had been most supportive of my house-buying adventure. His reaction when I told him had been exactly what I'd needed to hear: "Look, I see a lot of shite places in my line of work; you can turn anywhere around with a bit of graft."

I'd already had everything packed and ready for a week. Getting it all into the van didn't take us long. Paul did the driving and I sat in the passenger seat, feeling bad for my inability to make conversation. I'd been excited until the moment when I'd locked the flat door, and then panic had taken over out of nowhere. All during the journey it held me tight, and I hardly saw the streets we were passing through. For the first time, I thought I understood the scale of what I'd done, and that comprehension was like a weight crushing me.

As we approached the house, we could hear music. I tried to tell myself it might be coming from anywhere, but it wasn't. It was spilling from the property next to mine, the one with the broken windowpane – which was still broken. The music (and I felt bad about abusing the word) was a steady *dum*, *dum*, *dum*, loud enough to carry halfway up the road.

Paul gave me a sympathetic grin. "Don't worry," he said. "It's Friday night, right? Doesn't mean they'll always be like this."

I considered trying to return the grin, but I wasn't sure I could trust my face that far. What if it showed how I was really feeling?

We started to unload the van, moving the few heavy items first. Half an hour in, a man went into the house next door. He was wearing a grey tracksuit, the top open over a black T-shirt, and boots that looked like army surplus. His head was shaved to the skull. He watched us with suspicion bordering on outright hatred as he marched up to the door. He hammered with his fist, once, twice – each time peeking over his shoulder to scowl at us – and then the portal was wrenched open. The noise from within briefly amplified, and he vanished inside, the door slamming in his wake.

"What the fuck was that about?" Paul asked me.

I could only shrug. The whole encounter had left me with a sense of dread.

We were just carrying in the last boxes when Yasmina arrived. It was a good job we happened to be in the living room, because I wasn't certain I'd have heard the bell over the racket from next door.

I nearly hugged her, realised how disgustingly clammy with sweat I was, and instead said, "Yasmina, this is my friend Paul. Paul, Yasmina."

Paul grinned stupidly. "Hi, Yasmina. Heard a lot about you."

I could have punched him, but the awkwardness was basically my fault. Yasmina and I had slept together for the first time the week before, and I'd been foolish enough to mention the fact to Paul. Our upgrade in relationship status lay, too, at the root of my inviting her over that night, which had seemed like a romantic idea. Then again, maybe romantic wasn't precisely the word; I'd had fantasies of us tumbling onto a bare mattress, too dizzy with passion to care about our surroundings, and inaugurating my new life in my own home in the best way possible.

I glanced around the room, which had only grown dirtier and scruffier since I'd first seen it. I stared down at myself, and at my ragged Radiohead T-shirt, already black with dust. How could I ever have imagined this would be sexy, or anything but depressing? I looked back to Yasmina, dressed sensibly in black sweater and jeans and nothing like the version of herself I'd envisaged. She wasn't even trying to disguise her horror at the torrent of noise surging through the intervening wall.

"I'm sorry," I said helplessly. "I'm sure they'll pack it in soon."

"How long has it been like this?" she asked.

"Since we got here."

"Oh god, Ollie."

There was much in the way she said those words; a dismay to match my own. It would have been disproportionate to the events of just that night, but we both understood that there was more than a single night at stake.

"I'm sure they'll stop soon," I repeated – not because I believed it, only for something to say.

Paul left soon after, though both Yasmina and I made a show of asking him to stay. He claimed he had a date, which wasn't unlikely, knowing Paul. We spent an hour unpacking essentials: what little crockery and utensils I had and then some clothes. We didn't talk much. I couldn't tell if Yasmina was holding back because she'd picked up on how low I was feeling, or whether she was just wondering what she'd got herself into. Either way, my amorous moving-in night was going entirely to shit.

I phoned for takeout. Not trusting anywhere nearby, I ordered pizza from a place I knew, whose delivery range I was now on the very edge of. My head was starting to ache with the tectonic bass from next door; it felt as if the whole house was being shaken. When I put my fingers to the intervening wall, the vibrations were like the pulse of some monstrous animal. In desperation, I retreated to the kitchen and opened the sparkling wine I'd been trying to chill in the barely cool freezer, which I'd planned to save until our food came. I carried two glasses upstairs and pressed one into Yasmina's hand.

To my new home, I thought. But I couldn't bring myself to say as much. I offered her a dented smile instead.

"Fucker!"

The shout, and the accompanying crash, had come from downstairs and next door – though they were clear enough that for an instant I almost convinced myself they must have been from my side. It had sounded as if a body had been crushed up against the wall; more of a crunch than a thump. Something about the combination of noise, word, and tone of voice brought a moment's pure and primal terror. I looked at Yasmina, to find that her eyes were huge. Then there came laughter, loud and cruel – the kind of laughter only somebody else's pain could inspire.

Yasmina put her glass on a stack of boxes. I'd never seen her scared before; fear had washed all the colour from her face. "I'm sorry, Ollie," she said. "I can't stand this. I think I need to go home."

"What about the food?" I asked, appreciating as I spoke what a stupid, futile thing it was to say.

"I'm sorry," she said again. She looked desperate to be

gone; it would take more than half-warm pizza to keep her. "But why don't you come with me?"

I wanted to. God, I really wanted to. But an idiot voice insisted, *If you go now, then they've won.* "I can't," I told her.

Only once Yasmina's taxi had come and whisked her away – our goodbye swift, no noticeable affection in the kiss she gave me – did I realise: they had already won. Of course they had. There'd never even been a contest, and there never would be.

⋆   ⋆   ⋆

The pizza turned up eventually, and I ate a few cold slices sitting cross-legged on the living room floor. The rest I stuffed into the fridge. Then I went upstairs, to the room at the back I'd picked out for my bedroom.

I could tell from the way the noise had shifted that the party had spewed into the back yard. My window wasn't curtained; it hadn't occurred to me to buy any. I turned the light off, then stood and gazed out. There were half a dozen men penned within the small enclosure, illumination leaking over them from the kitchen door and window. They were all of a type, interchangeable with the thug who'd arrived while we were unloading. It was as if someone had tried to cross chavs and neo-Nazis, breeding for aggression without worrying much about appearance or athleticism. Still, for all that half of them had prominent beer guts protruding over jeans and tracksuit bottoms, they were every one bigger than me. I didn't doubt that if I considered anything as ridiculous as complaining, they'd be quicker to resort to violence as well – and more willing to see it through to a messy conclusion.

As though to prove my point, one of them chose that moment to bellow incoherently, and a plank of the intervening fence crumpled in two. I clearly saw his booted foot jut out, along with a few inches of trouser bottom, and then the foot wriggle and withdraw. For no reason I could begin to guess, one of them had chosen to kick a hole in my fence.

These people are animals, I thought. It wasn't an insult, more like a realisation. Asking them to keep down their shouting, their swearing, and their tuneless, pulsating music would make as much sense as confronting a pack of wild dogs for barking too loudly.

Instead, I went to bed. I lay in the sickly twilight cast by an overbright streetlamp somewhere outside my window, the pillow wrapped around my head doing nothing to protect me from the crushing weight of sound.

I understood that I'd screwed up. I understood I'd made a terrible mistake. But it was so much worse than that. Because I knew, too, that this was only the beginning.

CHAPTER TWO

I woke queasy, my stomach full of butterflies. I felt hung over, but I knew I hadn't drunk anything like enough for that. I didn't recall what time the revelry had ceased, or when I'd slipped from consciousness. My last memory was of lying there, certain the ordeal would never end.

I almost wished it was a work day. I didn't want to think about the previous night. I didn't want to think about buying the house, or any of it. When I came close, a sickly sense of horror worsened the turmoil in my guts.

At least the noise had stopped. I guessed that anyone left next door would have partied hard enough and late enough that they'd keep quiet until well after lunchtime. But this was only a reprieve. Tonight they'd start again, or tomorrow night, or in a week. I felt as if the brief glimpse I'd had of my neighbour and his mates had let me into a secret – an intimate understanding. I'd seen men who would do what they liked whenever they liked, because they knew no one was going to stop them. If I made myself the exception to that rule, it would end the worse for me.

Going into the bathroom, I remembered, with a jolt that was practically physical pain, that I had no shower. Not willing to waste time on a bath, I settled for what my dad had called a squaddie wash, scrubbing my face and armpits as best I could with soap and water from the sink. While the effort didn't make me feel any cleaner, the cold water brought me round a little.

I hated to admit it, but my first priority was to get out of the house. As long as I was in there, I'd never be able to think straight. Deciding that here was the perfect opportunity to explore my new stamping ground, I threw some clothes on and dashed out before lethargy and tiredness could get the better of me.

Outside, the sky was a solid ceiling of grey. The pavement was scarred by drizzle. The year was barely into August, and it felt as though summer had died on the vine. Every impulse told me to go back inside, but I pressed on, driving my feet past my neighbour's chipped front door, the roiling in my stomach reviving as my eyes strayed to the broken windowpane.

I felt better as soon as I cleared the end of the street. I could even see a sliver of blue in a gap through the rooftops; somewhere, however far away, the sun was shining. I turned left, trying to remember the lay of the land from the hour I'd spent tentatively reconnoitring in my battered Astra a couple of weeks before. I had hazy memories of a high street nearby; sure enough, after a couple more turns, I passed a pub, a seedy chain place imaginatively named the Hare and Hounds.

Somewhat farther on, the shops began: first a minimarket and newsagent's, then a bookmaker's, a hairdresser's, a Chinese takeaway, a second bookie's, and a small pharmacy. There were twenty or so in all, four of them boarded up and with 'To Rent' signs on display, another four devoted to gambling in various forms. There weren't many people around: a cluster of men in plain white kurtas and taqiyahs, three or four elderly couples, and a mob of bored-looking kids communing over their mobile phones. I carried on until the end, sparing each establishment a glance, finding nothing to hold my interest.

Then, right before the corner, I came upon a tatty hardware store, the kind of place I'd have assumed wouldn't exist anymore. A look through the window told me that they sold just about everything, crammed in without much order on high shelves: there were decorating supplies, which were what had initially drawn my attention, but also brushes and brooms, an astonishing variety of electrical goods, cleaning fluids in industrial-sized containers, books, children's toys, picture frames, rugs, cushions…an apparently unending stock of cheap crap. I went inside and bought a few odds and ends, and was glad to find a piece of board tucked in a corner that might do to patch my fence.

Feeling I'd achieved as much from exploring as I was going to for one day, I started back. Only as I drew close to my street did I realise that my walk had gone some way to shedding the tension I'd been carrying. Now here it was again, rising like dirty water around a blocked drain. I was reminded of the sensation of having had a week off work and knowing that this was your last day of release; that the next would return you to all the worries and stresses you'd come near to forgetting. Had things really got so bad so quickly? As I turned the key in the lock, I tried to persuade myself of how stupid I was being, and to rekindle some of the excitement I'd felt at the fact that this pile of bricks and mortar was entirely mine.

I paused inside the front door, considering the desolation of the living room. The only rational course was to try and make my home better in whatever ways I could. But the living room seemed too far beyond me to be an appropriate starting point. Instead, I decided to begin with the damaged fence.

There was no comfort in discovering that the reason the plank had been kicked through so effortlessly was because it had been half-rotten. The fence should have been replaced years ago. What were the odds, I thought, that my neighbour would agree to split the cost of a new one? And I almost burst out laughing. As a substitute, I scrunched my eyes and took a long, deep breath. Let the fence be a metaphor for my whole damned life: maybe I couldn't fix it, but at least I could patch it while I figured out what to do next.

However, even that proved beyond me. The wood was too decayed and dry to hold the nails I'd bought, and flaked under their pressure. As I worked, I felt a creeping sense of anxiety; what if my neighbour came out and discovered what I was trying and failing to do? Would he mock me? Attempt to apologise? Perhaps he'd kick the entire fence down, just to show he could. In the end I settled for propping the board as flush as it would go and tapping in a couple of nails to hold it.

I went back inside, and into the living room. Needing to do something, anything, that felt productive, I took the wallpaper scraper I'd bought and made an experimental stab at a seam. I was expecting resistance. On the contrary, the flimsy blade tore through the paper and ploughed on into the surface beneath. I tugged at the edge and it came away, trailing a great strip that freed a choking shower of powder. The paper had revealed a patch of plaster and the plaster was disintegrating, as though I'd uncovered the wall of some medieval church rather than that of a terraced house not even a century old.

I peeled a little more paper and it came easily, without encouragement from the scraper. I tested a different spot to confirm my results. Everywhere was the same: beneath the desiccated paper, the plaster was crumbling.

I collapsed onto the bare floorboards, dropped the scraper, and put my head in my hands. The dust was thick and clogging in my nostrils. I didn't need to check to know that the rest of the house would be the same. It would all need replastering before I could even begin to decorate, and what would that cost? A thousand pounds? Two? I had no idea, but it was money I didn't have.

I tried to tot up a total in my head: for the plastering, paint, a new fence maybe, and getting a shower fitted. The number made me dizzy. How had I convinced myself that the amount I'd save on rent would cover all that? It would be months, years, before this dump was anywhere close to habitable.

I felt ready to give up. Only, that wasn't an option; there was no walking away from this one. Yet I hadn't the faintest notion of what I *could* do. Even if I put the house back on the market, it might take months to sell, and what were the chances of anyone being stupid and desperate enough to make the same mistake I'd made? I sat there, wanting to cry, wanting to shout, too exhausted for either, and watched the daylight crawl across the floor.

I don't know how long I stayed that way. I don't know what changed. But suddenly I couldn't stand feeling sorry for myself anymore. I jumped to my feet, stormed into the kitchen, and made myself a coffee, which I gulped down far too hot. If I was no closer to answering the big questions, at least I understood that there were smaller problems I could deal with, enough to take my mind off things. Like, what was I going to do with the rest of my weekend? If I spent the remainder cooped up, I'd go crazy.

I wished I'd made plans to see Yasmina again − assuming she would even want to see me after the shambles of yesterday evening. I'd no desire for another night alone. I thought about texting her to apologise and nearly did, but a small part of me was smarting that she'd left, however unfair I knew that resentment to be. Instead I texted Paul and our mutual friend Aaron, suggesting the three of us meet for a drink. Then, when neither of them responded straight away, I wandered around almost in a panic, like a caged animal.

In truth, though, hardly fifteen minutes had passed before my phone began to chirrup. I answered at the second ring.

"Looking to hit the booze, eh?" Paul asked. "That bad, is it?"

I knew he was joking, but I didn't dare answer in case I told the truth.

"So what time did they pack it in?"

"Maybe four, I think. I was drifting towards the end."

"Fuck! Ollie, you can't be having that. I hope those arseholes didn't wreck your night in with your smoking-hot new bird?"

Despite myself, I couldn't help but laugh. There was something almost charming about how superficial Paul's perspective on the opposite sex was. "She left," I said. "I'm not sure she's talking to me."

"Shit." Paul sounded genuinely frustrated on my behalf. "You *do* need a drink, don't you? We'll find a decent boozer near you, then you'll have somewhere to sneak away to the next time that scumbag kicks off. Give me an hour, all right? I'll pick up Aaron on the way."

*　　*　　*

The wait turned out to be a little over an hour. I spent the interim unpacking, focusing on trying to make the living room tolerable. I set up the television, my stereo and the PlayStation, and then started lining a bookcase with games and the few DVDs I owned. In the end, the effort didn't do much to lift my spirits, only reminded me how fed up I'd been before I met Yasmina, and what I had to look forward to if I really had managed to blow it. Thankfully, there hadn't been a great deal of noise from next door – though every slight sound had set my heart racing. Was this how it was going to be, I wondered? Feeling constantly on edge, perpetually dreading the next onslaught?

When the knock came, I was so glad that I practically flung the door open. Paul entered first, slapping me on the shoulder as he passed, and Aaron followed. Aaron was a friend from university, one of the few I still kept up with; it hadn't taken long for the others to scatter around the country, most following the irresistible draw of London and London wages. His parents were Ghanaian, but you'd never have guessed from the broad

West Yorkshire accent he'd grown up with.

"So this is it?" Aaron grinned. "Needs a drop of paint, doesn't it? You going to give me the grand tour?"

"Am I hell," I said. "Let's get out of here, before the place collapses."

★   ★   ★

I led the way over to the Hare and Hounds. It was reassuring to have friends beside me. The streets, which mere hours ago had felt so alien and unwelcoming, now seemed no better or worse than anywhere else. When we arrived at the pub, however, the sight took some of the wind out of my sails. It hadn't looked so bad when I'd passed by earlier. With the overspill of raucous voices competing against some awful pop song I couldn't be bothered to identify, it had altogether less appeal.

"I guess this is my local," I said.

Paul appeared doubtful, Aaron openly distrustful.

"We can try and find somewhere else," I suggested.

"If it's your local, we should give it a shot," Paul asserted.

Aaron nodded in uncertain agreement. His tastes had always been more upmarket than mine or Paul's, and I suspected that this dingy boozer wasn't far from his idea of hell. Nonetheless, Paul was right; if this was to be my nearest watering hole, I had to give it a chance. I led the way inside, having to use more strength than seemed reasonable on the heavy door.

Beyond was a short T-junction corridor that led off into two rooms, one to either side, segregated by empty doorways. Glancing in, there wasn't much to choose between them, since the same rectangular bar served both, and they were each furnished with identical faded chairs and scratched, stained tables. The only meaningful difference was that the room to the right had a dartboard, where two paunchy middle-aged men competed intently, and the one to the left contained a half-size pool table, currently unused. Harried by Paul and Aaron piling in behind me, I picked left.

I regretted my choice. Just out of view within the entrance, hidden by the angle of the corridor, three skinheads were drinking, and they all looked up as we entered. One of them laughed a ponderous laugh, as though there was something funny about us coming in like that. Immediately I was assailed by memories of the previous night, and immediately I wanted to get out of there.

Instead, I forced myself over to the bar, and Paul slid in beside me. "I'll get these," he offered. "Why don't you find us somewhere to sit?" Beneath his breath he added, "As far from those tossers as possible, yeah?"

I picked out a spot towards the back and away from the pool table, with only a pair of elderly gents nearby, neither of whom looked round as we sat down. A minute later, Paul arrived with our pints, laying them before us delicately, careful not to spill a drop. Aaron and I had already started catching up – he'd just landed a promotion at the bank where he worked – and Paul slotted easily into the conversation.

For the course of that first pint, the night felt like old times. With each sip of too-fizzy, overly chilled lager, I was conscious of the worries of recent days slipping away. It was good to have mates, I thought, good to be drinking – and wasn't it that bit better for being in my new local, near my new home?

"Shall I get another one?" I asked, as Paul noisily drained his glass.

"Let me," said Aaron. "Save your money for some new wallpaper."

I forced a smile; his observation had hit too close to the mark. Paul stood up as well, and disappeared into a passage at the back signposted for toilets, so I checked my phone and then

– disappointed that there was nothing from Yasmina – turned my attention to Aaron. The three who'd been sitting by the window, the skinheads, had moved to barstools. As Aaron paid for his drinks, one of them leaned in and muttered something to him. Aaron didn't respond, only scooped up our pints and carried them over.

"What was that about?" I wondered.

Aaron gave me a look, as though he couldn't quite tell whether I was winding him up. "Are you serious?"

I shrugged, even more confused. Aaron lived on the far side of Leeds, in a nice flat in the suburbs, and I couldn't imagine why he'd know anyone here, let alone well enough to have made any enemies.

"Apparently," Aaron said, "I should watch myself, because this isn't a nigger pub. Whatever the fuck one of those is."

I almost choked on my lager. "Jesus. You're shitting me."

"Yeah," he said, "you know me. That's exactly the sort of thing I joke about."

"Jesus," I said again. I'd never exactly considered myself colour-blind, but nor had it crossed my mind that there were places I could or couldn't go with Aaron. In the past we'd done most of our drinking in the metropolitan areas around the university, or near to his flat, which was all family-friendly pubs and nice restaurants. Never once had Aaron had any bother that I knew of. It was like we'd suddenly stepped back fifty years.

"I'm really sorry," I said. In that moment, what had happened to him seemed a direct result of my hasty house-buying.

"Maybe we should finish up and head for somewhere else," Paul suggested. He'd got back from the toilets in time to hear what Aaron had said, and I could tell he was trying to be diplomatic.

"We shouldn't let those arseholes chase us out," I said.

I scrutinised the group at the far end of the bar more

carefully while doing my best not to seem like I was looking. This time, I realised something I couldn't believe I hadn't noticed before: I recognised them. The two nearest I knew from the party the previous night; they hadn't even bothered to change their clothes. The third, too, was familiar. Yes, now that I thought, hadn't he been the one who'd put a boot through my fence?

A part of me wanted to confront him there and then. But it was a stupid, suicidal part, one that had got me into enough trouble once upon a time, and I had more sense than to listen to it. "No, you're right," I decided. "We'll finish these and move on."

That second pint was subdued, the conversation overshadowed, as much as Paul struggled to cheer us up. We were about ready to go when we heard – even above the music and the babble of conversation – the front door slam. Then a man stamped through the doorway, and for the second time that night I came close to choking on my drink. Because I recognised him as well, and from the way the others had behaved towards him the night before, I'd felt certain the house must be his.

The other three bellowed at his arrival. "Chas, mate," one roared.

So now my neighbour had a name. All the memories of the previous night rushed back in a wave of revulsion. I studied him, transfixed like a rat in the path of a Rottweiler. His hair was dark and shorn short, balding on top, but not the full skinhead his companions had opted for. I guessed he might have been in his mid-thirties, and he looked older than they did by a good half a decade. His face was clean-shaven, which only emphasised how basically ugly he was: a prominent chin, blunt lips like wedges, and a nose that had been broken at least once and never properly reset. Yet his eyes fit badly with the rest of that face. They were restless, alert. Even as he talked, they were flickering about the room, and as they passed over our table, I glanced down quickly.

"Shit," I said.

"Don't tell me..." Paul began.

"Yeah. I'm pretty sure that's the prick that lives next door to me. I think I recognise the others too."

"That settles it," said Aaron. "You don't need any hassle. Let's get out of here. This is Leeds; we can always find another pub."

I nodded. No, I didn't need hassle. I'd spent the last two years drifting closer to the verge of a nervous breakdown, a combination of never having anything like enough money and trapping myself in a job I couldn't stand and wasn't much use at. Yasmina coming into my life, and then the money – for a while it had seemed as if I'd weathered the storm and come out on the other side. But now that life contained Chas and his charming mates, and I already felt like I couldn't escape them. Even a quiet drink with my friends was out of the question.

I didn't need hassle. That wasn't going to keep it from finding me.

Paul had finished up, and Aaron and I were down to dregs, when I heard the outside door again. Two men came in. One was very tall, well over six feet, with greasy brown hair hanging down past the furled hood of a worn grey running top and a dagger of beard protruding from his lower lip. The other was smaller, swarthy and sleepy-eyed, a new-looking leather jacket tight around his shoulders. If I'd had to guess, I'd have said they were Travellers; there was a site not far off that routinely cropped up in the local news.

The pair had hardly got through the door before one of Chas's thugs barked something at them. The cry was guttural, more noise than words. The taller man responded, not quite so loudly, and I couldn't catch what he'd said either. Then the skinhead got to his feet and heaved his half-full pint glass into the tall man's face.

It was so sudden. And the suddenness made it hard to believe. Surely nothing of any significance could happen in an instant, without warning. Yet the tall man was staggering back, his face streaming. He'd put one hand up to shield himself, and blood was dripping down his fingers and wrist.

Chas's mate had dropped the glass, what there was left of it. Now he was on his feet and bawling, a howl of raw pleasure. He lurched onward, leading with a crude left hook aimed at the tall man's jaw. But the smaller man stepped in, grabbing for his free arm, wrenching him round before the blow could land. And with that it was as though an invisible signal had been given: the other two skinheads were wading in with fists and feet, the tall man was flailing to defend himself, and the smaller man was trying to shield his companion while backing in baby steps towards the door.

Only Chas, I noticed, was staying out of the brawl. Indeed, he was keeping his hands conspicuously raised, as if to make clear that this was in no way on him. Yet his mouth gave him away: it was set in a rigid smirk.

I hadn't had much experience with violence of late; but when I was a kid, I'd had more than my fill. I'd seen things and done things that I tried hard not to think about. I didn't want to remember, and this was more of a reminder that I could handle. In a moment the panic was close to swallowing me whole.

Someone touched my arm, and I flinched, my fear instantly transforming into a readiness to defend myself – before I realised it was only Paul. "Come on," he said, perfectly calm-seeming, as though bloody pub fights were a hazard he navigated every day. "There's a fire door at the back, near the loos."

He was already on his feet, as was Aaron. I got up and followed. A small queue had formed in the corridor where the toilets were, with a half dozen patrons retreating from the fracas. More surprising was how many had chosen to stay behind and watch.

Outside was a car park, hemmed in by the backs of other buildings, a dozen vehicles sitting beneath toxic yellow lighting. The air felt shockingly cold, though it hadn't earlier. Paul led the way around the corner of the pub and onto the road. I was relieved to see that there was no one about. However, the noise from within, the shouts and grunts, was audible even over the unrelenting music, which was now some inappropriately innocuous bit of dadrock.

We turned right, Paul still ahead. At the end of the road, he slowed and looked at me. "It's okay, mate. Keep calm."

Keep calm? I saw then, as Paul probably had, that my hands were clenching and unclenching as if of their own accord. It wasn't just fear; there was anger there too. How dare these ignorant bastards ruin my first night in my new home, upset my girlfriend, keep me awake into the early hours, and on top of all that, disrupt my evening out with my friends? For every part of me that had wanted to get the hell out of there, another had desired only to wade into the midst of that abruptly exploding violence, fists flailing.

I took a deep breath and slowly unfurled my hands, to hold them flat at my sides. At the same time, I concentrated on walking straight; until then I'd been cutting a zigzag path across the pavement.

Paul clapped me on the shoulder. "Yeah. You're all right."

I nodded, not quite so all right that I felt ready to answer.

We walked the last distance back to the house in silence. Throughout I was anticipating sirens, as if they were the one thing that could break the tension. Yet minute after minute passed, and when they eventually came they were faint and distant-sounding, though we'd only travelled a few streets. By then we were almost at my front door. I paused to listen, trying to imagine the scene outside the pub.

Inside, Paul and Aaron sat on my ratty settee and, realising I had nothing stronger in the house, I made us all tea. Aaron seemed nearly as shaken as I was, and I thought I understood why: if the attack had been as pointless and unprovoked as it had appeared, he could just as easily have been the one on the receiving end. He drank his tea in quick gulps while I was still waiting for mine to cool. As soon as he was finished, he placed the mug at his feet and said, "I'd better be going. Lot to do tomorrow."

I didn't blame him. In fact, I was glad. "I suppose I've got things I should be doing too."

Paul looked at me with concern. "You going to be okay? Why don't you kip over at mine tonight?"

"I'm fine," I told him.

"You sure? You're white as a ghost. I'll make the sofa bed up for you, be just like old times."

"I'm sure," I repeated, too forcefully – not grateful to be reminded of the months I'd dossed rent-free on Paul's futon. Striving to sound reasonable, I added, "I've got some marking to get through. I need to be here."

I wanted them to leave; I wanted to be alone. Now that the worst edge of my fear was cooling off, I felt embarrassed more than anything. I hated that they were there in the shabby living room of my dilapidated house, trying to calm me down after a run-in with the nutter I'd been idiot enough to move in next to. It was as though my every failure was plastered across the walls for anyone to see, and here were my closest friends, soaking it all in.

Yet the minute they were out of the door, Paul assuring me he'd phone in a day or two, Aaron still clearly on edge, I wanted desperately to call them back. I wanted to confess everything, to admit every stupid mistake I'd made. I wanted them to tell me how I'd make it right. Wasn't that what friends did?

Too late. They'd gone. Even if they hadn't, I knew no one had any answers for me. I finished the last of my tea, hauled myself upstairs, and crawled into bed, and it took me all the energy I had left to bother to undress.

CHAPTER THREE

Yasmina rang me on the Sunday evening.

She didn't mention the night I'd moved in, so I didn't tell her how I'd done nothing all day, or about the sudden, causeless violence in the Hare and Hounds. I hadn't heard my neighbour get back the previous night, and I was trying to fend off the hope that he might be in a police cell. Probably that was a long shot, given how careful he'd been not to get his hands dirty; still, the fact that there had been no noise from next door had left me in a fractionally more positive mood. I managed to be cheerful, Yasmina was too, and within a few minutes I felt as though whatever slight breach had formed between us had knitted. We spent nearly an hour on the phone, talking about nothing much, and it was indescribably nice. Finally we agreed to meet for dinner at the end of the next week – with the implication, I was confident, of spending the night together afterwards.

But on Monday I was back to school. I was supply-teaching three days a week at a place called Lawn Hill, a split-site primary and secondary on the far side of Leeds. I was covering for a teacher on maternity leave and picking up other scraps of work where I could, not because I liked being there – I didn't, on any level – but because I desperately needed the money.

I taught history mostly, plus whatever I could turn my hand to at a push, primarily covering a Year Seven class and two Year Tens. The Year Sevens were just about bearable, in that they at least looked and behaved like kids. The Year

Tens were something else altogether. They had all the least appealing qualities of children and adults, plus a few generally associated with the more ferocious of wild animals.

The school was mixed-gender, and a perfect advertisement for keeping the sexes apart until age eighteen at the very earliest: I had one pregnant girl apiece among the Year Ten classes, which was apparently somewhat above the school average. The boys, meanwhile, focused most of their limited intelligence on finding imaginative ways to hurt each other, the only exceptions being the minority who soaked up the lion's share of that apparently limitless violence. On the worst days, I couldn't escape the feeling that if I stepped out, the scene I'd come back to would be like something out of a wildlife documentary, spotty adolescents screwing and killing each other with abandon.

Yasmina was a teacher too, not at my current school but at another, girls-only, considerably more civilised one where I'd filled in for a couple of weeks. I'd thought at first that the profession would be common ground for us; in fact, it had rapidly become such a source of contention that we'd both stopped mentioning the subject. The problem was that Yasmina was an exemplary teacher, whereas I was a terrible one. She basically loved the work, where I despised it to the depths of my soul. And she hadn't taken long to grow impatient with my defeatist attitude, telling me, "If you hate it so much, why not do something else?"

With the unspoken admonishment: *if you don't like these children, if you don't care whether you can do a good job for them, you really should.*

I hadn't argued. She was right. The truth was, teaching was a vocation I'd stumbled into and now found myself mired in, not knowing how to pull free or what I could possibly do if I did. And there were occasions, few and far between, when I actually did enjoy my time at Lawn Hill: moments of shared comprehension, moments when the kids would find some topic interesting enough to actually pay attention and when I remembered how much history had fascinated me at university.

That Monday, however, there was no such relief. I had both of my Year Ten classes, and by the end of the day I felt as if I'd survived a physical assault – and then by the skin of my teeth. I found it so hard not to see the boys, with their scrunched faces and constant air of pent-up anger, as miniature versions of my neighbour and his brutish mates. One in particular, Liam Sutcliffe – fourteen like the others but quite capable of passing for eighteen or older – struck me as every bit a Chas in the making. He'd already been nearly taken out of the school twice for violence, and nobody had any illusions that those two incidents had been exceptional; they were just the times when he'd been caught. He sat sullenly, staring at me with unveiled hatred, never answering questions or even pretending to do any work. I prayed for the day when he'd seriously injure someone, well away from school property, and be dragged off by the police for good.

The truth was that Liam Sutcliffe terrified me. All of them terrified me. I'd never felt truly helpless until the first day I stood in front of a class, knowing that if I so much as slapped one of them, I'd be up on criminal charges, while they could probably stab me to death and devour the flesh from my bones and suffer nothing more than expulsion.

Tuesday was easier: just my Year Sevens, who were in a relatively placid mood, and a last-minute cover for an English teacher who'd gone off with tonsillitis, having thoughtfully planned out his next week's classes before he did so. My first free day was Wednesday, and I spent it as fruitlessly as I had the weekend, already feeling like the week had sapped my energy. However, the Thursday passed almost as painlessly as the Tuesday, my Year Tens uncharacteristically docile, I had my date with Yasmina the next night to look forward to, and when I woke on the Friday morning, I found that a degree of my energy and enthusiasm had returned.

I'd made no progress with the decorating. I wasn't sure what progress I *could* make without an injection of cash to mend fundamentals like the decaying plaster. That morning, after breakfast, I performed another inspection, trying to convince myself that there were jobs I could be getting on with, money or no.

The psychological effect proved to be the opposite of what I'd intended. My first mistake was starting in the back yard, where I immediately noticed that the panel I'd fixed to cover the hole in the fence was now lying a good meter away. It could only have been kicked there and that could only have been deliberate, an act of malice to show how futile my attempts at repair had been. For a moment I was angry enough that I wanted to push the whole damn fence down. The bloody-mindedness was what got to me, but also the very specific vindictiveness: *If I want to smash holes in this fence*, that splintered gap said, *then I will, and there's not a thing you can do.*

I went back inside. I examined the peeling wallpaper in the living room and the crumbling plaster beneath. Both were exactly as bad as I recalled, and entirely beyond my ability to do anything about. Once again I was helpless, and already I could feel the good vibes I'd woken with evaporating, to be replaced by the lethargy that had dogged me all week.

I didn't want to surrender. There was one course open to me, and if it was about the least appealing task I could think of, there was no question that it would be productive: I could make a start on cleaning. Some effort had obviously been made before the property went on the market, but only enough to disguise the worst signs of neglect. And while mopping floorboards and wiping down walls wouldn't fix a thing, doing so might make me feel better, not to mention moving the house one step closer to a point where I'd consider inviting Yasmina over again.

But cleaning meant going out to buy cleaning materials. In the street, I crossed to the far pavement, so as not to pass in front of my neighbour's house. A couple of turns later and I realised I'd deliberately amended my route to avoid the Hare and Hounds. Was this what my life here was going to be like? Yet as much as I told myself I was being ridiculous, the impulse was stronger. If I had no choice about living next door to an antisocial headcase, avoidance was all I had left.

Easier said than done. I caught the whiff of smoke even before I turned the corner, not at all pleasant, somewhere between burned toast and roasted electrical appliance. My chest tightened. The reaction was absurd, but that stench alone felt like an assault. And as the high street came into view, I saw that it was – though not one aimed at me.

The smell was coming from the small newsagent's cum minimarket. Its front was a blackened hollow, the window shattered, a few stubborn shards turned to rotted fangs by the soot. I remembered that the glass had been blanketed in posters: adverts for products sold and services provided, along with cheaply photocopied notices for local events. Some clung as tattered rags; the remainder blew in scorched shreds about the footpath. With the window gone, I could see the inside of the store clearly, and the extent of the devastation. Its reach seemed strangely arbitrary: one set of shelves towards the back was untouched, where another near the counter had been heated sufficiently for the metal to melt and buckle.

I knew, somehow, that this destruction had been inflicted

by a petrol bomb. It was the way, I suppose, that the damage radiated from inside the window, and also the amount of burning. The attack must have occurred while the place was open, for I could see the protrusion of a security shutter just beneath the store's sign, one of those pull-down metal concertinas. Only then did I take in the ambulance, parked a short way up the high street, and the small crowd of gawkers loitering near its open doors. I caught a flash of a body lying within, and of a paramedic leaning over them, before a second paramedic slammed the doors and walked round to the driver's cab. A moment later, the ambulance was pulling away. No sirens, I noted – that meant the person inside hadn't been injured too badly. Or perhaps that no amount of haste was going to help them.

I stood there for what felt like a long time. The rubberneckers who'd been around the ambulance drifted off. Others passed by, pausing to stare and then continuing along their way, as though the incinerated store were an art installation put on to provide a little brief amusement. No one talked much; a few old people tutted or swapped grumbling observations. Nobody paid me the slightest attention.

Eventually I tore myself away. There was no reason to think this had anything to do with Chas and his mates. Leeds was like any modern city the nation over: it had its bad elements, its vandals. I was putting two and two together and coming back with the only number I was interested in. Yet I couldn't shake the certainty. I thought of the hole in my fence, of violence for the love of violence, and was irrationally, completely sure.

I should have carried on to the hardware store and loaded up on cleaning materials, just as I'd planned. I couldn't do it; I couldn't bring myself to walk past that charred cavity, which so resembled some scene from a warzone on the evening news, a glimpse of a terrorist atrocity before the report moved on. And wasn't this terrorism of a sort? Insurance would cover the damage, would pay for cleaners, glaziers, and ruined stock. But when all of that was done, still the fear would remain.

I couldn't face going straight home either. Instead, I set out on a route I was confident would loop around my house, hunting for another row of shops I'd driven by once or twice. It didn't take me long to start feeling lost: the interminable rows of back-to-back terraces all looked identical and all had the same forlorn air. I resorted to opening Google Maps on my phone and navigating by that, surreptitiously sliding the device into a pocket when I passed anyone I judged to be remotely suspicious. Nevertheless, nearly an hour had gone by before I finally found the street I was seeking, and by then any intention of cleaning had passed. I bought a few bits for my lunch from the Tesco Express there and headed back. The fact that the return journey took me all of ten minutes proved how far I'd managed to go wrong.

At home I sat eating and flicking TV channels, but nothing held my interest. I thought again about the cleaning, felt bad, felt frustrated that I should have to feel bad on my day off, and turned on the PlayStation. Four hours later, with the day well and truly wasted, I flung down the controller. I tried to assure myself that I'd needed to switch off, yet the attempt had only left me tense and short-tempered.

Yasmina had said she wanted to get some marking out of the way before the beginning of the weekend proper, and we weren't due to meet until late in the evening. Unoccupied and bored, I found my thoughts turning once more to the blackened hollow of the corner shop. I wondered if there might be any details in the local paper about it; eager for a diversion, I set off again to find out. The streets were busier than they'd been, congested with slow-moving traffic. I spent a couple of minutes in the Tesco skimming through the *Evening Post*, found nothing, concluded that the story would likely be in tomorrow's edition, and decided against wasting money on a copy.

On the way home, however, it occurred to me to find the newspaper's website on my phone. Sure enough, the incident with the shop was on there, though it warranted merely a carelessly taken photo and two brief paragraphs. The piece confirmed that the cause had been a petrol bomb, thrown by 'unidentified youths' from a moving car. No witnesses had come forward as yet, and nor was there any information about the car beyond that it was a four-door in a pale shade. Only the store owner had been hurt, with minor burns to his arms and torso, caused not by the bombing itself but by his trying to put out the resulting fire. At the end, the reporter hypothesised that the violence might have been 'racially motivated' and made vague reference to other, similar occurrences in recent months.

There was nothing in the article I didn't know or couldn't have guessed, except for the description of the car, which matched the rusted, off-white Ford Mondeo parked outside the house next door, but also thousands of vehicles within the city. Nevertheless, the suggestion of related incidents sparked my interest; the reporter had clearly invested little effort in the piece, and perhaps that implied that these recent events had been significant enough to stick in their memory.

Perhaps, too, there'd be more in the paper tomorrow. In the meantime, I resolved to push the matter from my mind, and to get ready for my date with Yasmina instead. I had a shave, a shallow bath — I was slowly learning to tolerate the absence of a shower — and dressed in what I considered to be my smartest clothes. By then, the hour wasn't far off the time we'd agreed to meet, so I decided I'd rather sit waiting in a restaurant than in my scruffy bedroom. It proved the right choice. Just as I was putting my shoes on, a blaring bass rhythm started from beyond the wall, and I felt a surge of overwhelming gladness to be escaping.

The restaurant was a family-owned Persian place called Artin's, a favourite haunt of Yasmina's that wasn't too far from her flat. I'd been once before and liked it. Fortunately, Yasmina was already there by the time I arrived, sitting at a table near the window, sipping from a glass of white wine. She smiled when she saw me approaching. Her face was severe in repose, a touch melancholy, and I never ceased to be surprised by the way that even brief happiness brought warmth to her features. I pushed through the door, leaned to kiss her cheek, and sat opposite, returning her wonderful smile with my own rather crooked one.

"It's good to see you," I said. It had only been a week, but seemed like ages.

"You too," she told me. "And this is on me. To apologise. I wasn't so nice to you last weekend."

"You were okay."

"No, I'm sorry. It was your moving-in day, and I wasn't supportive. I should have stuck it out with you."

I wasn't sure if we'd been dating long enough that supportiveness was something I had a right to expect. Still, I wasn't going to turn it away if she was offering, and nor was I about to refuse a free dinner. "I'm sorry too," I said. "I'd never have invited you over if I'd known things were going to be like that."

"Has your neighbour been any better?"

"Well, sort of. There've been a couple more noisy evenings, but not as bad as last Friday. And they knocked off in good time, so that was something." I was downplaying the reality; both occasions had been pretty miserable, and I'd spent each dreading a sleepless night, but I didn't want to put Yasmina off ever even considering another visit.

Then I realised I still hadn't mentioned the episode in the pub. I thought about not doing, but I didn't like the prospect of keeping secrets so early in our relationship. "There's been some other stuff, though." I described what had happened in the Hare and Hounds, and afterwards couldn't resist throwing in the petrol bombing of the corner shop. "Obviously I can't say for sure that was him, but—"

"It could have been anyone, Ollie."

"No, I get that. Only, what if it wasn't? And what I'm thinking is, maybe the police don't know about him. Or they don't know the full extent of— I mean, during the pub fight, he was careful to keep his hands clean. He's not brainless. He's probably not going to win *Mastermind* anytime soon, but he's no idiot. Maybe the police don't appreciate just how...." I ran out of words, unable to formulate a conclusion that matched the shape of my thoughts.

Yasmina's expression was carefully noncommittal.

"You think I'm being stupid?"

"I think it isn't your problem," she said.

"What? How is this not my problem?"

"In the sense that it's not for you to make everything right. All you have to do is look after yourself. And Ollie, stirring up trouble won't make your life any easier. If this Chas is as bad as you say he is, if he's involved in the kind of activities you suspect he might be involved in, what good is making him interested in you going to do?"

"Then what?" I asked. "What do I do, just ignore it?"

"As much as you can. Until you figure out something else." Abruptly she cupped a hand over mine. "Maybe you could stay over with me a little more."

On any other day, I'd have been glad of the offer. I liked

Yasmina's flat, and any solution that meant more time devoted to our burgeoning, still rather awkward sex life had to be a good thing. Yet in that moment, somehow I managed to find the prospect only another aggravation.

I sharply withdrew my hand. "You just...you don't understand what it's been like." The look she gave me jerked me out of my complacency.

"What I mean is—"

"I know," Yasmina said, "that I haven't told you much about my life before we came here."

"You hardly mention it," I agreed, caught between remorse and defensiveness. Perhaps it was foolish of me, but I easily forgot that Yasmina had been born in another country, one with its own exceedingly troubled history. Not that I knew much about Iran, no more than the dislocated snippets I'd picked up from news reports; I'd always intended to do some research to cover my ignorance and never found the time.

Yasmina stared out of the window, apparently at nothing. "Ollie, my father was killed in the war with Iraq when I was three years old, a month before the fighting ended. My brother died in prison. My mother raised me on her own for twelve years in a country where women have approximately the same basic rights as dogs." She looked back at me, and there was heat in her eyes. "Please don't tell me I don't understand what it's like to live with violence."

I could barely hold her gaze. "I'm sorry."

"It's all right."

"No, I'm really sorry."

This time she smiled. "It's okay. I get what you're going through. Your neighbour is an awful human being. You're finding that stressful. I just don't want you to do anything you'll regret."

*   *   *

The rest of dinner was an improvement: no traumatic subjects, not even the swapping of teaching experiences that our conversations often degenerated into. We joked and laughed, made affectionate fun of each other, talked about music and movies, and traded stories. It was exactly how I felt a date should be. And at the end, as the waiters were starting to make an obvious show of tidying up around us, Yasmina said, "Why don't you come back to mine tonight?"

"Sure," I agreed – trying to play it cool, not quite succeeding. I'd had more than my share of the bottle of wine we'd split.

Yasmina had walked, so I drove us the short distance to her flat in my car, careful to keep my speed down. When she let us in, I couldn't resist a pang of jealousy. Yasmina's apartment was so much nicer than my house, or than my own flat had been for that matter. Close on that thought followed the memory of what she'd said earlier: *Maybe you could stay over with me a little more.*

I felt guilty. Was the chance to get away from my home and all the problems involved with being there becoming a factor in how I felt about Yasmina? No, that wasn't true. I wasn't certain yet whether there was anything between us beyond the immediate affinity and passion, but I knew without question that she was currently the best thing in my life. That she had a tidy, attractively furnished flat that I could sometimes retreat to was a mere bonus.

Yasmina went into the kitchen and returned a minute later with two glass cups, each stuffed with brittle green leaves, a sugar cube dissolving amid the foliage: mint tea, her favourite beverage, and one I was slowly growing accustomed to. We huddled on the sofa, sipping our drinks in comfortable silence.

My mind wandered, through a rapid circuit of recent days viewed for the first time with something approaching dispassion, and then on to the last few hours and our conversation in the restaurant.

"You're right," I said.

Yasmina tilted her head enquiringly.

"About going to the police. It would make the situation worse."

She placed her cup on the pine coffee table, edged closer. "I'm sorry things have been so difficult for you."

I moved a palm to her neck and caressed her shoulder, enjoying the way that her fine, dark hair swept the back of my hand. "They're better now," I said.

"Good." Yasmina leaned in, maintaining her distance for one teasing moment, and then touched her lips to mine. I stroked my palm back up her neck, gently holding her there until the kiss became a proper kiss. I relaxed against heaped cushions and drew her after me.

They're better now.

They were. And they got better still.

CHAPTER FOUR

I got up late the next day and stayed until early afternoon, hanging around the flat while Yasmina finished up her marking and other odd jobs. It was nice to be there, normal-feeling and comfortable. I'd have gladly remained all weekend if she'd let me, but she was going to her mother's that evening and stopping over until the Sunday night, and however well our relationship might be going, we certainly weren't at the stage for meeting parents yet. I still didn't know much about Yasmina's life before she left Iran, and she didn't discuss her mother a great deal, though I got the impression they were close. When I offered to drive her, she said that it was quicker to cycle, so I kissed her goodbye and promised to call in a day or two.

I didn't want to go home. I thought about making an impromptu visit to Paul's, but he would probably be with a new girlfriend. Paul, who went through romantic partners like most people went through clean socks, was usually with a new girlfriend. Aaron had mentioned that his work was taking him away for a couple of weeks, and anyway, I'd have felt awkward just turning up at his after the incident in the pub. I even considered driving out to see my own mother, but I had no idea how she or my stepfather would react to an unannounced appearance. Unable to think of anywhere else, I drove back to the house – though by the most circuitous route I could invent.

When I pulled up, Chas's car was nowhere to be seen. I don't know what I'd been expecting, perhaps my front door to have been kicked off its hinges, but somehow that absence took the edge off my anxiety. I decided to make the most of my evening alone. I picked up a four-pack of Corona and ordered takeaway Chinese, a luxury narrowly within my budget. Yet my food had barely arrived when the commotion started next door: the tuneless, pounding music, the shouting, the harsh laughter. I put on my headphones and turned up the TV; regardless, nothing I did would allow me to enjoy my spare ribs and Kung Pao chicken.

The racket went on to sometime after two. I waited it out, dozing fitfully on the settee, as one late-night movie blended into another. When silence finally fell, I dragged myself upstairs, tumbled into bed, and slept restless sleep.

I woke late, no less exhausted for the lie-in. Through the whole day I felt tired, disconnected, and irritable, and even if I could have thought of some useful way to spend my time, I'd have had no will to do it. Though there was little noise from next door besides the occasional banging of a door or muffled words, I barely slept the next night either.

I'd agreed to take a bottom-set Year Ten class on the Wednesday, covering for a teacher away on holiday, which meant four days teaching in a row; good for my wallet, less so for my sanity. The week didn't wait till the Wednesday to start going wrong, however. It only took until the Monday afternoon and the second of my regular Year Ten classes, the one containing Liam Sutcliffe.

I was already on edge, the residual tiredness of three nights with negligible sleep making everything faintly unreal. Normally I kept my eye on Sutcliffe; the more closely I watched him, the sooner I'd spy him committing some cruel, revolting, or illegal deed and could send him out of class. This lesson, it was all I could do to keep any of them in check. I felt as if I were trying to hold back an avalanche with my bare hands, except that the avalanche was thirty raised voices, and whenever I managed to quieten one group, another would start up. In that maelstrom, one bad pupil hardly stood out.

Or so I thought. I should have known better. An out-of-control classroom leads to escalation. I was stupid to imagine Sutcliffe being content to fit in with the wider chaos; all it meant was that he'd raise the bar.

I was focused on one girl, Badria, who I'd caught in the act of surreptitiously passing a note to the girl in front of her – "Badria, unless that's something you think the whole class should hear, it can go in the bin," – when my gaze strayed past her, and I registered what Sutcliffe was doing.

The boy sat next to him, skinny, in glasses, face flecked with a few premature pimples – his name was Kristopher Peel, Kristopher spelled with a kicking K, as he'd insisted on explaining on my first day – had his arm outstretched across Sutcliffe's desk. Sutcliffe was pinning the limb in place with one hand, gripping just above the elbow. With the other he held a set of compasses. They were the kind you use in maths class to draw circles with and surely not his, because Liam Sutcliffe never even had his own pens. He was rhythmically, purposefully stabbing the metal point into the back of Kristopher-with-a-kicking-K's hand, and Kristopher had his eyes scrunched, as though he recognised that if he once began to cry, his ordeal might get much worse.

Almost before I knew it, I'd marched between the aisles of desks and leaned over to scream in Sutcliffe's face, "What the hell do you think you're doing? Stop that."

Sutcliffe looked at me. There was no expression in his eyes, no anything. "Why?"

"Because you're hurting him. And because I said so."

"S'not hurting him." Sutcliffe raised the compasses again, about to illustrate, as if I'd simply failed to appreciate the subtleties of what he was doing.

Before I could consider, and entirely forgetting the golden rule against touching students, I grabbed his hand, wrapping it in mine. "Let go," I snarled.

"They're mine."

He was strong, but he was sitting, and I had the advantage of weight. I put all of it into applying pressure to his fingers and wrist – knowing even as I did so that if he chose to complain, I would be out of a job or worse.

"Let go," I said again, striving to sound calm, as though this were just a minor altercation between teacher and pupil, and not something more akin to a wrestling match. Then I realised there was no way he *could* let go, because I was gripping his hand so tightly. I released him. At that, he jabbed the compasses into his desk, hard enough that they stayed erect. I snatched them, stuffing them inside a pocket.

"Go to the headmistress's office," I said. "I'll be along shortly to tell her what you've done."

Sutcliffe eyed me steadily. "Fuck off, Ollie," he said.

I froze. I'd never once used my first name in the classroom, always referring to myself as Mr. Clay. For a moment I couldn't think how he would know it. Then a dozen possibilities occurred to me, all together, and every one of them scared me.

Sutcliffe was sitting with his arms crossed across his chest. Our fracas was already the centre of attention for the entire room; they were listening with bated breath, amid the kind of silence I could never have hoped to impose on my best day of discipline. I knew that the repercussions of whatever I said next would last for as long as I tried to teach that class, and perhaps for as long as I taught at Lawn Hill.

But I had nothing. My mind was a blank.

"Class," I said, "I'm going out for a minute. I want you to sit in silence until I get back."

On any day, that would have been a futile thing to say. Just then it was absurd beyond words, and I was barely out of the door before the shrieks and laughter began. I trudged in a daze to the office of the headmistress, a woman named Jane Painter, wondering what I'd do if she wasn't in – thinking perhaps that I'd walk out and not return. But her secretary sent me through, and so I told Painter what had happened, omitting the worst excesses of my own behaviour, and tried to hide the shaking of my hands.

When I'd finished, Painter considered me fixedly over the rims of her glasses. Her eyes were the same pale shade of grey as her hair. It struck me that this was the longest conversation we'd had since my first interview. "What about the other boy?" she asked.

That threw me. Could I have explained so badly? Was she imagining some conspiracy of hooligans? "The other boy?"

"The one that Sutcliffe was hurting."

"Oh."

"Have you taken him to the nurse?"

Tending to Kristopher Peel hadn't even crossed my mind. "I don't think he was seriously hurt," I said. "It was just a...you know, a pair of compasses, from a maths set."

The look Painter gave me amply summarised the regard in which she held my medical opinion. She stood up. "Come with me, Mr. Clay," she said, "and let's see if we can sort this mess out."

★   ★   ★

That evening, Yasmina phoned me. I didn't tell her what had happened; she wouldn't approve of my behaviour, regardless of what had led up to it. Yet to hide how low I was feeling was impossible. Though nothing had been said, I was convinced I'd soon be hunting for another job. Even if I wasn't, I didn't know that I could get up in front of that class again, or try to face down Liam Sutcliffe.

Yasmina spent a few minutes attempting, unsuccessfully, to draw me out. I could sense her growing frustration at my terse answers and my lack of vitality. I wanted to apologise, but apologising would mean explaining, and that I'd already decided I couldn't do. I was scared she'd despair of the conversation, but every time I tried to become more engaged, my subconscious would throw up an image from the day: Painter's frosty gaze, or those compasses rising and falling, or Kristopher Peel's hand when I'd eventually bothered to examine it, a jumble of angry crimson dots.

I could hear the irritation in Yasmina's voice though, and in the end I couldn't bear it anymore. "I'm sorry," I said. "I'm being an arsehole. It's been a really tough day, you know? And I haven't slept much. It's not you."

A pause. "Okay." Another. "You could have told me."

"No, I realise. It's school stuff, mostly. Nothing interesting. But it's nice to talk to you."

"Next time," Yasmina said, "just tell me."

"I will."

"All right. Well, the reason I called was to see if you'd like to do something on Friday."

"Absolutely."

"Why don't I come over to yours?"

"You don't need to," I said. "What if that scumbag starts up?"

She didn't need to ask who I meant by *that scumbag*. "Then we'll come back to mine."

"It still pretty much resembles a bombsite."

"Maybe I can help."

"Do you have a flamethrower? That might do the job."

"Ollie, I'd like to come over. Unless you really don't want me to. Even if it's a mess right now, it's your home."

I nearly pointed out that the house didn't feel like my home; that it felt like a collection of bricks stuck together with mortar into a box I just happened to spend a disproportionate amount of time inside. I nearly kept arguing. I should have.

But all I said was, "Okay. If you're sure you're up for it."

★ ★ ★

When I got off the phone, I felt better. Yasmina had a way of doing that, of picking me up when I was down. If I'd made a mess of the situation with Sutcliffe, the school authorities knew all too well what he was like. And while my misstep might be a black mark against my name, it wasn't about to cost me my job. Of course, confronting that class again was going to be difficult, but I'd get through it. Maybe having seen me lose my shit would even make some of the less sociopathic ones a little more inclined to listen to me.

However, no amount of brief optimism could make the week go easily. My Year Sevens were a bigger handful than usual, and the more disruptive they got, the more I couldn't shake the worry that they were acting up because of what had happened the day before. The Wednesday, with a class who didn't care who I was and knew there would be no consequences, was every bit as bad as I'd anticipated. By the time Thursday came around, and the long-dreaded confrontation with my Year Tens, I was close to calling in sick. At least Sutcliffe wasn't there; that was something. I still felt as if I was herding cats, though – the kind that skulk in savannah grass waiting for an animal weaker than themselves to come by. It was one of those lessons that involved more policing than teaching, and by the end I had double vision and a headache rising like flood water.

That night, Paul rang. He was apologetic about having left it so long; he was, as I'd surmised, busy with a new relationship, one that had survived beyond the usual one-week mark and so become, by Paul's own definition, *a bit fucking serious.*

"It's fine," I said. "I've been pretty busy myself." I hadn't the energy for a conversation; I wanted to curl into a ball, to nurse that headache or try and sleep it off.

Paul must have caught the exhaustion in my voice. "Oh yeah? Yasmina keeping you up?"

"Nothing like that. Just work stuff."

"Oh well. Give it time, mate."

And Paul began to describe to me the many and varied ways in which his new girlfriend – her name was Lucy – had been keeping him from his recommended amount of sleep. Normally I couldn't help being amused by how candid Paul was about his private life, but that evening his anecdotes were so much noise. I did my best to tune him out, while a part of my brain struggled to calculate an escape route from the conversation.

"So anyway, that was – what? – the Monday morning. And then on Tuesday—"

I heard a loud crash from next door.

"Sorry, man, I've got to go," I said. I cut the call, not even giving Paul a chance to say goodbye.

My mind had immediately gone back to that first night, and what I'd envisioned, rightly or wrongly, as a body being flung against the intervening wall. There were other similarities too: once again shouting, and the word 'fucker' rising distinctly from the background din.

Yet that occasion had been brief, likely an altercation between pissed-up mates, whereas this went on. More crashing. More shouts. The scuffle seemed to continue for the better part of a minute – although, as the clamour ended abruptly with what sounded like a door slamming, I tried to persuade myself it could only have been seconds. Still, that was quite long enough. I could hardly dismiss what I'd just heard as a friendly tussle. So who would Chas be getting into fights with in his own home?

Put that way, I decided I might be making more of what I'd overheard than there was – because the answer was *anyone*. From what I'd witnessed, he wouldn't require much provocation. I hadn't seen any women around, but if Chas had a girlfriend, I couldn't imagine he'd think twice about roughing her up. Or maybe someone had come round to check his gas meter and looked at him the wrong way. Really, his motivation for violence could have been anything and anybody.

When ten minutes had gone by and I was certain the noise had died down, I texted Paul to apologise. I didn't explain, mainly because I couldn't work out an explanation that made sense, but I promised to give him a ring over the weekend and that I'd talk to Yasmina about the four of us meeting for drinks. Then, determined I wouldn't waste another day off, I went to bed early.

For the first night in ages, I slept deep and dreamless sleep. Too much so, as a matter of fact; I'd forgotten to set my alarm, and when I at last struggled into wakefulness, I was horrified to discover the hour was past ten. I hauled myself out of bed and ate breakfast while a shallow bath was running. Roused by my dousing, I made a start on the one job I'd determined to get done that day: making the house basically presentable.

I did my best, I really did. I spent the better part of two hours tidying, galled by the amount of mess that had managed to accumulate in only a couple of weeks, and after lunch I set to cleaning: scrubbing work surfaces and tiles, sweeping and hoovering floorboards, gluing peeling edges of wallpaper, and even wiping windows and the insides of cupboards.

My efforts made no difference. They made no difference at all. I'd been right in what I'd said to Yasmina; the sole thing that would make that hovel presentable was burning it to the ground.

Still, I'd tried, and I felt that, if you squinted, it was just possible to see how an attempt had been made. My endeavours had also helped the day pass quickly and kept my mind occupied, so that by the time I stopped I was satisfyingly weary, too used up to dwell on the problems of recent days. I got ready well before I expected Yasmina and hung around listening to music, bit by bit convincing myself that the house perhaps wasn't looking so bad after all.

Yasmina arrived about seven, a little earlier than I'd expected. I watched as her eyes roved the living room, tensing for any hint of a reaction. Finally she said, "You've been cleaning, haven't you?"

"Oh my god! I'm so glad you noticed."

"It looks...."

"Like a bomb site that someone spent the whole day trying to tidy?"

She smiled. "I was going to say, 'more homely'."

"Well, that's good. All the same, let's not stay here any longer than we have to."

I'd spied an Italian restaurant near the Tesco that gave the impression of being both decent and cheap. As we walked over, I felt I was viewing the cramped terraced streets somehow differently for Yasmina being there. I took in details I'd missed before, hanging baskets and gardens where people had tried to make good use of what scant land they had. These were folks with not a lot of money, but aside from a few isolated bastards like my neighbour, most of them weren't bad people. Maybe, given time, I could find a way to be comfortable there.

The Italian turned out to be all right. It wasn't as nice as the places we went to around where Yasmina lived, and I suspected the proprietors were in fact Eastern Europeans hoping their accents would pass for Mediterranean; nonetheless, the food was decent, and the location was quiet and cosy. Perhaps most importantly, the wine was cheap. Neither Yasmina nor I tended to be heavy drinkers, but it was a Friday night, I didn't have to drive us home, and our glasses seemed to be emptying of their own accord. The first bottle only took us halfway through our main course, so I ordered a carafe, and that lasted until we were tucking into tiramisu. I got the bill and, reactions somewhat dulled by alcohol, barely winced as I handed over my bank card.

In the street, the evening was cool. Summer was drawing

towards its end; a premature nip of autumn was in the air. I hunched within my coat, reaching instinctively for Yasmina's hand. She shuffled close and we walked like that, arms lightly coiled, fingers clasping within the pocket of her parka. It was nice. It felt right. I tried to pretend that my reaction was due to the wine, but it wasn't. I really liked her. I needed to avoid screwing this one up – and so far, maybe, I was managing not to.

Then I heard the footsteps.

They were distant, but closing rapidly. We'd been walking so slowly. I picked up my pace and Yasmina looked at me, mouthing words I could make no sense of. I didn't try to reply; I couldn't put what I was feeling into words. It was only that something about the sound of those approaching feet filled me with dread. I knew the particular crunch of boots on pavement.

We were moving faster. Those other feet were swifter still: two sets, not quite synchronised. We turned into my street. So did the footsteps – near now. I could make out my house in the distance, distinguishable by my car parked in front. We could be inside within a minute, through the door and safe.

Fingers clenched my bicep – firmly, but just for long enough to delay me while their owner stomped past us.

"Oi, mate."

There were two of them. And I recognised them both. They'd been in the pub that time: Chas's skinhead friends, the ones who'd started a fight with such enthusiasm and so little apparent provocation. So they weren't in prison. They weren't in prison, they were here before me, and there was no way we were getting past them, not unless they allowed us to.

That close, I could see that only one of them was actually a skinhead. He had a chubby face, oval and drooping, his eyes were heavy-lidded, and I knew him for the one who'd glassed the Traveller that night. He was wearing an unclean white T-shirt and dark blue jeans. His friend had at least the shadow of hair, like a birthmark stain under the sickly yellow of the streetlights. His face was slimmer, more active; his features gave the sense that there was some thought process occurring behind them, though the frown he wore implied that it was nothing pleasant. He had on a black jacket, zipped to the throat, and his hands were crammed deep into the pockets. I didn't like to speculate about what they might be holding when he pulled them out.

"Hold up. Got a question for you," Black Jacket said. He glanced at White T-shirt, as though this was a puzzle they needed to figure out between them.

"Yeah, yeah." White T-shirt nodded slowly. "We was wondering, right, what're you doing with a Paki bird?"

I knew I had to say something, but my mind was an utter blank, partly through fear and partly because I could think of no answer that wasn't ridiculous. I wanted badly to point out that Yasmina was Iranian, not Pakistani, as if that would make a difference to anything; as if their hatred was some rational topic that we could sit down and discuss. I got as far as opening my mouth and then was helpless to shut it.

"You know what," Black Jacket said, his manner abruptly philosophical, "up close, she's all right."

White T-shirt didn't look amused. "Are you fucking joking?"

"No, mate. For a Paki, she's all right."

"You are. You're kidding me."

"Nice pair of tits. And she's not wearing one of those…what is it? Those fucking tent things. So you know she'd be up for it."

He moved near to Yasmina, raising a hand towards her breasts, like he was testing fruit in a supermarket.

Yasmina took a step back. "Don't touch me." Her tone was angry, defiant, and I could find no fear in it.

"We don't want any trouble," I said. My own voice sounded garbled, as though I was out of practice speaking.

"If you didn't want trouble," White T-shirt said, "you

wouldn't have come down our road cosying up with a fucking Paki, now would you?"

And he put both hands to my chest and shoved me.

I struggled to stay upright. Then there came a moment of too-rapid indecision, as I tried to calculate which outcome would be worse. Did he want me to stay up so he could push me again? Did he want me on the pavement, where he could put the boot in? Either prospect scared me equally. I tottered, unsteady – and he dashed a fist into my jaw.

This time I went down. I had no choice. The gyroscope in my head was spinning, up no longer where it was meant to be. He got another punch in before I could even hit the ground, his arm driving downward almost vertically. I bounced off the tarmac, my shoulders straight away followed by my head, so that first the wind went out of me and then every thought hurtled apart. A kick made me curl like a poked woodlouse, trying to wrap myself around the toecap that had turned my stomach into a ragged carrier bag full of broken glass.

I'm going to die, I told myself. But that wasn't what frightened me, not really. Nor was I afraid for Yasmina, though I knew I should be.

No, what terrified me was just the pain. I was already hurting, and I had no doubt I was going to hurt much worse before this was over.

CHAPTER FIVE

I waited for the next punch, the next kick, to fall.

That it didn't come was worse. I'd taken beatings before, even given a few of my own, and maybe I was rusty these days, but I was confident that unless things got really nasty, I could hold up. So long as no one pulled a knife, so long as nothing vital broke or burst...so long as they understood when to stop. But the waiting, the blows not coming, the tension that felt like it was trying to scrunch me up until I vanished entirely, that I didn't know if I could stand.

Was it Yasmina? Were they hurting Yasmina? She hadn't cried out, or else I hadn't heard over the ringing in my head. Perhaps at this moment they were dragging her off or bundling her into a car. I had to open my eyes; but if I opened them, what would I see? It would be something bad and I'd regret my curiosity.

"What the fuck d'you think you're doing?"

A new voice. And now that I thought, there had been footsteps. Somehow I'd edited them out.

"Pierce, mate." That was White T-shirt. His voice had gained pitch, had become abruptly affable – almost deferential.

"Don't fucking 'mate' me, you backward little shite. What do you think you're doing?"

"Pierce, look, I don't know—"

"No, you fucking don't. I tell you what, you should have that printed on a fucking hat. *I don't know.* It could be your fucking catchphrase."

"Hey...." Then White T-shirt yelped: the exact noise a dog would make if you trod hard on its paw.

"You point that at me again, *mate*, and I promise you I will rip it off, and your whole bloody hand too, and I'll stick it so far up your arse that every time you gawp at yourself in the mirror, you'll end up giving yourself the finger." Then a pause, the shuffle of feet, and, "Are you all right, son?"

I sensed from the way the light had changed, the way the sulphur yellow wasn't so harsh against my eyelids, that someone had stepped in front of me. I got one eye open and saw a shape more than a person: big and bulky, with much of that bulk in the shoulders, the squarish head topped with stubbly dark hair. As his face swam into focus, I could make out narrow eyes, a fleshy, crooked nose, and thick lips. He might have been as old as fifty, but that face had seen plenty of damage and little care, so it was hard to judge.

He was bending forward to offer me his hand. It seemed like a trap. I would grasp that hand and then the beating would begin again. Yet I had no choice. I reached up and clasped his fingers.

He was strong; there was power in those broad shoulders. He plucked me to my feet with no noticeable effort. When I was upright, he clapped me on the arm. "There you go. No harm done."

No harm done? Pain was radiating through my jaw and up from my ribs in acid waves.

Once he was sure I was steady, the man called Pierce turned to White T-shirt and Black Jacket. "Now, both of you, you're going to apologise to these nice people." He leaned in closer to Black Jacket. "Aren't you?"

Suddenly these two men, with their shaven heads and their callous faces, looked just like big kids. For one absurd moment I imagined Pierce getting up in front of my class, imagined him leaning that way towards Liam Sutcliffe, and that same discomfort in Sutcliffe's dead marble eyes.

White T-shirt peeked at me for an instant and then hung his head. "Sorry, mate."

I thought Black Jacket was going to offer to shake hands. At the last, he decided against it. "Yeah. Right. Sorry."

"It's fine," I said. It was a stupid response, but nothing else came to mind.

"And to the lady," Pierce added.

Two more chorused apologies, Black Jacket going first this time. Yasmina just nodded, not even looking at them.

"Good," Pierce said. "Sorted." He was standing behind the two of them now. He looped an arm over each of their shoulders and drew them close, so that their heads were inches from his mouth. I evidently wasn't supposed to hear, but I did. "*Do you not know who that is?*" Then even lower, barely audible: "*You do not shit where you eat.*"

Releasing them, he started walking and looked back over his shoulder, apparently expecting us to follow. I waited long enough to be certain Yasmina was beside me and hurried to join him, stepping awkwardly around Black Jacket and White T-shirt, trying to keep my distance without being obvious about it. After a few steps, Pierce dropped back, so that Yasmina had to step aside and he was between us. Considering me, he said, "You're the bloke who moved in next to Chas, aren't you?"

I didn't want to admit it. I was still having difficulties accepting that this was anything other than another attack. But he was staring at me, and I couldn't say nothing. "Yes," I admitted, the word made into *yeth* by my already swelling lower lip. "A couple of weeks ago."

"Yeah? Well, Chas is all right. He might look like a bad sort, but he's got a good heart." Pierce coughed into his fist. "Mate, I'm sorry that had to happen to you. Dougie can be a bit of a prick, but he's not normally that much of a prick. He's been having some trouble is what it is. Not that that makes it okay. But he's been having a hell of a time."

Once more, he seemed to expect an answer. "It doesn't matter," I told him.

"Of course it bloody *matters*. I'm just saying. It won't happen again, you can trust me on that. So, you know, there's no need to go getting anyone else mixed up in this."

It took me a moment to appreciate what he meant. The police, he was warning me off calling the police. Well, it would take more than that, I thought, rage flaring so abruptly and so utterly that I had to fight not to shake with the force of it. Not only would I tell them about this, I'd ask about that night in the Hare and Hounds, and why these animals were out on the streets molesting me and my girlfriend, and not behind bars where they belonged.

I was walking slowly. Partly that was due to the pain, but mostly it was because – even though rationally I realised he'd just told me he already knew – I didn't want Pierce to see where I lived. When he glanced at me impatiently, I picked up the pace.

"How are you doing?" Pierce wondered. "Head all right? You're going to have a shiner in the morning, and that's a fact. But nothing'll be broken. My old grandma hits harder than Dougie does. Bit of ice on it, you'll be right as rain. I'm sure the lovely lady will take care of you. What do you do, love? Are you a nurse? You look like you could be a nurse."

"I'm not a nurse," Yasmina said. Her tone was frigid.

"No? Well, you'll figure it out. Smart lady like you." Pierce stopped – and I saw that, without my noticing, we'd reached my house. "Anyway, here we are."

"Oh. Yeah." I fumbled in a pocket for the keys, couldn't find them, and tried another, my fingers growing frantic. I forced myself to calm down, found the keys in the second pocket, took them out, and unlocked the door. I opened it and let Yasmina inside, attempting to place myself subtly between her and Pierce. I was suddenly fearful that he would invite himself in, and already trying to work out what I'd say if he did.

He didn't. Instead, he slapped me on the shoulder, hard enough that I felt it, and said, "In case you didn't catch it, my name's Pierce. Got that? If Dougie ever so much as looks at you sideways – and he won't, because he knows what I'll do to him – but if he does, you tell Chas and he'll tell me. All right?"

"Right. Thanks for your help."

"Mate. It's nothing."

"Well." I started to close the door.

He didn't put a foot in the gap; he didn't need to. Something in the way he shifted his mass, a subtle indication that he required my attention, made me pause, the door half-shut.

"You'll remember what I said, yeah?"

What he'd said? In that moment, I could barely remember my own name. Nevertheless, I nodded. "Yes."

"Course you will. Night, then." And he turned away.

It took every ounce of self-control I had not to slam the door.

Yasmina was sitting on the arm of the settee. Her back was stiffly upright; her legs were together and her hands were flat on her knees. There was nothing at all natural about the pose, only a radiating aura of tension. I passed behind her, into the kitchen, and took out the pack of peas I knew I had in my freezer. I put them to my cheek. The pain flared and then dulled as cold seeped into my bruised skin. I went back through to the living room. Yasmina was still sitting, exactly as I'd left her.

When I flopped onto the settee, she started and looked round, briefly wide-eyed. Then she took in the bag of peas I was clutching to my already swelling jaw. "Are you okay? Should we call an ambulance?"

I made a quick mental inventory of everything that hurt. Thanks to my impromptu ice pack, my face felt merely numb and bloated. The pain in my side was worst, but I'd had cracked ribs before and I didn't think this was that. Though I might be black and blue in the morning, I wasn't about to die of internal bleeding. "I'm okay," I said.

"Are you sure?"

"I'm sure."

Yasmina nodded. "Ollie, I'm going to call a cab. I need to go home."

I noticed for the first time that her hands were shaking – not fast but steadily. She was watching them too, and she didn't seem able to stop their movement.

"God," I said, "I'm sorry. I'm so, so sorry."

"No, Ollie. It's not your fault. I just...I can't be here. Do you understand?"

"Of course," I told her. I didn't understand at all. The only thing I wanted even slightly, the only thing I could imagine that would make me feel better, was for the two of us to hold each other.

We sat in silence while we waited for the taxi to come. One time I edged closer, thinking maybe that I would put my arm around her – but although Yasmina didn't recoil as I'd feared she might, she didn't respond either, and in the end my nerve failed me.

The blare of the taxi's horn knifed through the silence, making me flinch. Yasmina stood up, and I followed mechanically. I managed to walk to the door and, with concentration, to get it open. I stepped into the street so that Yasmina wouldn't have to brush past me, though out on the footpath I felt taut and unsafe. Yasmina paused as she went by, looked as if she'd say something and didn't. She opened the cab door. Then she put her arms around my neck, hugged me gently, and kissed my cheek on the side that wasn't bruised.

"Ollie," she said, "please don't call the police. Okay? Don't make things worse."

I wanted to ask her what she meant, how this could possibly be worse – but by the time I'd formulated the question, she was already within the taxi and drawing the door shut behind her. Then, as the car began to pull away, I thought of all the other things I could have said. If I'd begged her, would she have stayed? And why hadn't she asked me to go with her? Was I going to see her again?

I felt too exposed standing there in the road. I knew I was going to feel that way for a long time now, maybe for as long I was in that house. I went back inside. Sobs were clutching at my throat; tears stung the corners of my eyes. I wouldn't give in to either. I had no reason to be crying. I should be angry. I shouldn't be listening to what that creepy fuck Pierce or the girlfriend who'd walked out on me after I'd taken a beating had to say on the matter, I should be calling the police.

But I didn't. I had my phone in my hand, my finger hovering over the nine, and all it would have taken was a rapid tap, tap, tap – but I didn't. I just stood there near the door, watching the screen as it dimmed, as it faded to black, staring and staring at nothing. A minute or five minutes or half an hour later, I slipped my phone into my pocket and walked to the sofa, sat down, and placed my head in my hands.

I felt anesthetized, hollowed out. I felt as though my muscles had aged and turned to dust, as if my bones had calcified and fused together. I could happily have never moved again. But after a while, the numbness became a dull ache, and I grew more and more conscious of the pain in my jaw as my bag of frozen peas began to thaw. My stupor vanished by degrees, only to be replaced by a sensation that was even worse.

Finally I rose from the sofa. I was full of energy, but a horrid sort of energy, like static crawling up and down my limbs. There was no way I was going to sleep. Yet I needed to do something, and I sensed that trying to relax would just wind me up further. If I was going to be awake all night, at least I'd like to spend the time purposefully.

I thought once more about the police. I had a name and a description. I'd no doubt that they'd be aware of Dougie, that he had his share of priors. Would they arrest him? And if they did, what would he get? I had bruises, and I knew from my time off the rails that bruises would warrant a charge of aggravated bodily harm. I pulled out my phone and googled *Sentence for ABH*. The results were surprisingly comprehensive. Yes, there was a possibility of prison, especially for a repeat offender. Conversely, there was also the possibility of a fine. And hadn't Dougie assaulted someone in the last few days and walked away from it? But, all right, best-case scenario: I could get that arsehole off the streets and into a cell where he belonged.

Okay. Great. What then?

Then his mates would come and find me. His mates who, lest we forget, included my next-door neighbour. Then there would be another kicking, or a brick through the kitchen window, or being bundled into the back of a car to somewhere out of the way, where screams could go unheard…but my mind had no trouble coming up with possibilities.

My neighbour. Chas. He was the heart of my problem, of all my problems. He was already making my life hell, but he had every opportunity to do much worse. And maybe Yasmina was right; maybe, also, the police would be powerless to intercede. Not, at any rate, if his worst offences were playing his music too loud and having mates who thought nothing of kicking holes in fences or assaulting strangers.

Only, what if that was the least he'd done? What if he'd had a hand in far more serious offences? Wouldn't that be different?

I went back onto the *Evening Post* website and checked to see if there'd been any updates on the corner shop firebombing. All I could find was the original article. Reading over it again, I took away nothing new. However, I did notice this time that beneath were hyperlinks to similar articles. Most were older, references to random thuggery and the sort of petty crimes that afflicted every city everywhere, but one was more recent: *Police Seek Help in Finding Missing Youth Worker*.

I clicked on the link. The piece wasn't much longer or more detailed than the firebombing one. Just yesterday, a twenty-three-year-old man named Zahid Aziz, who worked part-time in a youth centre catering mainly to local Pakistani and Bangladeshi kids, had gone missing. His disappearance wouldn't have even made the news but for the fact that one of the children had claimed to have seen him being bundled into a car by two men. They'd told their parents, who had called it in, and sure enough, Aziz hadn't returned home that night. But there was no further evidence, so the police were asking for other witnesses to corroborate the story. They didn't even have a description of the car, or of the men, only the name of the road where the incident had allegedly happened. I checked on Google Maps and found that it was a couple of miles to the south-west, in an area I didn't know.

It was the kind of thing that would probably turn out to be a false alarm. The two men had been mates; Aziz had gone out on the piss and slept it off on someone's settee, or decided out of the blue that he'd had enough of living with his parents. Yet reading the terse account had left a sinking feeling in the pit of my stomach, one that wasn't going away. It took me a moment to realise why; then I recalled, with shocking clarity, the commotion I'd heard from the other side of the wall the night before.

It was a coincidence. It had to be. Still, for a minute I could hardly think for the blood rushing in my head.

There was another link beneath that article. This one led to an op-ed. Its broader subject was race-related attacks in the Leeds area, but the editorial focused mostly on one particular hate group, an organisation with the particularly clumsy name of the Britain for British Army. They had splintered from the BNP a few years ago, during one of its phases of trying to look respectable and to shed some of its more obviously racist elements, much like Combat 18 before them – a similarity the piece played up heavily. Yet there were significant differences. The BFBA had always been a fringe organisation, even by the standards of the BNP, and its activities were confined almost entirely to the north-east of England.

The author never actually stated that the group was operating out of Leeds, but the implication was hard to miss. They'd been linked with any number of small-scale disturbances and minor crimes, and also a couple of serious felonies, including a murder last year. In the closing paragraph, the article made reference to a spate of suspectedly hate-related disappearances that had gone on in the Eighties, drawing parallels that struck me as tenuous in the extreme.

Then again, was I any better? I was looking for a pattern where likely none existed, looking because it suited me that there should be one. Yet someone had firebombed the corner shop; someone, perhaps, had kidnapped the youth-centre worker. My neighbour was a thug with a taste for other people's pain and no apparent conscience. Even if he wasn't personally responsible, he still might be involved somehow.

I daren't get in touch with the police. But there was nothing to say I couldn't contact a reporter. The article was under the name Rebecca Ford; however, there was no link to further information. I searched for the name, and when that brought up too many results I tried *Rebecca Ford Evening Press*. Better. She had a personal website. Though there wasn't a great deal on there and I could tell the site hadn't been updated for a few weeks, there *was* an email address. I hadn't a clue whether it was current, but it was worth a shot.

Only, what to say? *Dear Ms. Ford, I think my neighbour may be a hate-mongering psychopath and I was hoping you might know something I can use to get the police to put him away for a long time.* Even in my fragile state of mind, I could see that wouldn't achieve much. After some thought, I settled instead for pretending to be a local writer. I was working on a non-fiction book about the BFBA and I was wondering, just between us, if she knew of any prominent personalities in the Leeds area that would make a suitable focus for my research?

I read over my email half a dozen times. It wouldn't stand up to serious scrutiny, but it might be enough to open a conversation – and once she responded, all I had to do was drop in Chas's name and see what she came back with.

I clicked *Send*. Maybe it was pointless. Maybe it was ridiculous. But at least I was doing something, and for the first time in days, I didn't feel altogether helpless.

CHAPTER SIX

By the end of the weekend, I had no idea what I'd done with the time. I had a dim memory of anger and frustration and not much else. I knew I'd texted Yasmina and that she hadn't replied. One minute things had seemed so good between us, the next she couldn't even answer my texts. It made no sense, and whenever I tried to make it make sense, the anger and frustration only got worse.

Monday morning saw the black bruises round my jaw faded to ghastly purples, reds and greens. There was no disguising them. I supposed I should count myself lucky that I could just about speak clearly, and that the pain was more or less gone, aside from the occasional twinge in my ribs when I twisted at the wrong angle. Nevertheless, the fact remained that I was going to have to try and teach with the evidence of Friday night plastered across my face.

I knew there wasn't a chance of my getting up in front of a class of Year Tens without someone pointing out my injuries. Indeed, it took no more than thirty seconds; I barely even had my jacket off before one of the boys crowed, "Been in a fight, Ollie?"

The cry caught me off-balance; I couldn't tell who'd been to blame. Not Liam Sutcliffe, I would have known his voice – but he *was* back in class, I noticed, and the awareness made my stomach clench.

I nearly fell back on that old cliché, *You should see the other guy*, but that would only have given them ammunition. The moment you let anything become a conversation, you'd already lost control, and I had little enough of that at the best of times.

"My name is Mr. Clay," I said, with all the authority I could muster, "as you know. Anyone else who forgets that will find themselves in Mrs. Painter's office."

It was a show of weakness more than of strength. Hiding behind the headmistress was never going to impress them. And sure enough, the damage was done. I spent the rest of the class in full riot-control mode, hardly even attempting to impart knowledge but only ensuring that they didn't tear each other, or me, apart.

Adding injury to insult, the constant effort of raising my voice brought back the ache in my jaw, until by mid-lesson I felt as though I was talking through a mouthful of cotton wool and marbles. My mumbling was like blood in the water: one girl, Anastasia, answered a question in adequate imitation of me, and after that they were all practising impersonations. Telling them off meant acknowledging it. I pressed on – and the sharks circled closer.

I made it to the end somehow. They trooped out, amid a chorus of mock stammering and stuttering. Liam Sutcliffe grinned at me as he went by, as if to say, *See what happens when you fuck with me.* I had to ball my hands and dig my nails into my palms to keep from slapping the smirk off his face.

I didn't want to go to the staffroom. It would be the same thing all over again, except with adults taking the piss rather than children. I gave myself five minutes of staring out the window, watching sullen clouds trudge across a dirty, lead-grey sky, and then told myself to pull it together. Though no one would want the classroom for another hour, staying there felt too much like loitering at a crime scene.

Normally I made myself lunch to save a little money, but I'd got too caught up in my research binge the night before to remember. I went out instead. Avoiding the chippy and the cheap Turkish burger place where the kids always congregated, I carried on until I found a corner shop that sold sandwiches and ate on the way back to school, wincing whenever a mouthful brushed the tender flesh inside my cheek.

I had the first period after lunch free, and by the time I returned, the afternoon classes had already started. I drifted towards the staffroom through empty corridors, munching crisps and feeling faintly rebellious. Halfway there, I heard a sound that I initially thought was someone laughing. Whoever they were, they surely weren't supposed to be hanging around the hallways, and I was wondering if I cared enough to intervene when I realised it wasn't laughter at all. The pitch was what had fooled me. Actually what I'd heard was a girl crying, in harsh, glutinous sobs.

My feet began to hurry, almost of their own accord. A small portion of the school was being refurbished after a water pipe had burst, and that was where the sound was leading me. I pushed past a half-hearted barrier of cones and hazard tape. The passage was a dead end. On the right were two doors into classrooms, closed off with more tape; on the left were girls' and boys' toilets, with 'Out of Order' signs Sellotaped across their frosted-glass windows. The crying was coming from the boys' toilets – and as I turned the corner, it rose to a scream.

Then the door was flung open and a girl tumbled out. She crashed past, barely missing me, toppling an orange cone and leaving tape fluttering in her wake. It was hard to tell, but I thought she was one of the Year Tens; I'd dimly recognised her. Her shirt had been torn open, or perhaps cut, revealing a white stripe of bra, which she'd been endeavouring to hide by holding the tatters of shirt in place with one hand. Her face had been puffy and mascara-streaked. She hadn't even glanced at me as she went by, and it didn't occur to me to try and stop her, let alone to get her name.

Because by then I'd seen Liam Sutcliffe.

He was in the doorway, shoulders locked in their perpetual slump, as though nothing that had happened could conceivably be of any importance to him. When he looked for the girl and saw me instead, his thin lips curled at the edges, into something resembling a smile.

I had crossed the distance that separated us and had my arm to his throat before I even knew what I was doing. My other hand had bunched around a fistful of cheap cotton and plastic buttons, and between the two, I had Sutcliffe a clean three inches off the ground. There were no coherent thoughts going through my head, just a looping white-noise roar.

"You little shit." My face was close to his. I could see my spittle splashing off his pockmarked skin, like summer rain on hot tarmac. "You think you're so big, huh? Hurting a girl?"

He didn't look scared. If he had only looked scared, I could have let him go. But he had all the power, and I had nothing. If I released him, he would make some insolent remark, or maybe he'd hit me. Or worse – hadn't the girl's shirt been cut? No, I couldn't let go.

He wasn't even struggling. And he was still smiling. It should have been impossible with my forearm clamped beneath his chin, but he was. He was holding my gaze and he was smiling, and so help me, he scared the hell out of me.

I unhanded him. The decision was every bit as unconscious as going for him in the first place had been. Somewhere in the depths of my brain, a calculation had been made, one that had offered only two possibilities: either I kill Sutcliffe or I back down and accept the consequences.

I thought he'd go for me. When he raised a hand, I flinched; I couldn't help it. But all he did was massage his throat, and then, with great care, straighten his tie. As though he were some city banker who'd been roughed up by yobs. As though he were the victim. And throughout, that smile never left his mouth.

Suddenly, all I wanted was to be out of there. I knew I was in the presence of someone who possessed not a glimmer of what I'd recognise as human feelings. There was nothing anyone could do in the face of a creature like Liam Sutcliffe. No, there was *one* thing – but I hadn't the backbone for it, and I never would have.

Still, the anger hadn't gone. I couldn't just walk away.

"One day, you sick little fuck," I said, "it's all going to catch up with you. Then you won't be smiling anymore."

*   *   *

I went to the headmistress's office. She wasn't in. Her secretary told me she would be back soon and I was welcome to wait. I sat in a badly moulded plastic chair, staring out of the window, watching ashen clouds drift. My mind was as close to empty as it had ever been.

I looked up and Painter was standing over me. "Shouldn't you be getting ready for class?" she asked.

I'd altogether forgotten about my afternoon lesson. I understood then that, if I was given a choice between trying to teach it and running out of the building, never to return, I was going to opt for the latter.

"I'm sorry," I said.

She stood there, regarding me for a moment. Then she went to her secretary, leaned close, and spoke a few words I couldn't catch. Back to me, she said, "Please come into my office, Mr. Clay."

I followed after and she shut the door behind us, waving me to a seat. "Tell me what's happened," she said.

So I did. I told her everything, leaving out no detail – except for my final outburst, which by that point seemed so absurd and melodramatic that I couldn't bear to repeat it.

When I'd finished, she sat watching me steadily, drumming the long fingers of one hand upon the lacquered surface of her desk. "If Sutcliffe makes a complaint..." she said.

"He won't."

"The young lady involved might."

I hadn't considered that. "Yes." And she had probably recognised me. If she spoke up, I'd be a witness. If I denied I'd been there, it would be my word against hers. At any rate, there was no way I'd lie to protect Sutcliffe, whatever the truth cost me personally. In fact, I realised – not without a certain relief – that if I'd known her name, I would insist that the incident be investigated, by the school, by the police, by anybody who'd listen. There was no way I'd let a girl be hurt like that, not by Sutcliffe or anyone, if there was a single thing I could do about it.

But I didn't know her. I doubted she'd come forward of her own accord. And I was unlikely to see and identify her, not in a school of almost a thousand pupils. Perhaps Painter would be able to unearth her name, either by asking around about the torn shirt or – if the girl had simply gone home, as was more probable – from a list of absentees.

"In any case," Painter said, "whether a complaint is made isn't really the issue, is it?"

"No," I agreed, "it's not."

"The issue is that you lost control and physically assaulted a pupil."

"Yes." That was the issue, all right.

"Not that it makes a great deal of difference, but do you have any explanation for your behaviour? Other than misjudged chivalry, I mean?"

I was tempted to say that I hadn't. That was the answer her tone demanded. But I was beginning to calm down by then, or else to lose the artificial calm I'd had. Either way, it had occurred to me that I would have to at least try and defend myself. So I told her, briefly, all that had happened in the last weeks. About Chas, about the fight in the pub, about being beaten up in the street and what might have happened to Yasmina if Pierce hadn't intervened. About my money problems, the trap I'd built for myself, and thinking Yasmina was going to break up with me. I told her not because I expected sympathy, help, or understanding, but because once I'd started I didn't know how to stop.

All the while, Painter kept up her finger-drumming. It was a habit she seemed unaware of. When she was sure I'd finished, she said, "We have support options that we can offer a permanent member of staff. Counselling. Sick leave. For you, Ollie...well, you're in a delicate position."

"I appreciate that."

"We next have you tomorrow and Thursday, yes? I think it would be better for everyone if you don't come in. Take a few days. Take the weekend. Come back on Monday." She flicked at a desk calendar. "Let's say eleven. And we'll talk again."

"I can't lose this job," I said.

She looked at me sternly – and, despite what I assumed was an effort to hide her true feelings, with the clearest dislike. "You may not have a say in the matter," Painter said.

★   ★   ★

That night I tried to phone Yasmina. I rang three times in a row. Each time the call went to voicemail. I wanted badly to throw my mobile across the room and watch it shatter against the skirting board. I wanted to text her, *I think I just lost my job*. Instead – moving slowly, as though the device might at any moment explode – I slid my phone into my pocket.

Half an hour later, I felt it vibrate. A message. It read simply, *Are you free tomorrow evening?*

When I wrote back, *Yes*, Yasmina suggested a bar that we'd

been to once or twice when we'd first begun going out. At that, my heart sank. Not her flat. Not a restaurant. A bar we hadn't been to in weeks. Wasn't there a sort of poetry, or at any rate neatness, to breaking up with someone in a place where your relationship had started? I told myself I should be glad she hadn't just done it by text, but I couldn't make that thought stick.

I spent the rest of the night trying to formulate arguments why Yasmina should stay with me, and the fact that I could come up with barely a thing only worsened my mood. I had no money, no prospects, and a temporary job that I was clinging to by the skin of my teeth. Sure, we had a good time together, but couldn't she replicate that with any number of other people? Arguably I wasn't bad-looking; maybe that counted for something. Could I tell her I loved her? Was it true? I was starting to suspect it was. Then again, it's easy to believe you love someone that you're about to lose. And even if I said the words, even if I meant them, would they change anything? Not if her mind was made up.

Finally, when my thoughts had become a whirlpool dragging me further and further into their depths, I considered phoning Paul to ask for his advice. But I could guess what he'd say: *There're plenty more fish in the sea*, or sentiments to that effect. For Paul, with his undeniable good looks, his own business, his easy charm, that was true. For me? That sea was more like a desert, and I'd already spent too long wandering it alone.

Before I went to bed, I checked my email. There was nothing from Rebecca Ford, the *Evening Press* reporter. I hadn't really expected there to be. Either the address I'd found was out of date, or she'd seen through my absurd ruse, or perhaps she was so barraged with messages that she ignored them all. Whatever the case, there was no hope for me there. And what had I imagined would happen? That she'd reply with a dossier of damning evidence against Chas that I could forward to the police? No, I was on my own, and the sooner I accepted that the better.

Or so I told myself. By the time I got to the bar the next evening, the phrase was rolling back and forth around my mind like a mantra. *You're on your own, accept it. You're on your own, accept it.*

Except that I couldn't. Not when it came to Yasmina.

The bar was quiet, though far from empty. Just right, I thought, for a breakup: loud enough to talk privately, not so loud that someone wouldn't step in if I lost my shit. She was already there, in a booth near the window, a brimming glass of white wine on the table before her. Another bad sign; Yasmina only ever drank during the week when she was on edge. On the other hand, would she have ordered a large glass if she was planning on a brief conversation? I wondered, should I get a pint or a half, and what message would each send? In the end, I settled for a bottle of Sol and carried it over. Not knowing if I should kiss her, I sat down instead, and then felt self-conscious, as though I'd immediately screwed up.

"Hi," I said. "It's good to see you."

"Thanks for coming," Yasmina told me.

"No, of course. I wanted to."

She nodded – slowly, emphatically. "I'm sorry I ran out on you. And that I didn't call. I just needed some time. To think, you know?"

"Sure. It's okay." I tried to sound sincere.

She took a sip of her wine, held up the glass and swirled its contents gently. "Ollie...the reason I don't talk about what happened to my mother and me before we came here is because those are parts of my life I don't *want* to talk about. We left to get away from those sorts of troubles. To find something better. To feel safe. Can you understand that?"

I pondered what I'd give to magically transplant my home to

a place where I didn't have to worry over the next loud noise, the next pub fight, the next beating in the street. "Yes," I said. "I understand."

"But Ollie, when I'm with you, I don't feel safe."

"Look, I know what happened was awful. I'm not going to put you in a situation like that again. If I'd imagined for one second—"

"It's not only that." Yasmina looked away – at her glass, or at the tabletop. "I mean, I don't feel safe with you. You seem so angry. Even when we're happy, I feel like underneath it there's this anger, just waiting."

I should have been stunned. I thought, distantly, that I should have been hurt, or offended. I couldn't be. When I sought for indignation, it was nowhere to be found. I recognised what she was referring to, all too well.

For an instant I wanted badly to tell her the horror stories of my misspent youth: about the black eyes and bruised knuckles; about the shoplifting, and the wrongs I was even more ashamed of, acts that when I remembered them in the middle of sleepless nights made me wonder if I was so much better than Chas and his depraved friends. How I'd hurt people. How I'd hurt people for the most idiotic of reasons. Because they were different from me. Because I'd needed an excuse, any excuse, to lash out.

For an instant I wanted to tell her all of it. How close I'd come to driving my future off a cliff, to following in my dad's footsteps and probably ending up in the same place. How I'd somehow veered away at the last moment, just in time – just enough to save myself. How when I looked in the mirror sometimes, I saw what she saw, what she'd described. Ugliness. Anger, barely contained. Like all I'd done was grow new layers of skin over the old, and occasionally they became translucent, revealing everything I thought I'd hidden or outgrown.

I wanted to say that I knew the anger was there, that knowing was what had taught me to control it. Because I didn't kid myself about who I was, deep down, and what I might turn into if I didn't hold myself tight.

But all I said was, "I'd never hurt you."

She nodded, though still without looking at me. "I know that."

"I mean it. Not ever."

"Not deliberately."

I wasn't sure how to take that. "No. Not deliberately."

"But *this* is hurting me."

"This?"

"Us. How your life is. Being a part of it."

I almost said, *You don't have to be a part of it.* But that would have been too easy to misconstrue, when we were already on a knife edge. "You shouldn't have come round that night. We made a mistake. We won't do that again."

"What? I won't come to your home?"

"No. *No.* I'll come to yours. I can split my life in two. A good half and a bad half. And the good half will be you. All the bad stuff – my house, Chas, my work – I'll keep that away from you."

Then Yasmina finally stopped staring at her glass. Her gaze was somehow imploring, though I couldn't tell what for. Maybe she only wanted me to see sense. "Ollie," she said, "that's your whole life."

You're my whole life, I thought, and cringed at how trite it sounded – and then, again, at how true it was. I could feel that I was close to tears, or worse, a rush of emotion that would sweep me from my feet and leave me who knew where.

"I'm sorry," I said. "I'm so sorry. About buying the house, about all of it. I did a stupid thing. I should have listened to you and…god, I really fucked everything up. And I don't know how to sort it. But I'll figure it out, I will. I'll find a way. So, look, I get what you're saying, and you're right, but please don't…just don't do anything drastic. That, you know, we can't take back. Just make it a break. And we can have a think, about what we both want, about how we could make things better. I'll figure it all out. Only—"

"Okay," Yasmina said.

"Okay?"

"A couple of weeks. Yes. We'll take a break. And see what happens."

"Yeah?"

"Yes. I don't *want* to break up with you, Ollie."

"I don't want you to either."

She smiled. "I know."

I smiled back. "As long as you do."

And suddenly we were close again, as close as we'd been. In that moment, I was sure she would change her mind – that somehow it was all going to be okay.

Yasmina stood. "I've got to go. I've got some marking to finish for tomorrow."

The moment was gone – or had never been, outside of my imagination. "Oh. Right."

She bent to kiss me on the cheek, and then turned the gesture into a brief hug, coiling her arms around my neck. It occurred to me that I should offer to walk her out – but I still had a third of my beer left. I tried to decide whether I should leave it or whether I should drink it down.

Before I was even halfway to reaching a conclusion, Yasmina was gone.

CHAPTER SEVEN

I don't want *to break up with you, Ollie.*

But people do all sorts of things they don't want to do.

By the next day, I was sure Yasmina had brushed me off. Of course she had. She'd said what she had to say to end the conversation, said what she knew I needed to hear. I hadn't won a reprieve, just two weeks of sitting around feeling sorry for myself until the axe finally fell.

Well, I couldn't live like that. I'd done nothing except feel sorry for myself ever since I'd moved into the house, and fair enough I'd had my reasons, but I couldn't stand much more. I'd been down that road, back in the days before I'd met Yasmina. I wasn't prepared to see it happen again.

I had nothing left to lose. So what if Chas kicked the shit out of me? So what if he burned my home down? Yasmina had been the only part of my existence that I cared for and valued, and now she was gone, and there was nothing in the rest that I could convince myself was worth fighting for. Yet at the same time, I was craving a fight. I was ready to lash out. And I didn't much give a damn about the consequences.

There was just one course I could think of – the one everybody had been telling me to avoid.

I settled for phoning the police non-emergency number. When a woman answered, I explained that I'd been attacked in the street a few nights before. I told her the details and answered her questions. Yes, I knew who one of the men was, his first name at least. And I knew the first name and address of one of his associates, because he was my neighbour.

A couple of hours later, my doorbell rang. I'd spent the

intervening time regretting my decision, knowing I couldn't take it back and unsure if I even wanted to. There were two of them on my doorstep, a white woman and a black man. They were smartly dressed but not in uniform.

The woman introduced them both. "I'm Police Constable Thornton and this is PC Sane." She waved ID that I barely registered. "Are you Oliver Clay? You called regarding an assault?"

"Yes. That's me. Yes, I did."

"May we come in?"

"Of course." I held the door open for them, immediately embarrassed that I only had the settee and a couple of folding wooden chairs to offer. "Can I get you a cup of tea?" I asked, falling back on that most British of resources.

"No thank you," Thornton said. Sane just shook his head.

I ushered them towards the sofa and unfolded one of the chairs for myself. Sat perched on its edge, I felt uncomfortably like a naughty schoolboy. Thornton had taken a clipboard padded with sheets of paper from a shoulder bag, and already had a pen poised. "When you're ready," she said, "why don't you talk us through what happened from the beginning."

The beginning? I fought the irrational urge to narrate a great swath of my recent life history, as I had with Painter: the entire stupid tragedy that had overtaken me ever since I'd come into the inheritance. Out of context, what had occurred that night sounded all the more pathetic. I resisted; I restrained myself to beginning as we left the restaurant. I was shocked at how a mere few days had blurred crucial details, by how hard it was to describe faces I'd assumed would be burned into my mind forever. Who had said what? And in what order? I found myself stammering, repeating and correcting myself. The more I went on, the more I was certain they wouldn't believe me, simply because my storytelling skills were so inadequate.

Eventually I got to the point where Pierce interceded. I told how he'd helped me up, how he'd walked us home – and how he'd warned me off calling the police.

Sane spoke for the first time. "Did you think about listening to him?" He had a distinct accent, rich and sonorous.

The question took me by surprise. "Yes. I thought about it."

Thornton exchanged a glance with Sane. "I can see from what you've told us that you already appreciate this, but you should consider your next step carefully. If you press charges and the case goes to court, then you, and Ms. Soroush as well, would most likely have to give evidence. With a charge like this, it's very probable."

"Yes. I get that."

Now Thornton looked uncomfortable, as if she was being forced to spell out something she'd rather have left unsaid. "As I understand it, you're not in any danger currently. The issue with the noise you'd have to take up with the council anyway; they'd want a record of incidents, and evidence. But aside from that, it sounds as though the situation…in a way…has resolved itself. And that pressing charges would stir it back up again."

I could feel myself growing more and more agitated. I was terrified that they would notice, that I'd give them yet another reason to dismiss me. "No, I see what you're saying. I should keep my head down, hope it all goes away. But that only makes sense if there's some end in sight. I can't carry on like this forever. I'm stuck here. I can't afford to move. I don't want this to be my life."

"I understand that, Mr. Clay, and I don't at all want to give the impression that I'm discouraging you from taking action. Just that, under circumstances like these, it's not a decision you should make lightly." Again Thornton hesitated. Then, leaning forward, she said, "And these things *do* often have a way of resolving themselves."

There was something forcible, almost intimate, in the way

she spoke the words. I knew what she was implying, and that I should leave it there, but my mind was full of doubt and the doubt was stronger than my certainty. "Do you know about him? Chas, I mean?"

Thornton leaned back. She and Sane looked at each other, and I could read neither of their expressions. Yet I was sure I'd blown it; that whatever confidence she'd been trying to let me into had snapped shut like a trap.

Then she said, "For obvious reasons, I can't discuss specific details of an investigation. But I can tell you that your neighbour has a history of offences, and that he's someone we keep a close eye on. He's been in prison before. Given his past record, there's a good chance he will be again."

I felt a rush of gratitude. Thornton had come clean with me, had stepped across a boundary just to give me a glimmer of hope. Suddenly I urgently wanted to tell her everything: about the fight in the pub and how Chas had held back, but in a way that suggested control rather than indifference; about the firebombing of the corner shop, and how the car that had been seen matched his. And from there I could lead into my suspicions – because someone like that, someone who hung out with people who'd start fights with anyone for any reason, who egged them on, what else might they be capable of?

PC Sane cleared his throat: a harsh, resonant crack. His eyes roved steadily up and down my face, as though he was noticing me for the first time. "What you should think about," he said, in that leonine purr of his, "is, what has actually happened? Not what *nearly* happened. Not what *might have* happened. You're okay. Your girlfriend is okay. Do you see? What actually happened. That's what we have to work on."

Oh god, he had seen right through me. Every word I'd wanted to say turned to ashes in my mouth. I coughed into my fist, as if that would expel them. But now I had nothing meaningful to respond with. I just wanted to get these two, who couldn't possibly help me, out of my house.

"I guess I'll need to give it some more thought," I said. "I'm sorry to have wasted your time."

"Not at all," Thornton replied, while Sane looked as though wasting his time was the least of it.

He got up first, leading the way to the door. I hurried to catch up with him and opened it. Sane paced out, hardly acknowledging me, and Thornton followed. As she passed me, however, she paused to open a Velcro pocket, drew out a sliver of card and offered it to me.

"This has my phone number and email. If you decide you'd like to go ahead and press charges, or if you have any questions or concerns, feel free to get in touch directly."

I made a show of glancing over the card, which had obviously been produced from a standard template: it had the West Yorkshire Police badge on it, Thornton's name, and as she'd said, a phone number and email address. "Thanks," I said. "I think, after everything we've talked about…well, I'll probably leave it for now…but, yeah, thank you."

Once I'd closed the door, I was tempted to rip the card to pieces. I desperately wanted to damage something. Instead, I stuffed it into a pocket. *For all the use it's going to be*, I thought. I'd have had as much luck phoning the Samaritans.

I tumbled onto the sofa. The cushions were still faintly warm; I'd happened upon the spot where Thornton had been sitting. I tried to find some hint of reassurance in what I'd just learned. At least the police were aware of Chas and were investigating him. The knowledge should have made me feel better. Shouldn't it?

Then again, maybe it merely raised a whole new set of doubts. Given the level of subtlety I'd seen Chas and his mates demonstrate, one of those had to be the question of how much evidence the police could really need. No, if they were that interested in him, it could only mean they had grander ambitions than a few ABH charges. Perhaps they weren't even after him; perhaps they were using him to get to someone else, someone worse, in which case it might be weeks or months before they made a move. And when they did, there was a very real likelihood that Chas would slip through the net or make a deal, that he would walk away scot-free.

The more I considered, the more every possibility led to the same inescapable conclusion: the police's interests were not the same as mine. The one thing I wanted was Chas gone, if only for a few weeks – long enough for me to sell the house. I didn't care about guilt or innocence, what he had or hadn't done, I just needed him gone.

Once again, I was back to being helpless – except that this time was worse, in that the sole avenue left open to me had been closed off. One thing Thornton had said had stuck with me: it wouldn't just be me who needed to testify but Yasmina, and given the way things were between us, there was every chance she'd refuse. Even if I did press charges, Dougie and his partner in crime were entirely likely to get off, and then I really would have dug myself a hole that there'd be no crawling out of.

I was powerless. Trapped. And I could hardly stand it. I didn't *want* to be a victim. I didn't want to spend the next months or years lying awake in the early hours of the morning waiting for a little peace, or being scared to walk my street, to bring a girlfriend home, to risk entering my local pub. This house was supposed to have been my new beginning, perhaps the foundation stone of a better life – not this hell of fear and indecision.

I got up. I roved into the kitchen, realised I had no idea what I was looking for, barged back through to the living room, glared at the peeling walls, and marched up the stairs. I started for my bedroom and changed my mind, stomped into the spare room instead. There was nothing in there beside the last few boxes I'd yet to unpack: books I'd never reread, CDs I'd never listen to, and other assorted junk.

My gaze fell on a small pile I'd kept separate from the rest. Yasmina's belongings. For someone so capable, she was curiously forgetful; on both of the occasions she'd stayed over at my old flat, she'd managed to leave without something. At the time I'd wondered if her absentmindedness hadn't been on some level deliberate, a subtle indication that our separate spaces were now shared.

There was a thin polyester sweater, dark green, with one of its large wooden buttons missing. A pair of underpants, black and plain; I'd always meant to ask if she'd gone out and taught a full day with no pants on and never quite dared. A pair of colourfully striped socks, which suggested it was more likely she'd brought spare underwear and forgotten that. A couple of hairpins and a bobble with plastic flowers, uncharacteristically kitschy. A compilation CD of North African blues that she'd lent me to listen to early on, and which I'd never got round to. A dog-eared copy of *One Hundred Years of Solitude*, her favourite book, similarly loaned and neglected. All things I'd meant to give back. And maybe there had been a deliberateness to my lapses of memory, too, for though I'd known we were a long way from the point of even talking about living together, there'd been something in those assorted odds and ends that teased the distant possibility.

Well, not anymore. Now it was just so much crap – and the sight of it there twisted my stomach. I carried the pile downstairs and dumped it in a plastic carrier bag from beneath the kitchen sink. I was half-ready to cram the bag into the bin, but some residue of sense restrained me. Still, I couldn't bear the notion of it being in the house. She'd dumped me, hadn't she? I wasn't about to be the pathetic arsehole who hung onto his ex-girlfriend's possessions in the hope that she might one day take him back.

My first thought was the cellar; but I hadn't replaced the

blown bulb down there, and I had vivid memories of cobwebs and choking dust. Then I decided to leave the bag out in the yard, at least until I'd calmed down, and got as far as opening the door before I was frozen in place – by raucous laughter from the opposite side of the fence. A moment later I heard voices, and was amazed I hadn't noticed them earlier. One I recognised as Chas's; the other two sounded familiar as well. Did they belong to Dougie and his accomplice? At any rate, I couldn't tolerate the prospect of them seeing me. I slid the door closed, locked it, and retreated until I was convinced the wall would hide me from view – as though a wild animal was out there and not three drunken louts.

My heart was drumming. Telling myself how ridiculous I was being to hide like a little kid didn't make that frantic beat settle. All the while, all I could think was, *You can't go on like this.* But thinking it was one thing, having any kind of a solution was another.

Finally, I slipped out of the kitchen. I took the carrier bag upstairs, intending to stuff it under the bed and try to forget about it. Then, as I climbed the last step, something caught my eye. I stood there, uncertain, not able to recall what I'd seen. Only when I glanced upward did I understand: midway along the yellowed ceiling was a square of plywood, carelessly painted to match and screwed at each corner.

My subconscious, obsessed with hiding Yasmina's belongings somewhere I couldn't possibly stumble over them, had guided me to the perfect place. Yet now that I was here, that petty quest didn't seem so important anymore. This discovery was more interesting than the motives that had led to it.

I had an attic.

Of course I had an attic. Didn't everyone? Only it had never occurred to me. Was there anything up there? Why had the makeshift hatch been screwed shut? Probably because the previous owners had been too miserly to fit a proper trapdoor, but still, the fact gave me pause. And more than any of those questions, I was glad of the diversion, of something to think about that wasn't Yasmina or my neighbour or my disintegrating career.

I didn't have a stepladder. Instead, I went downstairs for one of the folding chairs and then spent another five minutes hunting for my screwdriver, ultimately finding it deep in the bottom of a yet-to-be-unpacked box. The chair was rickety, totally unsuited to being stood on, and tottered at each slight motion. Fortunately, the ceiling was low enough that I could steady myself by jamming a palm against it. I set to work on the screws. They were cheap, the metal too soft, and at first all I managed was to gouge the heads. I pressed harder, almost lost my footing as the chair rocked onto two legs, and had a vertiginous vision of tumbling down the stairs.

When I was sure I was stable, I put all my strength into one screw. At last it surrendered. The second, however, was every bit as stubborn. Once I had a couple out, though, the going became easier. The wood of the frame was soft, and I found that with enough pressure I could simply lever the whole panel free. The final two screws gave up their hold with an unpleasant crack that showered splinters and dust.

I dropped the panel, clambered down, and stood panting. What had I been thinking? I'd nearly broken my neck for nothing. Above me was a quadrangle of utter blackness. All I'd achieved was to make a hole in my own ceiling, and I'd have a tough job ever fitting the cheap plywood back in place.

Still, the damage was done. To make myself feel better, I heaved up the bag containing Yasmina's possessions, watching with satisfaction as it vanished into the gaping darkness. That contentment lasted all of an instant, long enough for me to realise I'd done yet another stupid thing. What if Yasmina had meant what she'd said about taking a break? What happened when in two weeks' time she told me she wanted to get back together – or, for that matter, if she really had made up her mind and asked for her property? She would think I was a childish idiot, and rightly so.

Anyway, I was still curious. A fraction of the thrill I'd first felt at owning my own house had returned with this revelation of a space I'd never even known I had. I might as well go through with what I'd started – and I could retrieve the bag while I was at it.

However, unscrewing the panel had been one thing, climbing up would be another altogether. Eventually I decided the landing was sufficiently narrow that, if I could secure a hold above, I'd be able to support myself between the walls. But it didn't require much to reveal that plan as better in theory than in practice; as long as it took me to clamber back onto the shuddering chair and reach on tiptoes to grasp the flaking wood. Not for the first time, I regretted I wasn't in better shape. I jammed my left foot against a wall, forced a hand up for a proper grip, and, using that hold, contorted the foot as high as the lintel of the bathroom door.

The abrupt shift set the chair teetering. In a panic, I thrust up my right forearm and hooked it over the edge of the opening. I abandoned the chair, which tipped away beneath me, clattering to the floor. With all my strength, I dragged my upper body through, until I could wedge in both arms. Then there came another moment of terror, as I wondered if I hadn't just jammed myself in. I remembered the foot on the doorframe, and with that I kicked off, until I was far enough through that I could stretch my arms and slide onto the rough wood behind me.

I sat there, gulping air. Of all my recent, foolish ideas, this had to be high on the list. I couldn't even see the carrier bag. Once I had my breath back, though, and once my eyes had begun to adjust, the attic wasn't quite as dark as I'd expected; I could dimly make out the nearby wall and the outline of the roof overhead. Wishing I'd brought a flashlight, I suddenly recalled that I had my phone in my pocket. I slipped it out, selected the torch function, and a cone of light spilled before me.

I played my phone across the surfaces, slowly interpreting the surrounding space. What I saw was exactly what I should have anticipated: antique beams above, the occasional loose tile allowing slivers of illumination to penetrate; the air thick with ancient dust; a slender layer of insulation stuffed into the gaps of the floor, like mouldering candyfloss. There were a couple of disintegrating cardboard boxes in one corner, but even if I could have reached them, it was impossible to imagine them containing anything of value.

A typical loft of a typical two-bedroom house in a typically rundown area. Only, as I scanned my phone around, I couldn't shake the sense that something wasn't right. Maybe the darkness was just unsettling me, maybe it was the dust, maybe—

Then I understood. It was too big. My attic was far, far too big. Where there should have been a wall or partition to divide my roof space from Chas's, there was nothing.

All this time, the neighbour I was so afraid of had had a way into my house.

And I had a way into his.

CHAPTER EIGHT

Over the last couple of weeks, without entirely realising, I'd been growing steadily more attuned to Chas's routine. I had a fair idea of which nights his mates would be round, which nights meant music blaring through the wall, which gatherings would end up going on into the early hours.

But I'd never consciously given his habits much thought. I'd been dreading Chas's presence and looking forward to his absences, without fully appreciating what was playing havoc with my moods. It wasn't as if there'd been anything I could do, so the precise details had never really seemed to matter.

Now, though – now they mattered. Now they were the most important thing in the world.

It took me a minute of working up courage to drop down onto the landing. In the end, I descended by stages, using the doorframe once again for support, and still nearly managed to twist my ankle on the chair, which had folded just where I'd meant to land.

I stumbled onward and hurried downstairs. One detail I'd noticed about Chas's behaviour was that when he left home on a weekend, he would likely be out all day and into the evening. I'd come to unthinkingly value those hours of peace, but until this moment I'd never questioned them. I checked on the internet, to be sure. My theory was right. Football matches. Specifically, Leeds United matches. They'd played three weekends in a row, and the one Saturday when Chas had been especially late back had been an away game. I held my breath as I scanned the dates for the forthcoming Saturday. Yes, there it was. The first of November. Blackpool. And next to the team name, a single letter: A.

A as in Away. Chas was going to be out all Saturday. And I had a way into his house.

All the while, I'd barely admitted to myself what was going through my mind. But buoyed by that rush of exultation, I could no longer deny the plan – the insane, dangerous, unconscionably idiotic plan – that had come to me as I'd stared across that vacant roof space towards the distant far wall. So the police were investigating Chas. And they were happy to take their time about it. What would happen if I could present them with real evidence, something they couldn't ignore? Or if, even better, that evidence found its way into the hands of the local press? Yes, that would be the thing to do: let's see Rebecca Ford ignore me when I sent her an actual lead.

More and more, my intention didn't seem so insane, so dangerous, or so idiotic. In fact, it was all too easy to rationalise. I had a problem: my neighbour was wrecking my life, and as long as he was there, there wasn't a great deal I could do to fix it. No one was willing to help me, so I'd have to help myself. I had a way to do that. I was as certain as I could be that it was safe. What I was contriving was barely even illegal; it wasn't as if I was going to take anything, except maybe a few photos. The biggest risk was clambering up again into my attic, and I had a couple of days to figure out an approach less likely to leave me in the hospital.

Beyond any of that, though, I now had a plan. I realised then: I'd reached a point where any course was better than none. I'd rather do this and it be the wrong thing than sit around pitying myself, hoping Yasmina would call or that the police would finally leap into action.

For the rest of that day, my project was all I could think

about. My mind hadn't been so clear in weeks. For the first time since I'd made the decision to buy the house, there was no fear, no doubt.

As night fell, however, something resembling sense started to reassert itself. My buzz began to dissolve, regardless of how hard I clung to it. Its loss was like water draining to reveal the muck beneath, all the crap that infested the bottom of my brain.

I had a plan. I didn't want to talk myself out of it. But what by day had seemed risk-free and sound, by darkness appeared awfully close to suicide. There was so much that might go wrong, and while it was easy to assure myself I had nothing left to lose, that argument held scant weight against the threat of physical pain. I could remember precisely the sensation of Dougie's fist connecting with my face, and it took little imagination to fill in what might have happened after that, had Pierce not intervened. The truth was, it was always possible to make things worse, and maybe I was on the verge of doing exactly that.

I needed to talk to someone. Obviously I couldn't share what I was intending, if for no other reason than I didn't want to inadvertently make anyone I cared about into an accomplice. No, I'd just got too deep inside my own head; I had to find a way to back off and let my thoughts work themselves out instead of circulating uselessly.

Sat on the sofa, I cradled my phone, contemplating options. It seemed to me that my social circle had dwindled in recent weeks. The worse my circumstances had grown, the less willing I'd become to contact anyone but my closest friends, lest they ask questions I didn't want to answer. Yasmina wasn't an option, of course. I tried to remember when I'd last talked to my mother and how tense the conversation had been; too much so, I recalled, for her to be of any use now. Who was left? Aaron would still be away with his work, and his trip had sounded serious enough that I knew I should leave him in peace.

I called Paul's number. But by the third ring, it had occurred to me that if he didn't answer, there was no one else, and after that my stomach knotted fractionally more with each shrill note.

Just as I was certain the call would go to voicemail, Paul's cheerful voice intruded: "Hey, Ollie, good to hear from you! How are you doing? How's Yasmina?"

Not the ideal place to start. "We're kind of on a break," I said.

"Yeah? Shit. Whose idea was that?"

"Not mine." The words came out more bitter than I'd intended.

"Oh man. That sucks, I'm sorry. She seemed great. I mean, that's probably not what you want to hear...."

"No. No, it's cool. She *is* great. Everything was going okay, you know? But there was this thing with my neighbour's arsehole mates, and—"

"Wait, what thing? What the hell's happened now?"

I told him, as briefly as I could, what had transpired that night in the street.

"Christ. That's unbelievable." Paul sounded genuinely aggrieved. "Those fuckers! No wonder she got spooked, Ollie. But she'll come round. Just give her a bit of space."

Relationship advice from Paul, I thought cruelly, *Paul the serial monogamist*. "That's what I'm doing," I agreed. "So how about you? How are things with...." Unable to remember the name of Paul's latest fling and convinced it must surely have ended by now, I let the syllable drag out.

"Lucy? Bloody marvellously. At the risk of sounding like a dick, I think she might be the one."

"Okay, I don't know who you are or what you want, but whatever you've done with the real Paul...."

"No mate, I'm serious. I get that I've been a bit of a slag in the past—"

"There's an understatement."

"Well, it turns out I just needed to meet the right bird. Yeah, laugh if you want, but it's true. And you know what? I think you have too. I think you and Yasmina are going to figure things out, and a month from now we're all going to be having dinner together and talking about how bloody stupid this bother was."

"I hope you're right," I said. The way he'd described the scene, it had seemed so plausible; I could picture us sitting there around Paul's dining room table.

"I know I am. I'm *always* right, Ollie, you ought to listen to me a bit more. Actually, that reminds me...I was out with Lucy and this pal of hers, Katherine, and Katherine was saying that...."

But I tuned out the rest of the anecdote – and the one after. Paul loved to talk. He didn't really require an audience, and once he got started, he'd run until he'd worn himself out. I could guess what his topic would be, and as much as I was happy for him, I didn't need to hear how great his new relationship was, especially not in the kind of detail he tended to go into. I let his words wash over me, and my mind wandered. Just the sound of another voice made it easier to think, somehow.

Belatedly I caught the interrogatory hook, the expectant pause; Paul had asked me a question. There was no point in trying to bluff. All I could say was, "What?"

"I said, have you had any bother since?"

Attempting to piece together Paul's last couple of sentences, I realised he'd somehow circled back to the beginning of the conversation. "No," I told him, "not really."

"Not really?"

"I mean, no. Noise, the usual. But nothing like that."

"Mate," Paul said, his tone abruptly serious, "you just need to keep away from that prick. That's all there is to it."

"Sure, you're right, but—"

"No, Ollie, come on. I know it's getting on your tits. Still, you have to try and relax, yeah? It'll sort itself out. Things always sort themselves out."

"Yeah. Yeah, you're right."

"Course I am."

In that moment, I wanted so badly to tell him: *But the thing is, sensible as that advice is, I've been thinking about breaking into his house – and I've a feeling I'm going to anyway.*

I didn't say it; I had no need to. Because talking to Paul had achieved exactly what I'd hoped it would: it had made my mind up. If I could listen to my best friend telling me to do the precise opposite of what I'd planned, if I could agree intellectually with every word he was saying, and if that didn't force me to reconsider, then it was safe to say nothing was going to. I'd made my decision, and there was no use in second-guessing anymore. All I could do was try and minimise the risks as much as possible.

I hurried the conversation to an end, grateful to Paul but suddenly exhausted with the effort of talking to him. We agreed to meet for a drink sometime soon, Paul suggesting that maybe he would bring Lucy along and introduce us: "Honestly, mate, you'll think she's brilliant."

After I hung up, the silence I'd been longing for seemed dense and oppressive. However, it didn't last long. A few minutes later, about eight, the noise started up. It was a timely reminder that Chas's schedule wasn't as predictable as I might like to believe, for as far as I could remember, Thursday had always been a quiet night.

It soon became apparent that this one was going to be anything but. Tonight's assault involved the usual pounding crap that passed for music, only ramped up to barely imaginable levels; and still I could hear people crashing about, shouting, and the occasional swearword rising like a turd bobbing to the surface of a public toilet. This was a party, or whatever violent thugs did in place of a party, and there was no kidding myself that it would finish anytime soon.

I contemplated going out. I didn't. Instead, I soaked it up. Right then, I needed to be angry, and here was the perfect fuel. I sat there and I absorbed every thunderous bass note, every bellowed curse, every bang and yell.

I'm going to get you, I thought. *I'm going to fuck up your life, exactly like you've fucked up mine. I'm going to make you pay.*

⋆   ⋆   ⋆

The next day, the anger remained: complete and perfect as a polished stone.

The party had drawn to a close somewhere between two and three in the morning; it had been hard to judge, for I'd been dozing fitfully by then. I lay in almost until lunchtime, and still my tiredness was a dull ache, like the outline of a migraine.

The tiredness did nothing to affect the anger. It was simply the medium upon which it rested, like water supporting oil.

I had a day, a single day in which to plan. One thing was for sure, I wasn't going to rely on any rickety folding chairs again. I made myself lunch from what bits and pieces were in the fridge and set out, back towards the shops near the Hare and Hounds. I was impressed to see the corner shop well on its way to being repaired; the inside had been gutted, the walls repainted, and a new floor already laid. It was as if petrol bombs were an everyday business hazard, to be shrugged off and moved on from.

Walking by, I felt almost guilty. What strength did that shopkeeper and his family have that I lacked, to pick themselves up from so callous and senseless an atrocity and carry on as though nothing had happened? Then again, I didn't know the truth. Perhaps they were every bit as scared as I was. Probably all across the city there were hundreds of people afraid at that moment because of scum like Chas and his mates. And wasn't I standing up, at least? I'd let my fear get on top of me, but not anymore. Now I was pushing back, and maybe I wasn't only doing it for myself. If I could get some dirt on Chas, enough to put him behind bars, who could say how many lives I'd be improving?

Encouraged by such thoughts, my doubts already turning to righteousness, I went into the hardware store at the end of the street. Towards the rear, I found exactly what I was looking for: a compact metal stepladder that was ideal for my purposes and within my budget, as much as I hated to spend the money given the thread my livelihood was hanging from. On the way to the counter, I noticed a tray of small metal torches in various colours, attached to karabiners, and I picked up one of those too. Finally, passing a bank of cleaning materials, I grabbed a pack of latex gloves.

I was sure, somehow, that the young woman who served me would see through what I was planning. Why else would anyone buy a stepladder, torch, and gloves except to break into their neighbour's house? But she took my crumpled twenty-pound note with blank disinterest, barely even registering my presence. Then, back in the street, I became horrified at the notion of walking all the way home bearing the tools of my prospective crime. What if somebody saw and remembered? It was ridiculous, the more so because no one so much as glanced my way, yet I couldn't shake the sensation. It transported me back to the bad old days, and the nauseating tension I'd felt when shoplifting or about to start a fight I might not win. All the time, then as now, it had seemed to me that everyone could effortlessly see the inner workings of my mind.

I did my best to push such paranoia aside. But no amount of self-control could persuade me to parade past Chas's house, ladder in hand. So I took the long route round and approached my home from the opposite direction. Despite that precaution, I was convinced through every moment that I'd run into Chas or one of his mates. Yet when I eventually got in my front door, and had it closed and against my back, I felt at the same time exhausted and exultant.

I'd taken the first step.

The exhaustion passed quickly, but the exultation lingered. Rather than let it subside, I decided I should trial my new purchase. I hauled the ladder upstairs and set it up on the landing. Sure enough, clambering into the darkness above was almost easy; not once did I believe I was about to break my neck. I sat in the opening, dangling my legs, like a naughty child claiming a high wall.

And only then, as I stared at the floorboards below and the panel I'd propped there, did it occur to me: my attic hatch had been screwed shut. What if Chas's was too? Or not *if*…of course it would be. All my planning had been for nothing. Suddenly the situation seemed too ludicrous, and I wanted to beat my head against a rafter for the sheer rage I felt at myself for throwing away twenty pounds I couldn't spare on this fool's errand.

Still, I had to check. I drew my legs up and crawled on hands and knees, finding my way with the miniature torch, conscious that one slip would send me tumbling through my ceiling – or worse, through Chas's. Even the beams didn't feel altogether sturdy, and so I kept low, striving to distribute my weight.

I was a couple of metres from the opening above Chas's landing when my fears evaporated. I could see what was blocking it: a piece of board, just as with mine, but this one was resting on the raised surround and didn't quite cover the hole; I could make out a thread of light along one edge. In fact, it was conceivable that someone might be able to see up via that gap. I shut off the torch, sweat spontaneously beading on my forehead. I'd hardly even been trying to be quiet.

The crawl back to my own side took twice as long, as I crept with painstaking caution, navigating by the crooked square of brightness that marked the way into my home. I was dizzy with relief by the time I lowered myself onto the top rung of the stepladder: relief that I'd made it back in one piece, but also that my plan survived intact. So that was it, the final piece. Now there really was nothing left to stop me.

Strangely, my recce had also left me with a sense of calm. Or perhaps it was closer to resignation: the way someone might feel knowing that the next day would bring their execution and nothing could alter that fate. I went out to the Tesco on the main street and bought a four-pack of lager, then ordered takeaway pizza – it no longer seemed so important that I couldn't afford the extravagance – and turned on the PlayStation.

Friday night was one I associated with cacophonous noise from next door, but this brought only silence. It was another reminder that I was putting a great deal of reliance on Chas having a pattern of behaviour that I had ample reason to doubt. Nevertheless, I'd know if he went out, I'd know if he took his car, and I knew that Blackpool was a couple of hours' drive away. If the time coincided with the match, it would be a safe bet as to where he was headed.

In the morning, things no longer appeared quite so clear-cut. I woke fretful, though not able to remember why at first. As I drifted towards full consciousness, the memories returned – and I fought, endeavouring to will myself back into sleep. The more I tried, the more panicked I felt, until I had no choice but to accept my helplessness. I was awake, and the day was upon me.

I flung off the bedclothes, stormed downstairs, and scrabbled through cupboards for coffee. Mug in hand, I wandered into the living room. It was just past ten o'clock. According to the Leeds United website, the match didn't begin until three, and I reasoned Chas would want to arrive well in advance of the kick-off. Following that logic, if he left the house at any time before half twelve, and if he did so by car, then I was willing to take my chances.

That gave me two hours to kill. I should have watched a film or something, but there was nothing I could settle my mind to. I flicked at magazines, not absorbing a word. I rearranged my small DVD collection. I turned the TV on, and muted the volume when I became afraid it would mask any sounds from the street. I checked the time on my phone, again and again, and when I needed to piss I sprinted upstairs, fearful that my bladder would have picked the crucial moment to distract me. The minutes ticked by, agonising.

Twelve o'clock came. Aside from the occasional bang of a door and the shuffle of feet on stairs, I'd heard nothing from next door. So that was it. He wasn't going. I dragged myself to the sofa, slumped, and gazed at the silent picture on the television – a man in a chef's outfit chattering inanely as he whipped cubes of meat about a frying pan. I watched, dead-eyed. I felt at once numb and bowed by an intolerable weight. Chas wasn't going out, and my courage wouldn't hold for another week.

Then a front door slammed. The noise jarred me to my feet. I was sure it had come from close by, but still I had to fight the urge to peek between the curtains. I hovered, uncertain – until I heard Chas's voice. There came half a dozen muffled words, an answer from farther up the street, a third voice joining those two that might have been Dougie's, and laughter. Car doors opened, one and then a second. More conversation. Engines started, grumbling, badly tuned. They pulled away. I checked the time: 12:16.

They were going to the match.

Should I wait, to be positive? Or should I hurry, while I had my chance? Yes, I'd delayed enough, and there was no way Chas would have driven off with his mates unless he intended to be gone for some time. I started towards the stairs.

At the last instant, I thought about letting somebody know.

I felt a spiteful urge to text Yasmina: *If you don't hear from me again, I hope you have a happy life*, or some drivel to that effect. More rationally, I wondered if I should set up a scheduled email to the reporter, Ford, or to PC Thornton. But I didn't entirely trust my technical skills, not when the consequences of a mistake would be so great; the last thing I needed was to inadvertently confess to breaking into someone's home.

In the end, I wrote a brief note and left it on the coffee table, secured with a scrap of Sellotape. It outlined briefly what I was going to do and why, and emphasised that if anyone was reading it, that meant something appalling had happened to me, most likely at Chas's hands. Strangely, doing so made me feel better – if only because my note seemed so absurd and melodramatic. Was what I was about to do really such a big deal? I was simply sneaking into somebody's house. It wasn't exactly normal behaviour, but nor was I plotting murder. I'd have a quick look around, and probably I'd be in and out in less than half an hour.

With that, I darted upstairs, grabbed my torch, and was up the stepladder and into the attic before I had time to formulate any more doubts. No longer worrying about being quiet, I crossed the roof space standing, a foot on each of the two central beams. I knelt and manoeuvred Chas's makeshift trapdoor aside, rousing billows of dust.

Below I could see a square of patterned brown carpet, surely three decades old at least, and the corner of a cheap set of shelves, the lacquer over the chipboard cracked and flaking. They didn't look too sturdy, but I thought they'd take my weight when it came to climbing back up, especially if I used them in conjunction with the doorframe as I had the folding chair. The only alternative was figuring out a way to haul the stepladder up after me, and who knew how long that might take? No, the bookcase would have to do. Before I could talk myself out of it, I slithered down into the gap until I was held by my elbows and forearms, then slid to hang by my fingers and dropped the remaining distance.

I landed with a thud that set my heart racing. I'd done it; I'd actually done it. Unbelievable as it seemed, I was inside Chas's house. And there could be no going back.

CHAPTER NINE

The stench had struck me even in the roof space. Now that I was down there, it was much worse. At first I couldn't get past the stink of pot, which was rampant and noxious. I was no expert, a couple of bad teenage experiences having left me siding firmly with alcohol, but I thought maybe I was smelling skunk or sinsemilla — something seriously strong. Either way, the sweet vegetable reek of it nearly knocked me from my feet.

After a few seconds, however, other odours managed to work their way through. Sweat. Old food. A hint of mildew. I tried to shut it all out, hard as that was, and to let my eyes do the work instead. Looking around, the layout was clearly identical to mine. From where I was standing below the attic hatch, the stairs descended to my left, the bathroom was ahead, the larger of the two bedrooms was to my right and the smaller was behind me. I decided to ignore the bathroom, and at the last minute changed my mind. Who knew what might be in there? It wasn't as if I was dealing with a rational human being here; for all I knew, there'd be a bag of heroin in the bath or a bloodied machete in the sink.

But as I pushed through the door, it occurred to me that I wasn't expecting to find anything. I was just being nosy; I wanted to see how someone like Chas lived. And perhaps that had been an unconscious element in this whole scheme all along: an impulse to understand the monster who'd been making my life insufferable, not to sympathise but as scaffolding to give my hatred clearer shape.

By that measure, the bathroom was a solid place to start. It was truly revolting. The shower curtain was black with mould; the toilet was crusted with shit. There was a cabinet above the sink – which was cleaner than the toilet, though only marginally – and in there were a browned toothbrush, a mostly empty tube of toothpaste, cheap plastic razors, and shaving foam.

None of that could be considered useful evidence. I was about to move on to the bedroom when it struck me that I couldn't say for certain Chas lived alone. Wasn't it possible he had a girlfriend? Or an elderly parent maybe, one deaf enough to tolerate the unbearable volumes of noise he produced? Unlikely on both counts, but nonetheless I teased the door open, sneaking a glance before I committed to putting a foot inside.

The precaution was futile, as I'd known it would be: there was no one in there, and really, I had difficulty in conceiving how anybody could live in that room.

Inside, it was even harder to separate out the smells than in the hallway. A dozen odours, all repulsive, warred for my attention. Some came from the fast-food containers scattered on the floor, many of which still contained leftovers; I could pick out stale lager too, from the many cans and bottles. A few of those had doubled as ashtrays, though there were a couple of the conventional sort also, cheap plastic dishes filled to overflowing.

The smell of cigarette smoke, however, had almost been buried beneath the stronger fetor of marijuana, and I noticed a glass bong on a set of shelves, its innards nearly as stained as the toilet had been. It shared space with a handful of books and magazines, the only element in the room that surprised me even slightly. But when I checked them, they turned out to be a mix of tatty porn mags – which I was careful not to touch – and extreme right-wing propaganda, not all of it in English and none of it giving the impression of having ever been read. There was more pornography plastered across the walls, mostly topless blondes with breasts large as their heads, and more hate paraphernalia as well – including, to my astonishment, an actual swastika flag pinned over the bed.

My god, I thought, did people really do things like that? The sight knocked the wind right out of me. Despite my intentions, a part of me did feel faintly sorry for Chas. There was something desperately lonely about that room, with its floor lined with unwashed clothes, its rancid bedding, its well-thumbed wank mags, and its unread, unreadable propaganda. It was the student flat from hell – or perhaps more like the bedroom of an abandoned child.

Then again, was my own home that much better? A little tidier maybe, a little cleaner. But I had no doubt that a stranger would react with a similar mingling of revulsion and pity if they were to look around my house. I was living better than Chas, but not by much, and I had no reason to feel sorry for him. After all, he had chosen this, where I'd only stumbled into it.

I wavered over how careful a search to make. If I was genuinely hoping to find evidence I could use against Chas, I was going to need to be thorough; on the other hand, every moment I spent in his house increased my risk of being discovered. Perhaps I'd do better to consider this a recce, to get the lay of the land? Now that I'd made my way in here, it would be easier a second time.

No – that was the fear talking. Either Chas had popped out and could be back at any minute, in which case my neck was already in the noose, or else he'd gone to the match like I thought and there was no chance he'd be back before evening. Just because I'd done this once, I had no intention of making a habit out of it.

So I started with the books, easing each ragged volume out to make sure nothing was hidden behind, taking pictures of spines with my phone camera so that I could google the titles later and get a sense of precisely what Chas was into. I picked a route between the filthy garments layering the carpet, checking beneath any that suggested they might be hiding something, finding only balled socks and grubby pants. I knelt to peek under the bed – and saw the shoebox carelessly shoved there. When I drew it out, I had half an idea of what to expect. Inside were three chocolate-coloured blocks tightly bound in plastic film, one of them open at the end, where a portion had been crumbled away.

Cannabis resin. And while I was hardly an expert, I suspected there must be a few hundred pounds' worth there. There was also a smaller piece of desiccated vegetable matter that I guessed was skunk, and a knife with a plastic grip, its serrated blade about the length of my hand. I thought for an instant of taking the box, realised immediately what a stupid plan that would be, and settled on snapping more photographs instead. Then I resealed the box and pushed it back to where I'd found it.

I'd looked everywhere I could think to look. The drugs and the knife were a decent start, though I doubted either would lead to more than a few weeks' jail time at most. I returned to the landing and stuck my head into the smaller bedroom. Like mine, it was a box room, scarcely big enough for a child. Regardless, Chas had chosen to fill the space entirely with a double mattress; it was yellowed and blotched, and I supposed that it made this the guest room.

There was nothing else in there, so I started downstairs. Even though I was sure by then that the house was empty, I couldn't help tiptoeing. The sensation as I descended was a strange one, at once exciting and somehow almost sexual, but in that ashamed way that makes your balls want to scrunch into your stomach. To be somewhere I knew I shouldn't be, doing something I knew I shouldn't be doing; there was a sour, dizzying thrill to it.

The downstairs was better than the upstairs, if only fractionally. There were more empty cans, and a tumbling stack of pizza boxes in one corner. The carpet, once green, was now mostly grey; the walls were decorated with incongruous flower-patterned paper that someone had begun to cover over in light blue paint, before giving up halfway around the room. There was a scruffy couch and an armchair, both too big for the space, but the television was what dominated: the screen must have been fifty inches. It occurred to me that there was a good chance the set was stolen, so I took a photo of the serial number on the back. Other than that, though, the room was disappointingly lacking in evidence.

I was nervous of going into the kitchen. What if someone should spy me from one of the houses opposite? But when I looked in, there was a tatty blind across the window. Peeking through, I saw that the yard was awash with yet more empty beer cans and bottles, and an uncountable number of cigarette butts; two overfull rubbish bags were crammed into the far corner. The kitchen itself, meanwhile, was every bit as revolting as the bathroom had been. The sink and work surface overflowed with greasy plates, and the smell of a blocked drain was overpowering. Out of interest, I inspected a few cupboards, and found nothing that could legitimately be described as food. The bin, however, was wedged open with takeout cartons and the black plastic trays from oven dinners, no doubt prepared in the soiled microwave on the worktop.

I returned to the living room. I'd checked everywhere. And while I'd found plenty to warrant suspicion – that Chas had a serious class B drug habit, enough so to imply he was dealing too, and that he was devoted to the worst extremes of far-right politics – I had nothing that would persuade the police he was a genuine threat, and probably nothing they didn't know about already.

Then it hit me: no, I hadn't checked everywhere. One place remained, and it was literally staring me in the face. Right in front of me was the cellar door.

I didn't want to go down there. Yet I had no reason for the violent aversion I felt, or none that made any kind of sense. In fact, there was something almost primal about my reaction. Eventually it dawned on me that part of my fear was of exploring in pitch blackness with only my small torch to aid me, and that there was every chance I wouldn't have to. Sure enough, when I hunted, there was a switch just within the doorway — and as I flicked it, the dark retreated.

Chas's light worked, which was one improvement his house had over mine. The stairs were stone, the wall naked red brick streaked with cobwebs. I could smell damp rising from below, and worse, a revolting burst-pipe stink. The light hadn't done a great deal to counter my resistance; maybe the darkness hadn't been the issue after all.

Bad things happened in cellars. Everyone who'd ever watched a horror movie knew that. And even putting that perhaps-irrational concern aside, I'd seen what a state Chas had made of the portions of the house he actually lived in. I hardly dared imagine what he'd have done with somewhere that was *supposed* to be a mess.

In another sense, though, all I was doing was convincing myself. Wasn't I looking for evidence? And now I was afraid to go down a few stairs in case I *found* something? Having come this far, I couldn't possibly give up because I was too cowardly to see my mission through. Nothing I told myself made my dread go away, but the argument was sufficient to get my feet moving. And once I'd put a couple of steps behind me, progress grew easier; past the halfway point, it actually felt less intimidating to keep going than to climb back up. All that still deterred me was the smell: it was like someone had been using the place as a toilet, and given what I'd observed elsewhere, that seemed a real possibility. Covering my mouth and nose with a sleeve, I tried my best to ignore it.

The stairwell was walled on either side, so that only when I reached the bottom could I see what I was getting myself into. One half of the space, that farthest from the stairs, was relatively uncluttered. The other, the area directly before me, had been used as a dumping ground. There was so much stuff crammed in there that it was all but impossible to catalogue: I recognised a washing machine, its door removed, an armchair leaking tumours of white wadding, a bicycle frame, crusted tins of paint, an old-style CRT television. Stacked around and amid the jumble were twenty or so cardboard boxes in various shapes and sizes.

The presence of that junk made all the more noticeable how much effort had been put into keeping the other part of the floor clear. The prospect of searching that accumulated rubbish filled me with despair, and in any case was surely pointless, so I threaded my way through the narrow pathway left open as access to the vacant portion. The unfinished ceiling was low enough that I had to duck, and made more hazardous by overhanging pipes and the occasional protruding nail. The smell grew worse with each step. The bulb was approaching the end of its life, and its mealy light only deepened the shadows.

Remembering my torch, I took it out, flicked it on, and scanned its beam about the cramped space. A muted glint caught my eye; I paused. Yes, there it was: dull metal, low against the wall. Stepping nearer, I saw that a length of chain had been bolted into the brick, its end coiled on the ground. My heart skipped a beat. Well, *that* was suspicious. Who had a chain in their cellar? Then again, on closer inspection I could see that it was far from new; many of the links were dull and scabby with rust. I was almost ready to discount it – for all I knew, every cellar on the street had a rusty old chain bolted into its wall – when the torchlight picked out another detail. Around the point where the excess chain lay in loops were dark stains upon the concrete. I saw, too, what looked like shards of glass, as though a bottle had been smashed.

At that, the fear won out. I wasn't even certain what had got to me so badly. I only knew I couldn't bear to be in that claustrophobic, stinking hole a second longer. I staggered through the breach in the piled junk and tumbled up the steps, remembering at the last moment to turn the light off after me.

Rather than wait, I kept going, dashing up the stairs to the landing. There, I stopped to get my breath – and cursed myself for forgetting to take any pictures. I considered going back, admitted that there was no way I'd ever convince myself to. No, I was getting out while I could.

I studied the bookcase. Much like the cellar, it was being used as a dumpsite for assorted crap. There were cigarette filters, cheap plastic lighters, and at least five half-empty packets of Rizlas, a tattered copy of the *Sun*, small change, a pair of headphones, phone books, assorted magazines, a pile of letters – mostly bills and junk mail – and a few odder items, such as a none-too-clean pair of Y-fronts draped over one shelf.

Nor did the bookcase look half as sturdy as it had from above. It was a cheap, flat-pack affair, and hadn't even been well put together; from in front I could see that it slanted in one direction. Still, it wasn't as if I needed the shelves to take my entire weight. I'd use the frame of the bedroom door, just as I'd planned. I cupped a hand tentatively over its edge, testing one foot on the first ledge of the bookcase. Yes, it would work. All I needed to do was get that foot up to the third, push off and—

The shelf gave way. I slid backwards and it came after me, disgorging its contents across the revolting carpet.

I stared in disbelief. Only sheer luck had prevented the shelf from dislodging the ones below, but still the carpet was strewn with scattered rubbish. In that moment I saw the sight through Chas's eyes as he came home – to this. The chaos might as well have been a smashed mirror for all the hope I felt of piecing it together. One careless mistake and I'd as good as killed myself.

Something clicked inside my mind. It was just like that: the flicking of a switch. The panic didn't go away, but it retreated, giving way to other instincts. In an instant I'd shoved the shelf back into place and was scrabbling on my knees, reclaiming a pack of cigarette papers here, a ten-pence coin that had rolled the length of the landing there.

I spent a frantic five minutes replacing the contents of the shelf and then rearranging them, again and again, desperately striving to remember where everything had been, all the while knowing that my recollections were getting more and not less muddled. In the end, I crumpled to my knees and stared, trying to think through a fog that seemed on the verge of overwhelming me.

"Calm down," I told myself out loud. "You need to calm down."

I contemplated the shelf one more time. It looked like a mess. It had looked like a mess before. It had looked like a mess because Chas didn't care; because it was where he threw things he had no need for. Hell, I'd probably paid more attention to that bookcase in the last few minutes than he had all year. I'd done the best I could. I'd have to hope it was enough.

Still, what had I been thinking? There was no chance I was getting back up that way. If I took a running jump, I might be able to boost myself against the wall and get a handhold. But what if I left a footprint on the flimsy paper, or worse, tore it? And the same went for the bookcase: if I was careful I might be able to make use of it, but the risk of inflicting further damage was too great.

No, I needed another way – and surely exiting had to be easier than entering. After all, no one designed houses not to be broken out of. The more I considered, the more that made sense. My keys were in the pocket of my jeans; I could get back into my own home the traditional way, so all I needed to do was make it outside. Indeed, if I was careful that nobody saw me, was there any reason I couldn't leave by the front door?

There was: the fact that it was locked. I'd anticipated a latch, but no such luck. I hurried into the kitchen, only to find that the back door was the same. So I'd been wrong; escaping a house was every bit as difficult as breaking in. I could feel my fortitude slipping once more. Then, just in time, I realised the door wasn't my sole option. The window would do equally as well, for unlike at the front, this one wasn't barred. I tried the handle and was almost overcome with relief when it gave.

Of course, getting the window open was barely half the battle. I still had to reach it, and there was hardly a spot around the sink not piled with plates and glasses and mugs. Ultimately I settled for clearing a small gap, enough for a foot. As much as doing so set my nerves on edge, I reasoned that no one ever memorised the arrangement of their unwashed crockery. That done, I managed to clamber up and get my other foot onto the window ledge – which, thankfully, was free of clutter.

The window would only open halfway, but that sufficed. I squeezed through and hopped down into the yard. Then I reached back and closed the pane, as well as I could from the outside – which still left it noticeably open. Yet again I'd have to rely on Chas's faulty memory, and hope he'd assume he'd left it ajar himself, or that one of his incessant guests was to blame.

Anyway, my problems weren't done. Because, crappy as Chas's security might be, he *had* taken the time to secure the gate of his yard: it was bolted, and reinforced with a padlock the size of my fist. I could climb over, but there was an obvious risk of being seen. And I didn't dare try the same with our shared fence, which was as likely to collapse entirely as it was to bear my weight.

That did give me an idea, though. I inspected the hole that had been kicked all those nights ago. Then, gritting my teeth,

I did the same to the adjoining plank. Sure enough, a length broke off with a dry crack. The resulting gap was, I thought, just barely adequate for my purposes.

Again, if I was seen, it would raise all sorts of questions I couldn't answer, but by that point I was past caring. I lay on my side and pushed my head and shoulders into the space. For a moment I had horrible visions of getting stuck, or of tearing an even larger hole. Yet somehow I scraped my way through. I lay gasping, scratched and smarting, in the muck of my backyard. Finally, I crawled to my feet and staggered to my own back door. I jabbed the key into the lock, stumbled inside, and made it as far as the living room before I collapsed onto the sofa, not caring about my dirty clothes.

I was home. I was bruised, filthy, exhausted, and ready to throw up with stress and tension, but I was in one piece. The last hour had been a nightmare, but I'd got through it.

Now all I had to worry about was what would happen when Chas got back.

CHAPTER TEN

Was I insane? Perhaps I was. This was not the behaviour of a rational person.

Not only had I broken into my neighbour's house, I'd made a suicidally lousy job of it. I'd left evidence a blind idiot could follow. One slip-up, maybe two, I might have got away with, but between the rearranged shelf, the kitchen sink, the open window, and the busted fence, it was inconceivable that Chas wouldn't notice something and get suspicious – and how much deduction did it take to trace all those clues back to me?

As I lay on the settee, staring at the ceiling, I realised: I hadn't truly believed my own theories about Chas, not until I'd seen that chain bolted into the wall. I'd been throwing accusations at him because I was angry, not because I was genuinely convinced he might be responsible. It had suited me to think that he or his mates might have been involved with the firebombing of the corner shop and the disappearance of the youth centre worker. I'd been like a kid with a jigsaw, cramming pieces in whether they fitted or not, caring more about getting the result I wanted than whether I was right.

But what if I really had been? What if Chas had had a hand in those crimes, or worse? And this was the person whose house I'd taken it upon myself to break into, leaving behind a trail that would lead him straight to me. Mentally I replayed each careless mistake, tormenting myself over every moment of stupidity.

I froze. Stupidity was the least of it. Jolting to my feet, I dashed upstairs, flung myself up the stepladder, and struggled through the attic opening. I crawled across the beams, oblivious to the threat of splinters, barely even managing not to thrust a foot through the ceiling in my haste. When I was over the hole that let onto Chas's landing, I stared for an instant; seeing the bookcase, my stomach did a horrified flip. Then, remembering what I'd come for, I scrabbled for the panel and slid it into place, careful to leave a sliver of space along one edge, just as there had been.

By the time I'd climbed back down, I was calmer – more calm than I'd been since I'd first entered Chas's house. Perhaps I'd only exhausted every drop of adrenaline in my body. At any rate, once I'd returned to the living room, I tore up the note I'd left and tossed the fragments into the bin, and my hands were steady all the while. Then I sat on the sofa again and went through the last hour in my head, piece by piece, cataloguing what I'd seen, what I'd found, and what I'd done.

Viewed like that, there was no denying that I still had far more supposition than proof. All I really knew was what I'd had good reason to suspect already: Chas was a thug with a taste for far-right politics, he had at least one weapon, and he liked to get shitfaced on cheap lager and stoned on expensive weed, which he probably paid for by dealing to friends and acquaintances. Strip all of that away and there remained the chain in the cellar, but that might have any number of explanations. By far the most plausible was that he'd been keeping a dog down there, which would certainly explain that faecal stink. No, on its own it meant nothing.

I was no further on. All I'd done, in fact, was make the situation worse. Now that I was more composed, I didn't actually believe Chas would trace the trail I'd left back to me; judging by his apparent drug and alcohol intake, it was hard to imagine he'd even notice the signs of disturbance. Nevertheless, I couldn't discount the possibility, and at best I was going to spend the next few days with it preying on my mind while I waited for the axe to fall.

Only, the next few days were the least of my worries. I still had the rest of that one to endure. I wouldn't be able to think straight until Chas got back, and until he'd had time to look around his home. If I got through that night, then maybe, just maybe, I was in the clear.

In the meantime, the waiting was intolerable. Eventually it occurred to me that I hadn't eaten all day – it was approaching four o'clock by then – and so I heated some oven chips I discovered in the bottom of the freezer. I sat propped on the arm of the settee, forcing myself to nibble at them, hungry and yet without an appetite. Would the match have finished by now? Even if it had, they weren't likely to come back immediately. There was bound to be drinking, and was it a leap of imagination to suppose that they might be football hooligans? It wasn't at all. So, drinking, fighting, perhaps a little property damage, and only after that would they drag themselves back here.

A small piece of good fortune – or just a symptom of the toll that the day's events had taken – was that by five I was beginning to get sleepy. Not in a pleasant way, though; rather, I was beset by sickly lethargy, the sort that's so difficult to pull free of, as if your brain has decided you'll sleep whether you want to or not. I fought for a while and found myself drifting, until I wasn't certain what had happened and what I'd dreamed. Had I really gone into Chas's house? Had I seen the things I recalled seeing? The memories blurred with others, with scraps of conversations, and then with nothing at all – until I registered, groggily, that night had fallen and that I'd been entirely asleep. What had woken me was shouting from the street.

No, not shouting. Chanting. Singing. They were back.

The room was dark. The only light was a sickly amber radiance oozing through the thin curtains. I checked the time on my phone – it was nearly nine – and used the glow from the screen to guide myself to the light switch. As I clicked it on, the too-bright bulb made me want to vomit; the hours of half-sleep had left me feeling grimy and ill. I heard a door open, almost drowned out by the raised voices. Inside, they were louder and yet more muffled; I traced their movement from the street to Chas's front room by the ebb and flow of sound.

On impulse, I flicked the light switch off again. The darkness felt safer. If I hadn't already given myself away, then better that they should assume I wasn't in. I stood there, head against the wall, trying to interpret the background patter and intermittent bursts of noise, to separate out which might relate to Chas. Was he going upstairs? Was he going into the kitchen? Which would he see first, the open window or the disturbed shelf? Yes, the kitchen – the voices had moved there. I followed, striving to pick out words. There was laughter, an explosion of it. One of them bellowed something, any meaning buried by sheer volume. I just needed to hear two syllables. Window. *Window.* But it was all nonsense, infuriating nonsense. They sounded like dogs yapping at each other over garden fences.

Yet I couldn't tear myself away. Back in the living room, when it became apparent that they'd settled, I slumped with my spine to the wall, cheek pressed against fraying wallpaper. Even when the music began, even though I could feel its thundering beat upon my skin, and though it drowned out all but the loudest peaks of conversation, I didn't move.

I'd been doing my level best to ignore Chas's parties. This one I was determined to experience every instant of. Because weren't tonight's festivities the perfect cover? After this, there'd be no way Chas could tell who was responsible for a few subtle changes around his tip of a home. There was a significant chance one of those charmless pricks would open the kitchen window while they smoked a fag, or that someone would stumble against the bookcase on the way to taking a piss. For that matter, if Chas was drinking, if he was on the weed, how likely was he to remember by the morning whether he'd done those things himself? No, this night would decide my fate.

So I stayed where I was. When, an hour later, the doorbell next door cut through the cacophony and more revellers barrelled in to fill Chas's living room, I stayed. When the music got even louder, smothering almost everything, I stayed. When my head began to ache, when my back grew sore, when my fingers and toes went cold and numb, I stayed. My mind wandered. At points I wasn't sure I hadn't somehow slept – the lightest sleep imaginable, more like a trance. I got hungry. I ignored it. My headache worsened. I ignored it. I was waiting for a sign – for anything.

Finally, it came.

The music dipped, to a nearly tolerable level. The front door opened and closed once more. Next came footsteps in the street; people were leaving. And those that remained were moving. I lurched to my feet, fighting pins and needles, and reeled through to the kitchen.

Yes – just as I'd suspected, the dregs of the party had shifted into the yard. I thought I could separate out five or six voices: Chas and his closest hangers-on. But I could hear them no better than before; the intervening fence and window stifled utterances, and the pulsing pain in my head didn't help. When I'd convinced myself that, with the light off and the blind down, I couldn't possibly be seen, I rooted in a drawer for paracetamol and washed a couple of tablets down with a can of shop-brand cola from the fridge. I found a packet of crisps and some biscuits and wolfed them hurriedly.

As I was about to resume my vigil, it struck me that I'd be able to hear more from upstairs. I dashed to my bedroom, grateful that the painkillers were already kicking in. As I crossed the threshold, next door's doorbell sounded again. I checked my phone; it was well past twelve. There came a brief exchange from the front of the house, and then the music was turned down further. I used the opportunity to creep on hands and knees to the window and open it a crack, fervently hoping no one in the yard chose that moment to look up. I was starting to dare believe I'd got away with what I'd done, but that didn't mean I wanted Chas to know I was spying on him.

Just as I was reaching for my quilt, thinking to curl up against the cold from the open window, I stopped, transfixed. Two people were talking over the others, and I recognised both speakers. The first, of course, was Chas. The second, the new arrival, was Pierce.

I was sure of it. I'd spoken to him for no more than a couple of minutes, but his accent was distinctive and not local. There was an edge of Cockney abruptness there, and something else I couldn't place; he'd evidently moved around a bit. Regardless, I had no doubt it was him. I noticed, as well, how he'd immediately taken over. The others, who before had been bawling incoherently, were now listening with remarkable patience to whatever he was telling them. I only wished I could hear. Presumably he and Chas were speaking from the kitchen, for their voices were muffled to incomprehensibility.

Then Pierce said something I caught plainly: he must have stepped into the yard. "Why don't you lot fuck off inside for five minutes?"

There was a chorus of muttered agreement and the rumble of booted feet. Who was Pierce, I wondered, that he got to talk to Chas's mates this way? And I remembered, too, the dressing-down he'd given Dougie and his companion that night in the street.

The back door slammed shut. Now it was just Chas and Pierce out there in the yard. Chas mumbled a short phrase, the words distorted more by inebriation than distance, and Pierce responded. Apart from his order, it was the first sentence I'd heard distinctly – and it paralysed me.

"You need to have a word with that arsehole next door."

Though he was speaking quietly, his voice carried. Here I was, the arsehole in question, overhearing while my heart hammered iced water around numbed muscles.

Chas said something, and Pierce spoke again, his voice lower. I couldn't catch it all this time, but one word I made out clearly. *Police.*

I tried to piece the fragmentary sentence together. Yet the writhing in the pit of my stomach made me certain of what he'd said. *He's been talking to the police.* The more I played it over in my mind, the less doubt I felt. *He's been talking to the police.* Not at all what I'd been dreading all those hours, and every bit as bad as my worst fears.

Pierce was still speaking; his voice had sunk even further. Twice Chas put in comments, and once he laughed – nervously, I thought – but I couldn't get any sense of the conversation. Then, abruptly back at his normal volume, Pierce said, "So, we all good? You're not going to be a wanker about it?"

Chas laughed again, and this time it was a happy, drunken burble, as at a shared joke. I heard the back door open once more, followed by footsteps as they went inside.

Half an hour later, the last of Chas's mates headed off. A minute or two after that and the kitchen light blinked out, bathing the yard in darkness. I could just follow the erratic thump of Chas's feet as he climbed the stairs, as he tramped into his foul pit of a bedroom.

The time wasn't much past one. This was going to be an early night by his standards.

I wished I could say the same.

Sleep was an impossibility. All that my head contained,

reverberating like a rubber ball in a sealed room, was Pierce's words: *You need to have a word with that arsehole next door.* Whenever that hushed for even an instant, my mind went back to translating the second sentence, the one I was less sure of. *He's been talking to the police.* Could I have imagined it, or got it only partly right? Perhaps Pierce had suggested I might be thinking of reporting Chas to the police. Conceivably he'd happened to be passing that day, and had seen them arrive or leave and not been fooled by their plain clothes.

No, that was beyond unlikely. And I was reasonably confident of what I'd heard. So what did it mean? Obviously Pierce knew Chas, knew Chas's hooligan mates. But he also had access to information that nobody except the police should have.

My first conjectures were sheer paranoia, mad theories of a conspiracy that took in thugs and coppers both. Or perhaps Thornton and Sane hadn't been police officers at all; really, they could have been anyone. Yet as I began to calm down, I saw how ridiculous that was. Whatever I was dealing with here, it wasn't some scheme concocted by malevolent geniuses. The obvious explanation, maybe the only possible one, was bound to be the truth – and it was that Pierce had connections on the force.

Could he be an ex-cop, now hanging around with exactly the sorts he'd been supposed to protect against? Perhaps he'd been bent all along, and having got out, considered himself free to exploit the contacts he'd made. Whatever the case, it explained why Dougie and his friend had been so respectful. A tough-as-nails ex-copper, still with solid contacts ready to feed him information: if your hobbies included assaulting strangers and firebombing corner shops, then that was a useful man to know.

It was certainly a more rational theory, and also accounted for why Pierce would have stepped in to protect Yasmina and me. Except, why would he have gone to the effort of defending us, and of warning me, only to make trouble now? That part didn't make any sense.

No. It *did* make sense.

Because he had told me not to do something and I'd done it anyway. It made sense if Pierce was punishing me.

Yes. Pierce had somehow found out that I'd gone to the police, and that had pissed him off, because he wasn't the kind of man who expected to be disobeyed. At the time I'd thought that the fear and adrenaline were what had made me so dislike him, that maybe I wouldn't have trusted anyone just then. Looking back, though, there had been something genuinely bullying in Pierce's solicitousness. It didn't take much imagination to believe a man like that might mess with someone to prove a point. And the notion terrified me; such harassment was personal in a way that the threat I'd felt from Chas, or even from his pals in the street that night, had never been. Chas hadn't been consciously screwing with me, but Pierce – I was on his radar now.

The prospect was the sole thing I could think about as I lay there. I'd been worrying over the act of craziness I'd committed, the clues I might have left, and all the while my call to the cops had been what had tripped me up – just like everyone had tried to warn me it would.

*   *   *

I must have slept at some point, though I remember watching the sky begin to lighten through a crack in the curtains. But I must have, because I was jolted awake by the ringing of my doorbell.

The sound was more shocking for the fact that the bell was used so rarely; I'd almost forgotten I had one, and there came at first a moment of disconnect, *I wonder whose that is*, which made the final recognition all the worse.

It was mine. And I knew whose finger was on the button.

My initial instinct was to ignore him. Aside from my car parked outside, what proof did he have that I was in? Only, all I'd be doing would be putting off the inevitable – and giving myself one more thing to live in fear of. Anyway, the noise was lacerating my brain; the bell was ringing and ringing, and who could say how long he'd keep it up for?

I rolled out of bed, glanced around for some clothes, and realised I'd slept in my jeans and T-shirt. As I staggered downstairs, I pondered distantly if I should hunt for a means to protect myself – a kitchen knife maybe. But I'd read that, unless you knew what you were doing, arming yourself was the absolute last course to take in a hostile situation. At best I'd be facing charges for going overboard in my self-defence; at worst I'd end up giving Chas a weapon to use on me.

At any rate, by the time I'd reached the bottom, I felt the decision had been taken from my hands. I'd made enough of a racket as I tumbled down the stairs that Chas was sure to have heard, and probably he'd also seen me through the frosted-glass pane in my front door.

As if as proof, the bell clattered once more, and kept up an insistent, waspish drone. I steeled myself, so much as I could, and opened the door.

There was Chas on my step, looking impatient, poised to press the button yet again. "Hello, mate." He shifted awkwardly. "I'm Chas. I'm your neighbour."

I was aware of my mouth opening and closing uselessly, and I hadn't a clue how to stop it. I wanted to say, *I know who you are.* On the heels of that thought came, *I know why you're here.* And then – fear, fear that urged me to shrink into a ball or somehow try to hide. But I could see from his expression that with each passing instant I was only making matters worse; I could see I was just pissing him off.

"I'm Ollie," I managed, in a croak that sounded nothing like my usual voice.

"Yeah," he said. "I heard that. Ollie." He scratched idly with a blackened fingernail at a spot on the side of his nose. "Heard something else too. You had some bother with a couple of my lads. Dougie and Rick." He gave the spot another vigorous scratch, and this time drew blood. Inspecting the finger without interest, he wiped it on his tracksuit bottoms. "Pair of twats."

"It's not a big deal," I said. "Just a misunderstanding. I'd pretty much forgotten about it." I was babbling, my voice a full register higher than it would normally be, and so I shut up.

"Yeah?" Chas nodded. I couldn't help but stare at the thin trickle of blood and pus now leaking around the rim of his nostril. "Okay then."

"Well," I said. "Thanks for coming over, though. I mean...." The sentence petered out. I didn't know *what* I meant.

"No bother," Chas said. "No one wants trouble. Do they?" He considered, head aslant, as if he'd raised some philosophical conundrum. Perhaps he was questioning the validity of his own statement; for wasn't he living proof that there were people who did, in fact, want trouble – so long as it was happening to others?

With the back of his hand, he smeared a greasy stripe of yellow-red from his lip to his cheek. "Just leads to more trouble," he decided. "So, you have any more problems, right? You come talk to me." He leaned in closer. The smell of pot that rose off his skin and clothes was at once nauseating and intoxicating. "You get me?"

Absurdly, I almost wanted to laugh at him – at his sheer lack of subtlety. Even with his face up close to mine, a part of me wanted to laugh. In that moment, I wasn't afraid of him. In that moment, the memory of his home was clear in my mind – his pathetic, filthy, lonely little home – and he wasn't frightening but funny.

"I get you," I said.

"Yeah. Good." Chas turned away with no goodbye, as though in that same instant he'd utterly forgotten my existence.

Seconds later and he was back inside his own house and the door was slamming behind him, more loudly than could possibly be necessary.

I stood in my doorway, staring across the street. I had no idea what to think or feel. There had been something childish about the entire scene, something in Chas's behaviour that echoed the kid tapping at a neighbour's door: *Can I have my ball back, mister?* I realised: Pierce had told him to come and so he'd come.

Pierce. Pierce, who knew I'd spoken to the police. Pierce, who knew I'd gone behind his back. Pierce, who had just sent me a warning.

Finally I found the strength to shut the door. Because suddenly I understood what my next move should be, and who I had to talk to.

CHAPTER ELEVEN

Somehow, I all but succeeded in putting the whole business out of my mind throughout the rest of the Sunday. I was too tired to think, too tired to worry. I'd made my decision and it seemed straightforward. What had Thornton said? *If you have any questions or concerns.* Well, I had plenty of both. *Here's a concern for you, officer: how the hell does my neighbour know that I nearly pressed assault charges against his mates?*

All right, I hadn't heard Pierce speak those precise words. If the lone piece of evidence I'd had was that barely overheard sentence, I could perhaps have dismissed my misgivings. Except, wasn't it funny how Pierce had let so many days go by without saying anything to Chas? And how only after I'd involved the police had he felt the need to suggest that Chas might want to have a reassuring word with me – a reassuring word that could easily be mistaken for a threat?

No, I'd made my decision. The way I saw it, the police owed me one, and Thornton was my best bet for collecting. And since I could barely think straight through the tiredness anyway, and yet was too wired to go back to bed, it was easy not to analyse my resolution. I played video games, watched a movie, wandered out early in the afternoon to buy food, and then resumed doing not much of anything. By nine I was quite ready to crawl into bed.

I woke in the depths of the night, sweat dripping from my brow, hardly able to draw breath for the dread closing my throat. I sensed more than remembered the nightmare I'd crawled out from under – or rather, the anxiety dream, for I knew without recalling the details exactly what it had been about. A worry I'd managed to push out of my conscious mind, to distract myself from with the greater trauma of Chas and my near-disastrous excursion into his home. My interview. The meeting with Painter. And the matter of whether I'd still have a job by the end of the day.

I'd given it so little thought that I hadn't even set an alarm. To be on the safe side, I arranged three in close succession on my phone, and then got up to make myself a drink. Maybe, I told myself as I sat perched on the end of the bed sipping tea, I was finally losing my grip. Maybe I was having a breakdown. I should have spent the weekend coming up with a strategy, planning answers for the questions I'd known were coming. I should have found somewhere else to be, so that at least I could have got a couple of adequate nights' sleep and eaten some sensible meals. I couldn't possibly have been less prepared.

But four in the morning wasn't the time to do anything about that fact. All I had left was to make the best of my predicament and face the consequences. I even felt a numbed sort of acceptance. And somehow, that and the tea together were enough to usher me back into sleep – albeit fitful, miserable sleep.

As such, the insistent beeping of my phone alarm, when eventually it came, was almost a relief. I rubbed the grit from my eyes, stared for a moment at the drab light filtering between the curtains, and lurched through to the bathroom. I wasn't certain of the last time I'd had a proper wash, so I ran a bath and, while the tub was filling, shaved.

The bath made me feel a little better, a little more normal. Afterwards I wondered what I should wear. What message did I mean to send? Should I go in as though I was expecting to teach? But if Painter had considered that a possibility, she wouldn't have scheduled our meeting over one of my classes. In the end,

I settled for a suit; smartness seemed politic. I just wished I had a decent shirt to go with it. I picked out my best and spent a good fifteen minutes trying to iron the rumpled fabric, a process that only appeared to introduce fresh creases. I worried over which tie to wear and opted for something plain. When I looked at myself in the mirror, the effect was of someone who'd scarcely slept in days wearing a cheap supermarket suit. If the call had been mine to make, I'd probably have fired myself.

Nevertheless, I was as ready as I was going to get, and it wasn't yet ten. I wouldn't need half an hour to drive to the school. Even taking into account the fact that I should aim to arrive early, I still had time to kill.

Then I recalled the day's other crisis-in-waiting; it was as though my brain refused to cope with more than one dilemma at once. I rooted around for a whole minute in my pockets, steadily growing more frantic, until I remembered that for the first time in days I'd changed my clothes and that I'd been wearing my jeans when I talked to the police. I dashed to my pile of dirty laundry, and sure enough, Thornton's card was there in the pocket. I read it over, asking myself if I dared go through with what I'd planned. Then again, after yesterday, was that even a question? Clearly I was past the point of worrying what I did or didn't have the courage to do – or how deep a hole I was willing to dig before I flung myself in.

So I dialled Thornton's number. It rang and rang, and I was convinced that it was about to cut off when a crisp female voice said, "PC Thornton."

She sounded different on the phone – more intimidating. I came close to hanging up. "Hello," I said, fighting the quaver in my own voice, "this is Ollie. Ollie Clay. You interviewed me and, um, you gave me your card."

"Oh. Yes. Mr. Clay, how can I help?"

"There's something I'd like to discuss with you," I said,

striving to seem normal and not as if I was some crazy.

"I'm off duty today," Thornton said. "But if you're able to go into the station, I can arrange for someone else to—"

"I'd like to talk to *you*."

"Well," she said, her voice now distinctly colder, "as I say, I'm off duty today, so—"

"I'd like you to tell me," I cut in again, "how my neighbour could have found out that I'd talked to the police."

A drawn-out pause. I was sure she must be about to cancel the call or tell me to stop wasting her personal time. I braced myself. Then she said, "Are you going to be near the centre of town? I might be able to meet with you for a few minutes."

"I could be," I said. "I mean, yes, absolutely. I've got an appointment in an hour; I'm free after that."

"Do you know a cafe called Lucio's? On Greek Street?"

"I can find it."

"I'll be there at one."

"Okay. Great. Look, I really—"

"Goodbye, Mr. Clay," Thornton said, and the line went dead.

Well, that was one problem down – or else one problem created. At any rate, the deed was done. If I was honest with myself, it was more of a result than I'd expected, and an outcome I wasn't certain how to rationalise. All right, I had my reasons for being frustrated with the police, but I could hardly hold Thornton personally responsible. On the other hand, logic dictated that if someone truly had talked to Pierce, the leak had begun with either her or – what had his name been? – with Sane. At the time I'd felt less trust towards Sane, who'd seemed more concerned with deterring me than helping; yet he wasn't the one willing to meet me on his day off. Why would Thornton go out of her way for me? For a moment, my paranoia surged again. Maybe this wasn't about her being prepared to help. Maybe it was about ensuring I kept my mouth shut.

However, even at my most sceptical, I had trouble making that one stick. Perhaps it was just that I desperately wanted to put my faith in someone; perhaps I simply didn't have the time to wind myself up over another unsubstantiated worry. Already my mind was teetering back towards the clear and present danger of my interview with Painter, the puzzle of Thornton's motives fading into the background.

It was still a little early to be setting off, but I couldn't bear to stand around getting more and more worked up. I hurried out, and had the car open before I realised I'd left the front door ajar. I dashed back to lock it, and then slipped in behind the wheel and nearly clipped the vehicle in front of mine as I pulled away from the curb. Slamming on the brake, I sat there, gripping the wheel with whitening fingers, willing myself to calm down. I'd never knowingly had a panic attack, but I sensed that was what I was on the verge of – if it wasn't happening already.

"Get it together," I told myself out loud. "Get it the fuck together."

I was parked across the middle of the road. If another car had appeared, if someone had honked their horn at me, that would have been it: I'd have tried to punch my way through their windscreen, or else collapsed in a sobbing heap. But no one came. A minute passed, and another, and by then I had enough control back to restart the engine and reach the end of the street.

Driving was soothing; doing something so undemanding and mechanical let instinct override the thinking parts of my brain. By the third corner, I felt I had myself in hand. Maybe this was how I'd get through the day: road by road, step by step, not even trying to contemplate what came next. Because hadn't that always been the problem? I'd spent weeks agonising over what might happen, what the next catastrophe would be, and not one moment of that fretting had stopped my world from crumbling around me.

The traffic was light; I'd missed the morning rush. In the end, I got to the school a whole quarter of an hour early. It was strange to be back there. Though I'd only been away a matter of days, the absence felt like a lifetime. There was a part of me that would have been happy never to have returned; was that why I'd somehow managed to forget about this interrogation until it was almost too late? Gazing over the ugly, prefabricated buildings and the litter-strewn playground, I could easily believe it.

I considered lingering for a few minutes and arriving dead on time, but it never did to loiter outside schools, and in any case, that probably wasn't the attitude I should be trying to present. No, I was better off working the desperation angle, the *See how badly I need this job* angle. Frankly, given what a subpar teacher I'd become, that was about the one argument I had left.

As it turned out, however, when I got to Painter's office and told her secretary who I was, she asked me to wait – and when the clock on the wall behind her read eleven, I was still waiting. So far as I could tell, the secretary hadn't even communicated to Painter that I'd arrived. Were they screwing with me? Was this Painter showing me who was in control? As though I didn't already know that; as though there could be any question.

It was ten past eleven when Painter's secretary glanced up and told me, "You can go in now, Mr. Clay." I couldn't guess what secret signal had furnished her with this information. I felt a brief, bitter surge of resentment as I stood up, but before I reached Painter's door it had dissolved. I had to remember that I didn't get to be angry. This was Painter's show, and the most I was allowed was to play along.

She looked up as I entered. Today she had her silvery hair gathered in a tight bun, and she wore a metallic grey suit – no doubt vastly more expensive than mine – that complemented its shade perfectly. She exuded authority, just as I was surely giving off the scent of raw, shambling defeat.

"Thank you for coming in, Ollie," she said, as if this was an interview for a job instead of a conversation to decide whether I still had one.

Was that a good or a bad sign? But if I read into every word Painter spoke, I'd do nothing except tie myself in knots. "It's good to be back," I replied, hoping I'd struck the correct balance between contrition and hopeful eagerness.

"How have you been?" Painter asked, with a fair approximation of genuine concern.

Realising she was expecting me to do so, I took the seat before her desk. "Yeah. Not bad." I felt as though something more was needed; *not bad* did not explain why I looked like such a walking train wreck. So I added, "A little stressed, you know." I tried for a nervous laugh, which came out choked.

"Well then, let's get straight to it," Painter said. "You should know that we found the girl who was involved in the incident. Mrs. Bonham identified her from the state of her clothing. Her name is Lindsey McDermott."

"Is she all right?" I wondered, with what I thought was about as good an impression of interest as Painter herself had managed.

"She was shaken. She hasn't been very forthcoming, but we don't believe that anything seriously untoward happened."

It took me a second to grasp what Painter was implying. The girl hadn't been raped. It had never occurred to me that she had – I'd assumed she'd fled when things had begun to get out of control – but for Painter, the possibility must have been a serious worry. Any disturbance that brought the police into the school did nothing to aid its already dubious reputation.

"I'm glad she's okay," I said.

"Yes." Painter considered me carefully, slate-grey eyes boring into mine. "And Liam Sutcliffe hasn't come forward to make a complaint."

Again, the likelihood had barely crossed my mind. Admitting

he'd been in that corridor for me to pin against a wall meant explaining why he'd been there at all, and after that it would have been his word versus mine and the girl's. Anyway, knowing Sutcliffe's extracurricular activities, he'd doubtless prefer to deal with our disagreement in a more personal manner: maybe by waiting for me with a baseball bat one dark winter's night.

"So the good news," Painter said, "is that we shouldn't need to take the matter any further."

The good news? In that moment, I'd have clamped my hands around her jaws if it would only have stopped her from speaking.

"The bad news, Ollie, is that I don't think we're going to be able to keep you on. At this stage, it would be difficult for me to even give you a positive reference. I can see you're going through some challenges right now...."

"You don't know the half of it," I said. I wanted to spit at her, but the words sounded pathetic as they spilled from my mouth.

"No, I'm sure I don't. Nonetheless, the fact remains that you are not my, nor this school's, responsibility. You aren't a permanent member of my staff. Having said that, if you'd come to me with your problems before this escalated to the extent that you were behaving violently towards students then—"

"Not students," I said. "Liam Sutcliffe. A nasty little sociopath who shouldn't even be—"

"I'm afraid that's just it," Painter interrupted in turn – and her voice was like a sheet of steel descending between us. "That you've arrived at this point, where you think that it actually matters which student it is you're threatening in the corridors of a school. If you'd come to me before you reached that point, then perhaps we might be having a different conversation."

And I had no answer to that. Intellectually I understood what she was saying; emotionally I had no doubt in my mind that she was wrong. Nothing I could have done to Sutcliffe would have crossed a moral line, because people like him had no such line.

He would hurt anyone, for any reason, and never feel an instant of remorse. As far as I was concerned, that excluded him from all recourse to social decency.

I stood up. "Well," I said.

"Your outstanding pay will be settled at the end of the month." Painter offered me her hand. "The best of luck, Mr. Clay."

I considered the hand as if it were a cobra waiting to strike. Then I turned and walked out of her office.

★　　★　　★

It was everything I could do to find my way through the once-familiar corridors of the school. I felt that they were all identical, that they'd become a maze set to trap me. But eventually I stumbled upon an entrance, though not the one I'd come in by. I wandered around the outside of the building, moving on autopilot.

As I happened to glance in through a window, I saw him. For an instant I was surprised, and then it seemed inevitable. Perhaps he sensed my gaze, because Liam Sutcliffe looked round, and even at a distance I could see the deadness in those dark eyes, as though something inhuman and cold-blooded sheltered behind them.

I could find you, I thought. *I could cut your throat and drop your body in a ditch, and not one person anywhere would care.* As much as the idea horrified me, there was a sort of comfort to the raw hatred surging in my veins. It was the knowledge that I'd never do such a thing and that I could, and the way those convictions balanced each other like kids on a seesaw. Rationally I knew that I'd never see Liam Sutcliffe again. Irrationally I knew I could if I wanted to. And that awareness made me want to smile, so I smiled at him, and all of what I was thinking and feeling must have been in my face for that fraction of a second — because

Sutcliffe's eyes grew wide and he quickly looked away.

A reaction. I'd got a reaction from the evil little shit. It was a tiny, meaningless victory that didn't go one iota of the way towards redressing the day's defeats, but a victory all the same.

I rounded the next corner and there was the car park. By the time I got to my car, however, my hands were shaking. I opened the door, got in, grasped the wheel, and my fingers juddered visibly against the plastic. I sat there for a full five minutes, certain the tremors would pass, that at any moment they'd pass – but they didn't. I got out, locked the door, and checked my phone. It was barely half past eleven. I could walk into the city centre and still make my appointment with Thornton.

The walking helped; enough to distract me from whatever seismic processes were going on within my head, the aftershocks of which were grounding in my fingers. I wasn't thinking anything very much, but I could tell that on some level I was reacting – even if that reaction looked a lot like shutting down completely. I was sufficiently detached that it all seemed almost interesting, as if I was observing with curiosity as these malfunctions occurred in someone else's brain.

After a couple of miles, I passed a pub, so I went in, bought a double vodka, and drained it in one go. The landlord watched me with vague distrust. Outside once more, suddenly concerned that Thornton would smell the alcohol on my breath, I bought mints from a corner shop. I'd emptied the entire packet by the time I reached Greek Street. Lucio's, when I found it, was small enough that I could see all the tables inside through the window, and though I wasn't sure I'd recognise Thornton out of uniform, no one in there could possibly have been her.

Then again, when I checked my phone, it wasn't quite ten to. Not wanting to sit alone, I settled for waiting outside, trying not to appear as if I was loitering.

Fortunately, Thornton arrived early too – though from the

direction I wasn't looking, so that I started when behind me she said, "Mr. Clay."

She was wearing jeans with a dark blue sleeveless top, and her hair was down; I remembered that it had been tied back when she was in uniform. She was wearing very little makeup, and its absence suited her: she had that just-out-of-the-gym air that seems to come naturally to some people, like a faint inner glow, and although I didn't find her particularly attractive, that alone was appealing.

"Ollie," I said, "please."

"Shall we go inside?"

I nodded, and followed her through the door. "What can I get you?" I asked – recalling as I spoke that I was down to my last twenty and practically at the limit of my overdraft.

"A latte, please," Thornton said, sliding in beside a small table against the wall.

At the counter I ordered the latte, pondered getting just a glass of water for myself, realised how that would look, and finally requested an Americano, the cheapest item on the menu. I carried the drinks over, placed them on the table, and sat opposite Thornton. "Thanks for taking the time to talk to me."

"I only have a few minutes," she said, sipping foam from her coffee.

"Okay. Sure."

"And I'd like to get to the bottom of what you said on the phone. That your neighbour knew you'd spoken to us."

"So would I," I agreed.

"The probable explanation is that he saw us come to the door and assumed—"

"No," I cut her off. "It wasn't that. Someone told him. A man named Pierce." Thornton froze, lips parted – and it struck me that I'd just contradicted a police officer to her face. I should have apologised; instead I pressed on. "I told you about him.

The man who stopped them, Dougie and the other one, in the street that night."

"Yes, I remember." There was a note to Thornton's voice, but I wasn't certain it was anger – and it had vanished when she spoke again. "Did you actually, specifically, hear this man Pierce say that he had knowledge of your having spoken to the police?"

I tried to recollect, or rather to separate out the actual memory from the scaffold of fears and fantasies I'd constructed. "I don't think that's how he put it."

Thornton tore the corner from a sachet of brown sugar, spilled the contents into her cup and stirred it, then watched the resulting whirlpool thoughtfully. "Mightn't this Pierce have been trying to protect you?" she asked, eyes still on her cup rather than me.

"He's got a funny way of going about it."

"What I mean is, was it possible that all he was doing was advising Mr. Walker—"

"Wait," I said, "who?"

For the barest instant, she looked confused. Then she said, "Your neighbour. Charlie Walker."

Of course. I'd even seen the name on Chas's mail, though I'd barely registered it at the time. But thinking about that was a reminder of what I'd done, what Thornton mustn't know I'd done, and suddenly I felt as if my face was flushed, that I was sweating, that half a dozen symptoms were announcing my guilt in ways any cop was sure to recognise. In the dim hope of distracting her, I mumbled, "Sorry...I interrupted you."

Thornton hesitated, retracing the thread of her thoughts. "What I was saying was, is it possible this Pierce was only advising Mr. Walker that he should come over and talk to you, to try and make things right?"

Strange that the possibility hadn't even occurred to me. "Yeah," I said, "I suppose it's possible."

"Is it likely?"

I considered. "I think it's likely that it was both. I mean, whatever Pierce had in mind, I still think Chas meant to threaten me."

"And did he? Did he specifically threaten you?"

Had he? I couldn't remember, only that I'd *felt* threatened. Everything that I'd been so convinced of was starting to slip away, evaporating under the glare of Thornton's rationality. And a part of me would have been glad to believe her: that Pierce wasn't gunning for me, that Chas hadn't come to my door to warn me off, that maybe all of this was like a scab that, if I once stopped picking, would heal of its own accord.

Yet I'd already tried accepting that, and the effort hadn't made it any truer. Every time I'd turned my back on the situation it had grown worse, and now I had no job and no girlfriend. If I dared to disregard Chas and his circle of hooligans again, what did I have left to lose? My sanity? My life?

"What if I had actual evidence?" I said. "That he was a criminal? What if I had something concrete?"

"Then I'd tell you to take that evidence into the station." Thornton sipped from her coffee and observed me steadily. "Why, do you?"

My initial impulse was to lie. Perhaps that was because, for the first time, she seemed to be paying me genuine attention. But which lie to tell? Should I claim I knew more than I did? Should I downplay my theories, lest she suspect what I'd done? With either option as bad as the other, I fell back helplessly on a version of the truth: "I know for a fact that he has a serious drug habit, and I'm pretty certain he's dealing." There were any number of ways I could have found that out that didn't involve breaking into his home. "I have… well, strong suspicions about some other things. Things that maybe I could prove."

"If you have evidence, then it could potentially be an offence to not bring it to the attention of the police," Thornton said.

"It's not that I do. Just that…I've good reason to think it exists. And if, somehow, I did get it, I'd want to know…." But what exactly was I asking her for? I hardly understood myself. "I'd want to know there was someone I could trust," I tried.

Thornton looked uncomfortable. She had a great deal of self-control, I realised, more than most people, and I felt almost guilty that I'd managed to dint it. "Ollie," she said, "the reason I met with you like this – which, I'm sure you appreciate, isn't something I'd normally do, or even should have done – is that I wanted to tell you that you're dealing with some dangerous people. It's clear you're under a lot of stress. And in situations like yours, sometimes bad decisions get made. In a completely unofficial capacity, I'm advising you that you should back away from this."

I did my best to hold her gaze – and couldn't. "I get that you're trying to help me," I said, "but I think I'm past that point. I have no one to turn to. I've nowhere to go. I…shit, I wasn't going to say anything, but I lost my job today. Because of Chas. Because of all this. Because I can't deal with it. It's all just getting worse and worse, and I can't stop it. So I guess what I'm saying is, I can't back away because I've nowhere to back away *to*."

I was close to tears. Not dignified, manly tears either; I felt as if acid was burning its way up through my throat, was seeping into my skull, and at any moment was about to erupt from my eyes. I didn't want to break down in front of Thornton. She'd come here to do me a favour, and I found her attractive enough that some sad part of me was desperate to salvage a good impression – but mostly, I felt I'd already humiliated myself sufficiently for one day. I stared at the Formica tabletop and willed down that threatening geyser of emotion.

When I looked up again, Thornton had a sleeve peeled to consider her wristwatch. "I need to be going," she said.

My heart sank. So there it was. I'd blown my last chance.

Thornton got to her feet. "But you've got my number," she told me. "Take care, Ollie."

"Goodbye," I said. "And thank you."

I didn't watch her leave. I stayed and drank my Americano. It had, after all, been one more stepping-stone towards my total bankruptcy. And even once the coffee was finished, I still sat there, empty cups on the table before me, staring out the nearby window at the passing human traffic.

I felt numbed and giddy at the same time, tired out and wired. I was certain that something significant had happened, yet I couldn't quite get the memory to play out right in my mind.

Had Thornton really meant what I'd thought she meant? And if she had, what happened next?

CHAPTER TWELVE

By the time I left the cafe, I'd made my decision.

Thornton might be a long shot, but she was all I had. I had a feeling I could trust her; that if push came to shove, she wouldn't let me down. Perhaps that was stupid. Perhaps I was building our brief conversation, and particularly her final comment, into something other than what it had been. But the more I went over it, the more I assured myself that there had been hints I'd originally missed.

The first, the biggest, was that she'd met me at all. Despite what she'd said, she'd had no reason to do that. So maybe she was a crusader. Maybe she had a grudge against Chas, or Pierce, or another of that cluster of thugs. Who knew, maybe she just liked my face. In the end, her motives hardly mattered. She had tacitly agreed that I could contact her again, and I didn't need to know her reasons. What mattered was that, if I could unearth some solid evidence, I wouldn't have to formally approach the police with it, and risk questions I had no hope of answering or even word once more reaching Pierce.

So I'd go back into Chas's house. I'd find something. I would have a proper search in that cellar, a proper look at that chain that had freaked me out so badly, and if it was all innocent, then at least there were the drugs. A sample, a couple of photos – that might be enough to edge Thornton into calling a raid, or whatever the police did in these situations. I didn't want to think the scenario through too hard; it felt like the right thing, the only thing, to do.

And this time there wouldn't be any foolish mistakes. I definitely wasn't going to be climbing out of any more windows. Since I was already in the city centre, I took the opportunity to have a hunt around for the one item of equipment I knew I'd need: a length of rope.

Within half an hour, I'd discovered that the purchase was going to be more difficult than I'd have guessed, cheap rope not being in particularly high demand in the twenty-first century. And after an hour of fruitless searching, I was close to giving up. Then I stumbled across an independent hardware store, not altogether different from the one near my house. Just within the door, they had what they'd billed as old-fashioned washing lines. They could call them what they liked; as far as I was concerned, they were selling ten metres of rope for under a fiver.

Only once that was done did I remember I'd left my car at the school. I wanted desperately to get a taxi back, but if I did, then it was hard to say when I'd be able to afford to eat again. I supposed I was going to have to sign on for benefits; in the interim, I'd need to get by with what little I had. So, on foot, I retraced my route from earlier in the day. It came as no surprise when, a few minutes in, rain began to fall. It seemed, in fact, entirely appropriate.

Fortunately, I arrived in time to miss the kids leaving and not so late that the gates were locked, though my car was almost the last one left. I took a final look at Lawn Hill School and vaguely wanted to smash a window, as if I were a pupil who'd been expelled and not a teacher. Instead, I got into my car and drove home through the increasingly foul weather.

The remainder of the afternoon and evening passed in a blur. I was beyond the point of reflection or emotion, and I even managed to sleep that night, a black, numbed torpor that left me no less tired when I woke the next morning.

The prospect of having to wait until the next time I could

be certain Chas was out of the house was like a weight around my neck. It might be Saturday, but what if it was in two weeks, or three? Even getting by until the weekend seemed an impossibility.

I muddled through to the late afternoon by milling about the house, starting small projects and then abandoning them, generally without noticing I'd done either. The only job I succeeded in settling on was preparing my makeshift rope: I spent ten minutes making knots big as my fist at half-metre intervals, so that I'd stand a decent chance of climbing back up. Once I'd finished, I tied one end to the back door's handle and pulled with all my strength, until I was leaning halfway to the ground. My rope held just fine; it was sturdy stuff. Then I thought that I should hide it. If someone came round and happened to see, what would they think? Only, I didn't much care, and no one was likely to visit anyway. Nevertheless, in the end I spooled the clothesline and bundled it beneath the sink.

After that, I felt even more aimless than before. I wanted badly to talk to Yasmina, more than I had at any point since we'd last spoken. How long had it been now? I couldn't concentrate to count the days, except that I knew our two-week break was nowhere near up. Not that she'd explicitly said we couldn't speak in the meantime, but the thought of her not answering, or worse, answering and being angry, was enough to deter me. In any case, she would be working, I realised; already the notion that other people had jobs to be at and I didn't was beginning to seem unreal.

Then I recalled someone else I hadn't spoken to in a while. My mum. And there'd been a good reason, too, one of the classics: for of course it had been money we'd fallen out over. Or maybe not fallen out, as such; there'd been no cross words spoken on either side. Still, I knew she was angry with me for keeping the whole of the inheritance. And I was angry that she was angry. She had ample money these days; she hardly needed any more. What would she have spent it on? A world cruise? Another extension? I'd put a roof over my head when I desperately needed one, and she had no right to resent that.

Then again, the fact that I'd got it so badly wrong only made matters worse. And suddenly, urgently, I really did want to speak to her. I dialled before I could second-guess the impulse. The line rang and rang – and went to voicemail. There followed a brief message in my stepdad Alan's voice, which I knew by heart because they hadn't changed it since the wedding nearly a decade ago.

So that was that. There'd be no reconciliations today, no apologies, no ambiguous attempts to say goodbye in case something went awfully wrong. But just as I was putting my phone back into my pocket, I decided I might as well give it one more try – and this time, it picked up on the fourth ring.

"Hi? Mum?"

A pause. "Oliver?"

"Yeah, it's me."

"Oh." Another, longer pause. "Oliver, I'm a little busy right now. Did you ring a minute ago? I'm packing, and there's no phone in the bedroom."

"Okay," I replied, more irritated than anything she'd said could possibly warrant. "Maybe some other time, then."

My mother wasn't listening. "Hold on," she said, and again, "hold on." I heard her shout, the words muffled by her hand cupped over the receiver. "It's fine," she said, the hand removed, "it's just that we're getting ready to go away. To Gran Canaria. I'd meant to let you know, but it's been so last-minute."

"Okay," I said. "At least I know now."

I could hear muted noises; I guessed she was still packing with her free hand. "Are you all right?" she asked.

"I'm not great," I admitted. "Things have been…well, not so good."

"Is it that house? I knew the moment you told me about it that was a bad idea."

I wanted to be irked by her judgment, but it was hard when she was so obviously correct. "I suppose it's the house," I said. "I mean, it all started with the house."

"I'd say I tried to warn you, but you didn't give me the chance."

"Look, I get it. I had no right to spend the money. I should have...I don't know, split it with you or something. I'm sorry. It was a shitty thing to do."

"Is that what you think?" she said. Her voice was cold, and the sounds of one-handed packing had abruptly ceased.

"Is *what* what I think?"

"That I was upset because of the money?"

"Well...yeah, I guess it is. Are you saying you're not?"

"My god, Ollie, sometimes I wonder what you take me for. I just wished you hadn't rushed into a decision without talking to me. I was glad for you to have that money; you need it far more than we do. But maybe if you'd asked our advice and actually listened, Alan and I might have been able to help you."

Then, finally, I understood. And I knew, too, that I'd recognised the truth all along and kept persuading myself I didn't. My mum and I might not always see eye to eye, but she wasn't the sort to fly into a sulk over money. If she'd wanted a share, she would have simply told me. "I'm really sorry. I've made a mess of everything."

"Oh, don't be melodramatic. I'm sure it's nothing that can't be fixed. Ollie, why don't you think about selling that place? I appreciate that it means a lot to you to have—"

"I'd sell it this second," I interrupted. "There's...there are problems."

She went quiet for a moment. "Alan and I don't have a lot of surplus money."

"What? I know—"

"But perhaps we can help you out a little, just this once. I'll talk to him, all right?"

"I'm not asking for—"

"Are you still working?"

I didn't want to confess the truth, but what would have been the point in lying? "I lost the job I had. I'm...I'm looking for something."

"If you haven't found anything by the time we get back, come and stay with us for a few days," my mother said – and I could tell she was making decisions as she spoke them. "Ollie, you sound terrible. I don't want to be worrying about you. So will you do that? Come and stay and we'll talk this all through."

It had been years since my relationship with my mum had been anything but strained, and even a month ago the idea of spending more than a day or two with her and Alan would have filled me with horror. Now it seemed like the best offer I'd ever had. I could feel a lump forming in my throat at the prospect, gratitude and relief congealing.

I was about to tell her something to that effect when I heard the noises from next door. There'd been a faint current all through the day – of raised voices, a TV blaring, and occasional barks of laughter – but I'd more or less been managing to tune it out. This was different: the voices were louder, and I knew it was because they were coming from the street. I made out scraps of words, and then car doors opened and an engine grumbled into life.

"Mum, I've got to go."

"Well, me too." She sounded faintly annoyed. "But let's have a proper talk when we get back."

"Sure. That'd be great."

I cancelled the call before she could say anything else. Though I was dimly aware that I'd upset her yet again, I barely cared.

For, as I'd heard that engine starting, a memory had flashed into my mind, clear as if the image had been right in front of my eyes: the match fixtures I'd looked at on the Leeds United website. I had no doubt, but I got them up on my phone anyway. And there it was: a home game against Nottingham Forest. While the match didn't begin for a couple of hours, I was convinced that must be their destination; likely they were planning to get a few pints in first. That gave me the rest of the afternoon and the early evening.

This time, I didn't hesitate. I was almost eager; strange how the simple fact of having set a precedent made things much easier. I had no difficulty getting up into the loft space. I had the technique down by then. Crossing the beams in the roof was just as straightforward, and I didn't need the torch to find my way. It was as if this had become a second life, one I was more comfortable in than my everyday existence. Easing my fingertips under the panel that let onto Chas's landing, I felt a dizzy surge of anticipation.

I'd crammed my makeshift rope into a backpack, along with the torch and gloves I'd bought last time and forgotten about; I reasoned having a pack with me might prove useful once I was inside. I took the rope out, tied it firmly to the crossbeam above the opening, and let it fall: it more than reached to the floor. I gripped the highest knot with both hands, applied all my weight, and then did so again with my feet barely off the ground and my heart in my mouth. The rope held.

I hadn't planned to use it for anything besides getting out, but one more test couldn't hurt. Tentatively, I slid my feet over the edge. The cord stretched taut, and for an instant I was sure that it, or the beam, would give. They didn't. It really was good rope; to have used it for its intended purpose would have been a true waste. Putting all of my weight on the knot again, I prepared to clamber down.

This was it, I promised myself. No more screwing up. Today, right now, I was going to start turning things around.

Yet at the last moment a fresh uncertainty intruded. Could I be any less discreet? All right, I was an amateur at this sort of behaviour, but leaving a rope dangling from Chas's landing ceiling was as unsubtle as I could get. I wrestled with myself, doubt warring against convenience; in the end, I coiled the rope on the edge of the loft opening, leaving a couple of inches dangling. I was confident I'd be able to jump and grab it, and if anything should go wrong, it might pass unobserved unless someone happened to look directly upward.

Satisfied, I lowered myself through the opening, taking care not to dislodge the rope. I easily dropped the final distance. Chas's upstairs was about as I remembered it; definitely no tidier, maybe a little worse, but I struggled to tell amid so much clutter and chaos. Certainly the smell was every bit as overpowering. I checked his bedroom first, going straight for the shoebox, concerned that its hiding place under the bed might have been a temporary measure while Chas thought of somewhere less obvious.

I needn't have worried: the box was still there and its contents were largely the same. One of the dark brown bars of resin was gone, however, confirming my suspicion that Chas was likely dealing, at the very least to his own circle. But dealing cannabis was small potatoes, a conviction wouldn't get me the result I was after, and that meant the box was my last resort. If I couldn't find anything else, I'd take some fresh pictures of the contents and where it was and send the lot to Thornton, hoping she was sufficiently on my side to overlook how I'd got them. Anyway, I'd reached a point where I was nearly beyond caring. If she chose to drop me in it, could prison really be a whole lot worse than what my life had become?

Well – perhaps. Yeah, probably. When I went to Thornton,

it needed to be with something persuasive enough that she would overlook my own misdemeanours.

Then I noticed the knife again, wedged beneath the two remaining resin bricks. It was a vicious-looking implement, small but obviously sharp. If Chas had bought it for cutting his stash, it was entirely disproportionate to the task. Thinking of cop shows I'd seen, I wrapped my hand in my sleeve before I took it out. The blade was hardly what you'd call clean, but there were no distinctive marks there either. If I'd been hoping for bloodstains, I was disappointed. Still, couldn't forensic scientists find them whether they were visible or not? Again, I was going off things I'd seen on TV, but if that knife had been used on another human being, and if Chas's fingerprints were on the hilt, as they surely must be, maybe it would be just what I needed.

That added up to a lot of ifs. I put the knife back, careful to replicate the position I'd found it in. No, the box was definitely a last resort.

I didn't bother with the spare room or bathroom. I wasn't confident I had time to waste. I did spend five minutes hunting around the living room; like the bedroom, it remained a disgusting mess, but there were enough subtle differences to persuade me that rechecking might be worth my while. However, there was nothing obviously incriminating among the discarded fast-food containers, empty beer cans, overflowing ashtrays, and general, ingrained filth. And I knew in my heart that I wasn't expecting to find anything; I was looking there because it was better than looking where I should be. The truth was, I just didn't want to go into that cellar.

Strangely, admitting my cowardice gave me the courage I needed. At any rate, it got me as far as opening the door and switching on the light. I stood staring into the gloom, feeling the hairs across the nape of my neck prickle. If there was something to be found, then it lay down there. And I'd be stupid to even imagine I could turn back now; what would I turn back *to*? I stepped through the doorway, descended the first step, and refused to let myself stop.

This time, I flicked my torch on straight away; I wasn't going to rely solely on a knackered light bulb. As far as I could judge, the cellar was exactly as I recalled. I gazed at the great stack of heaped trash. Was I really thinking I'd search that tip, and what did I hope to uncover? I'd begin with the other area, I decided, the clear part at the farther end that had given me the jitters so badly before. I was feeling it again already, every instinct telling me I should be getting the hell out of that close, lightless space. But I wasn't about to listen; if I'd been braver the last time, then maybe I'd have had proof to show Thornton, and maybe I wouldn't be here now.

I determined to take things slowly. If I was playing detective, I ought to make a proper show of it – and whatever my instincts told me to the contrary, I wasn't in any hurry. First of all, I made a general inspection of the empty section of floor. I thought I could discern scuffed footprints, but even kneeling and with my torch I couldn't tell much from them. They might have been from multiple pairs of shoes, or they might have been my own, from my earlier visit.

Once I was satisfied I wouldn't be disturbing any clues, I took a couple of paces away from Chas's piled junk. The smell was loathsome. Partly it was a mingling of damp and decay coming off the mound at my back, partly the stink of what I guessed to be a leaking sewage pipe buried in the foundations, but there was another ingredient I couldn't place. I covered my nose and mouth with my free hand, though doing so didn't make much difference. Then I searched with the torch for the suspicious stains I'd spotted previously. They took some finding; the concrete was dark with a patina of primeval dust. But eventually the beam picked out half a dozen splotches, one the size of a side plate, the others smaller and less defined. It could have been blood. It could have been engine oil. It could have been Marmite for all I knew, and I wasn't about to taste it to find out.

Perhaps, though, I could take a sample? If the scrapings looked suspicious under the cold light of day, then they might be something else to pass on to Thornton. If only I'd planned better, I'd have brought tools and a container for the purpose.

I decided I'd return to that particular problem. Careful to stay well clear of the stains, I advanced a couple more steps. I knew it had to be the chain next, the matter I'd been putting off. And I couldn't but notice how the closer I got, the worse the smell grew: the stink of a rarely cleaned toilet in a seedy pub, it almost made me gag.

I shone my torch up and down the chain. Really, it didn't look like much. Now that I considered more calmly, there was no getting around the fact that the likeliest explanation was also the most plausible: Chas had been keeping a dog down here. That would account for the chain and the stains on the floor, and it would certainly account for that powerful odour of shit.

Nevertheless, that didn't mean he hadn't committed an offence. If Chas had been keeping a dog, it was a safe bet that dog was the most vicious mutt he could lay his hands on. Weren't there illegal breeds? If he was dealing drugs, then dog fighting wasn't such a stretch; or maybe he just liked the idea of having an animal he could set on anyone who pissed him off. Probably he'd got rid of the beast before I moved in and never bothered to clean up or try and address that obstinate faecal stench.

So perhaps the chain was a dead end too. I thought for the first time of the conversation with my mum. I thought about how I'd believed a lie of my own making – that she was angry with me over the money – because to do so was easier than admitting the truth. Finally I had someone willing to help me, yet I'd chosen to ignore that offer of support and come here anyway.

Given a choice, would I always make the worst one? How much of this was genuinely Chas and how much the impulse towards self-destruction I'd cultivated all those years ago, the last time I'd nearly derailed my life for good?

Suddenly I was ready to abandon it all. Whatever had been driving me, I could feel it evaporating, as if it were pouring up out of my skin. What the hell was I doing, creeping about in my neighbour's cellar, hunting for evidence that didn't exist so I could give it to a policewoman who wouldn't care? I'd had enough. For the first time in weeks, acting like a nutter had lost all appeal.

I'd kip on Paul's sofa for a few days, until my mum came back. Then I'd go visit and talk everything through with her, just as she'd said. If I really dropped the price, someone was sure to take the house off my hands; a developer would buy it at a rock-bottom price. And perhaps my mum would put me up in the meantime, or loan me the money to rent a little flat somewhere. At that moment, the future seemed so clear, and I couldn't believe how screwed up and convoluted I'd tried to make it.

I was ready to walk away. I was actually turning aside – and I suppose it was sheer dumb luck that, as the torch beam scudded across the dirt-encrusted brickwork, I distinguished a feature I'd missed before. The rear wall, the one the chain was bolted into... something there wasn't right. But it was difficult to see. The harsh white of the torchlight scoured any detail, and without the torch there was just shadow. The more I concentrated, though, the more it became apparent that someone had interfered with a patch of bricks. I could make out cracks – some hairline fractures, some quite distinct – and the damage appeared too focused to be subsidence. The overall impression was that the wall had been deliberately damaged and carelessly repaired.

I couldn't explain it. And I didn't like it, even more than

I didn't like that chain – which by comparison seemed almost innocuous. I didn't like the prospect of investigating either. But could I afford not to? A part of my mind was screaming at me, insisting on how near I'd been to forgetting about all this, how near I could still be. Yet it was fading with each passing second, becoming easier to ignore. I took a step closer to the broken brickwork, holding the torch steady....

Then I heard it. The noise was instantly recognisable, even though I was underground: the rumble of a car pulling up. I was forcing down a first wave of panic, telling myself that car might belong to anyone, when the familiar voices followed: Chas and Dougie, and immediately after, the second man who'd been in the street that night.

Moments later, I heard the front door open. Their footsteps sounded impossibly heavy. Dust shivered from the rafters in ghostly clouds. Their conversation was loud, though muffled. That was when the fear began in earnest, a black smog that filled my eyes and clutched into my throat. I urgently wanted to dash up the stairs, even as I knew it was precisely the wrong thing to do. But running straight into them seemed no worse than being caught in that oppressive, shit-smelling cave.

Then I paused long enough to truly imagine what would happen, embellishing my mental picture with recollections from my beating in the street, and the result wasn't better at all. I couldn't let them find me. And on that front at least, I had a little luck left: foul as the cellar might be, it wasn't shy of hiding places. I dashed to Chas's junk pile, searching for an entrance into its depths. Against the wall adjoining my house was a narrow gap, hemmed about by an ancient washing machine and disintegrating cardboard boxes. I squeezed in, feet first – even though the act of trapping myself in a confined space only made my panic climb.

Behind me, I felt the gap open out. There was a cavity amid

the rubbish, sufficiently large to cram myself within if I curled on my side. Above me was a filthy old sheet, and I dragged at its edge, striving to disguise the fissure I'd crept in through. I could hardly move a muscle; I was pressed on all sides. Clicking the torch off, I tried to make myself small. I was breathing far too fast and far too loudly, so I jammed a fist into my mouth and bit down hard.

There was no reason to think they'd come down to the cellar. All I had to do was wait this out. It would be bad, really bad. But I could do it.

I'd be okay. I just had to keep it together. There was no reason to think they'd come down here. No reason....

Not until I heard the creak of the cellar door opening.

CHAPTER THIRTEEN

"What tosser left the light on?"

Chas's voice was at once horridly familiar and distorted by the tight environs of the staircase.

I tensed, more than I'd have thought possible, certain that at any instant they'd realise why the light was on and start searching. But as the seconds passed, I began to understand that the enquiry had been wholly rhetorical. And I saw, too, that I'd been an idiot for ever worrying about the window I'd left open or the other traces of my presence. Chas was so perpetually drunk or stoned that he'd never notice a detail like that, or if he did, would never think to find it suspicious.

No, what I should have been worrying about all that time was this. It was doing something so crazy that I wound up getting caught red-handed in my vicious thug of a neighbour's house.

"This is bollocks," one of them grumbled. I recognised the voice as that of my second assailant from that night. They were at the base of the stairs. I felt as though they were right on top of me – and I couldn't believe they hadn't already spotted me. I couldn't see them, or much of anything, yet imagination made the assorted crap piled around me transparent as glass.

"What?" Chas said, in a way that made clear he wasn't asking a question.

"I mean, missing the match...."

"If the boss says he wants this doing, it gets fucking done. If he says now, it's now. Have you forgotten what you owe him?"

"All right, sure, but another few hours—"

"Rick, be fucking quiet." That was Dougie.

"Yeah, Rick," Chas said, with unmistakable menace, "shut the fuck up."

So I had a name for my second attacker; and I remembered that Chas had even told me it, that time he'd come to my door. Now I could see the three of them. They'd pressed past the heap that composed my hiding place, to gather on the vacant square of concrete beyond. If I could see them, they could see me. Their backs were turned, but they were hardly more than a metre away. I could practically have reached out and touched them. In those pent confines, how long before I made some sound that drew their attention?

"So," Chas said. "You two going to gawp or are you getting on with it?"

Rick gave a resigned shrug. With Dougie, he crossed to the rear of the cellar, where the chain was. But it wasn't the chain they were approaching; it was the patch of broken wall. I could just tell that Rick had something in his hand – a penknife, I decided, as the dull light reflected off smooth metal. He shoved the blade into a crack and worked it back and forth with grunts of consternation. Within a few seconds, he had a brick out. He turned around – and I was sure he'd spy me. But all he did was carry the brick a couple of paces and lay it on the concrete. Meanwhile, behind him, Dougie was already working another free – or rather, four together, held by a residue of mortar. He placed his piece next to the brick that Rick had removed.

Like that, they worked together, and the whole undertaking had the air of a well-practised ritual. It struck me that the reason they were being careful to keep the pieces together was so that they could be easily reconstructed later. This was something they'd planned, prepared, perfected. And that scared me, somehow, more than the question of what might be behind there, of what they'd gone to all this trouble to keep concealed.

I'd been quick to write off Chas and Dougie as mindless thugs, but what they were doing now wasn't mindless.

They took about ten minutes to clear the gap altogether. It was obvious by then that this was some deliberately constructed hidey-hole; the brickwork had been carefully broken and weakened, so that it could be dismantled and yet appear relatively normal under anything but close scrutiny. When they'd finished, there was a patch of darkness in the wall, nearly a metre high and maybe a third of that in width. The meagre light didn't penetrate it even slightly, and I'd no way to judge how far back it went. For all I could tell, they'd hollowed the entire underneath of Chas's yard.

They hadn't. I knew that when Dougie reached in and pulled out what they'd stashed there. The space didn't need to be big; not when all you wanted to hide was a human being, and you didn't care how damaged they got in the process.

I could make out a man in a filthy, stained kurta that might once have been white. There must have been another chain bolted into the wall inside the cavity, because a metal restraint was locked around one of his ankles. His hands, too, were tied, and over his head was what I thought was a dirty pillowcase. Having flopped onto his side when Dougie hauled him out, he lay foetal on the concrete, close to those dark splashes I no longer doubted to be blood.

Chas had been leaning against the leftmost wall, watching his two lieutenants work. Now he strode over and crouched above the prostrate man, and I heard a faint metallic rattle. In a moment he had the ankle restraint off. That done, he spat at the pillowcase. "Wake up, twat."

The man shuddered, and lay still again.

Chas gave the pillowcase a hard, open-handed slap. Then he drew it off and tossed it into the nearest corner.

At first I couldn't see the man's face, not until Chas stood up and stepped aside. Yes, it could be, probably was the youth worker whose disappearance I'd read about: slightly built, Asian, surely no older than twenty-five. Despite the distance, I could tell that he'd been badly beaten. Even if I'd clearly remembered the photo I'd seen and even if the light had been better, I wasn't convinced I'd have definitely recognised him – for his face was like so much raw meat.

Chas dug a foot into the man's side. "Stop fucking faking."

The man opened one eye, the one not gummed shut with blood. He tried to rise, made it halfway to his knees. He was nursing one arm, which wasn't hanging right, with the other.

"Well," said Dougie, "he sure as fuck looks softened up to me."

Chas nodded slowly, as if this were some academic problem they were discussing. "So you get him over to the farm. That's what the boss says. He's ready. No more fucking about."

"We can't just waltz him across the street," put in Rick. "It's still light out."

Chas considered. "We'll take him upstairs. The minute it gets dark, you can bring the car round back and get him in the boot."

"So we could've stayed for the kick-off—"

Instantly Chas was up close to Rick's face. "You need to shut the fuck up about the fucking match."

"Someone's going to see," Dougie pointed out.

"Not if you're bloody careful."

"And it's Tuesday, the roads are gonna be—"

"You're not going to sit him in the backseat, are you, you daft prick?"

Dougie gave that due thought. "No. But."

"Take the A65 past Kirkstall. And don't get fucking lost this time."

"The 65."

"Remember, it's Woodhead, not Wharfedale. I don't want you two driving around all fucking night again."

"The 65. Past Kirkstall. Woodhead," Dougie parroted.

"And what are you going to be doing?" asked Rick.

"What am I doing?" Chas looked disgusted at the question. "I'm going to be staying here is what I'll be doing. Watching some bloody telly. Having a can or two."

Dougie and Rick shared a glance, and then both shrugged in unison, with all the world-weary insouciance of some crap comedy double act. They hoisted the young man to his feet and half led, half carried him between them; I could hear them cursing as they tried to manoeuvre him up the stairs. Chas hung back, peering around the cellar like a monarch surveying his kingdom – and for one awful moment I was certain he was about to order me out of my hiding place. Then he shrugged, and clomped up the stairs after the other two. Seconds later, the light blinked out.

I lay there in the total darkness. I couldn't altogether explain what I felt. The fear had vanished the instant that Chas had. In its absence, I was angry; I'd never been angrier. And at the same time, I was absolutely calm. It was as if the fire in me had been turned up like the flame of a blowtorch, to a precise and incandescent heat.

It was all I could do to make sense of what I'd just witnessed. My worst suspicions had come true – yet I hadn't really believed them. Oh, I'd had no doubt that Chas and his mates were vicious scum, bigots that got a kick from preying on anyone different from and weaker than themselves. But this? Torture? Bricking people up in cellars? This was something else entirely.

And it had to stop. Chas had to be stopped. But no matter what the police did – if they did anything, if they didn't take me for a liar or a madman and actually investigated – he wouldn't be. If they found proof, then what would he get, life in prison?

Not even that. Because the youth worker had been alive when he left, and whatever was going to happen to him, Chas would have no hand in it. Just like in the pub, he was letting his lackeys do the dirty work while he stood by.

No. No more. He had to pay. And there and then, I could make sure he did. No one else was going to. This was my responsibility. And I wanted it; I understood that, finally. I wanted Chas Walker gone from the world. I was ready to be the one to make that happen.

Only, I wasn't a murderer. I didn't have that in me. Rage, hate, spite, I could see now that I was full to brimming with those things and had been for years. But to commit cold-blooded murder? I wasn't prepared to step over that line – and even if I had been, I wasn't willing to face the consequences.

Anyway, whatever action I took would have to be done soon, before this white-hot fire in me faded. So maybe I'd accomplish nothing, and Chas's punishment would fall to the authorities after all. But I refused to relinquish my anger just yet. Perhaps there was still some way to make good on it, some opportunity I hadn't seen. At any rate, I couldn't do a thing hiding in the cellar. And I couldn't do anything until Chas went to bed. Anger or no, for the time being I was trapped.

The next few hours were the worst of my life. I thought about the youth worker, or whoever he'd been; the beaten, broken human being who a certainty in my gut told me would be dead before the night was out. If only I'd had my phone, I would have called the police. Even if it meant admitting how I knew, that would be better than being aware I could have saved him and hadn't. But I'd left my phone at home, and to get it I'd have to wait until a time that would almost inevitably be too late. So regardless of what I did, it looked as though his death was going to be on my conscience anyway.

After a while – an hour, two? – I was cramped from head to

toe and sure I was going to wet myself. It wasn't the prospect of leaving evidence but only a childish sense of shame that had kept me in check. Yet I couldn't stand the discomfort any longer. I crawled out through the gap between washing machine and wall and stretched my aching limbs, feeling intolerably exposed.

I'd hoped that moving might take some pressure off my straining bladder, but it made no difference at all. In the end, I managed to pick out a paint tin with my torch, levered the lid off with a scraper I discovered nearby, pissed in it, and sealed the can back up. Afterwards, I considered creeping into my hiding place; if Chas were to come down again, I probably wouldn't be able to make it in time. But even knowing that, I found I couldn't bear the possibility.

Instead, I used the torch to navigate my way to the bottom of the stairs and then switched it off. In the darkness, I could see a faint sliver of light from beneath the door at the top.

When that vanished, I told myself, it would mean Chas had gone upstairs. When that light went out, I was free.

*   *   *

I must have slept, though I never at any stage felt as if I had. There in the blackness, staring at that slender ribbon of yellow until the world was only a blur, sleep would have been a lot like wakefulness anyway. All I knew was that there had been light and now there wasn't.

I wasn't ready to believe it at first. Maybe my eyes were playing tricks; maybe Chas had turned the light off for a minute while he went into another room. I counted to a hundred, then to two hundred, and still the gloom was impenetrable. Steadying myself with an outstretched hand, I crept to the top of the stairs. I couldn't even see the outline of the door.

With sudden courage, I fumbled for the handle and opened

it a crack. When I listened and heard nothing, I stepped out. The darkened living room was empty. Standing there, I wanted to sob with relief. Just being on my feet, working my muscles, felt like the best thing I'd ever experienced after those hours of forced immobility.

Yet through my entire ordeal, at no point had my anger gone away. On the contrary, it had only grown hotter and more focused. The fury in my mind was like a tiny, superheated tumour, which scorched any thought that strayed too close. I should have been escaping, perhaps clambering out the kitchen window again, but the anger held me in place. The desire to rid my world of Chas still burned brightly, and I'd never get another chance like this. What's more, I had a vague impression that there in the living room might be a means to make my intention real.

I wasn't willing to use my torch. After some deliberation, I drew one of the living room curtains partway and opened the kitchen door. Between the illumination from the street and the fainter glow from the rear of the house, I found that within a minute I could see quite clearly. I stared around the room, searching for I knew not what.

Then my eyes fell on the gas fire against the far wall.

I felt as though instinct had guided me. I must have already registered the fire; maybe all the time I'd thought my brain was doing nothing coherent, my subconscious had been digging through the dilemma of what to do about Chas. Either way, in that moment I was filled with a rush of tension that was totally unlike what I'd endured down in the cellar – that was much closer to excitement.

The fire was one of those monstrosities from the Seventies or Eighties: ugly brown plastic at the top, a chipboard surround, a grille of flimsy-looking wire, and at the bottom, synthetic logs resembling nothing ever produced by nature. It was a relic, and I doubted it had been serviced even once in its decades of existence; in short, that fire was a death trap waiting to be sprung. I had a hazy memory of reading that household gas was no longer poisonous, but I was pretty certain it wasn't breathable, and the house would have all night to fill up. Surely that would be time enough for Chas to suffocate, so long as he didn't wake – and if tonight's intake of alcohol and pot had been up to his usual levels, there wasn't much risk of that.

I inched to the head of the stairs on hands and feet. When I glanced round the corner, I could see a scrap of light beneath Chas's bedroom door, though I couldn't hear anything. I crouched for a minute, and another, and still there wasn't a single sound. I was ready to bet that he'd fallen asleep and left the light on.

For an instant I almost convinced myself to get out of there. I could jump and grab the rope, and even if Chas heard, I'd be gone before he could stop me. After that, it was just a case of reporting what I'd seen to the police and dealing with the consequences. I didn't have to do anything else. I didn't have to touch the gas fire. I didn't have to make one more mistake I might regret for the rest of my life.

Except, as I gazed towards the ceiling and my barely visible escape route, I saw faces against the darkness: memories superimposed. I saw Dougie and Rick, looming before me as they had that night in the street. I saw Chas and Pierce, and I saw Liam Sutcliffe. Especially I saw Sutcliffe. I thought about what they'd done to me, between them – what they'd taken.

I didn't have to touch the fire. But I wanted to. I really did want to.

I tiptoed back downstairs. Suddenly remembering, I reached into my rucksack, drew out the latex gloves I'd bought, and slipped them on. All right, I'd probably left enough evidence to convict me ten times over, but I didn't have to make matters worse. Anyway, wasn't the point of fixing something to look like an accident that there'd never be much of an investigation?

This time, I did take out my torch, though I cupped the beam with my hand. Keeping the light close to the fire, I inspected every speck. I wasn't sure what I hoped to find; some sign of wear, perhaps, that I could worsen. But while the fire was decrepit, nothing was obviously wrong with it.

Okay, so the answer wouldn't be that straightforward, not a case of further weakening a dented pipe or detaching an already loose screw. Maybe there was something else, then, maybe...but no. How many objects did the average house contain that might inadvertently cause a fatal accident? And every second I spent in Chas's living room made me that bit more likely to be discovered.

There was a plastic dial on the side of the fire. I set it to the two-thirds point. Immediately I heard the faintest hiss. There was a button beside the dial. If I pressed that button, the gas would ignite and the fire would light. If I didn't....

It wasn't subtle. But it *might* happen by accident. The night was a cool one. Chas could have begun to turn the fire on and been distracted. Hell, he could have been so stoned out of his gourd that he'd confused it with the microwave. The how and why weren't for me to explain. All that mattered was that, whoever's job it was, they didn't come to perhaps the least probable conclusion: that Chas's neighbour had broken into his house, realised he was a monster with blood all over his hands, and decided to take justice into their own.

I closed the door to the kitchen, which looked to be a tight fit. I reclosed the curtains. I considered the front door, and could see no glints around its edges. I waited at the bottom of the steps until I was satisfied that I could smell gas; until the odour was beginning to make me woozy. Then I crept back upstairs. There, I waited again. Perhaps it was stupid, but I needed to be certain. And sure enough, within a couple of minutes I was positive that the gas smell had followed me.

I tiptoed onto the landing. By the faint glow emanating from the bathroom window and beneath Chas's door, I could just make out the opening to the attic, and the couple of inches of rope I'd left hanging over its edge. I had to hope Chas was a deep sleeper, because there was no way I was doing this silently. And whatever happened, I needed to get it right the first time.

I stretched to my full height, grateful that I cleared six feet. I raised my arm up ready. I took two quick steps and leapt.

For a moment I thought I'd missed; my fingers barely brushed the rope's tip. But that, along with gravity, was enough. A loop of washing line slid into view, and abruptly, with a ragged *wumph*, the rest followed. Almost overwhelmed by relief, I put a tentative hand on the line, as if to persuade myself that it was genuinely there.

"What the fuck?"

Chas was standing in the doorway to his bedroom. He wore nothing but a grubby pair of boxer shorts. Even in the dim light, I could see that the expression on his face was one of pure astonishment, as though he'd just stumbled across Bigfoot going through his bins.

"What," he repeated, "the—"

I hit him.

At least, I tried to. My attack turned out more like a shove. It was pathetic, really, and Chas didn't look impressed.

"What the fuck?" he said, yet again. I was starting to think that was all I'd get out of him. Then he came for me – and his punch wasn't pathetic. On the contrary, it felt as if he'd torn my jaw clean off my face. I lurched away, rebounded off the frame of the bathroom door, and almost lost my footing.

By that time, Chas was on me. His next punch was off-target and came up against the side of my head. It probably hurt him more than it did me – though it still hurt like hell – and I managed to get a swipe back in return. He responded with a solid blow to my gut, good enough to double me up entirely. I reeled sideways, striking the bookcase – and of course its shelves tumbled free, spewing their contents across the floor and me.

I crouched, gasping for breath. I couldn't believe that piece-of-shit bookcase; it was like the thing wanted to fall apart. Then my brain registered what was lying at my feet, and I picked up the shelf and swung it edge first into Chas's face. The heavy board landed with a satisfying smack that left him teetering on his heels. I thought about hitting him again, but the shelf made a clumsy weapon – and I'd already seen something better. It was a glass ornament, the kind of knick-knack a child might buy as a holiday gift. All the same, it looked solid and, when I hefted it, had real weight.

Chas was looming back over me by then, his face contorted with hatred. The shelf had left an ugly welt across his temple. I waited, let him come close, let him think I was getting my wind – and when he was near enough, I slammed that cheap piece of crap into the bridge of his nose.

This time, he went down and didn't get up. He'd fallen hard, sprawled at the top of the stairs. I wanted to check whether he was breathing, but I didn't dare. Anyway, hadn't I been planning to kill him? Only, Jesus, not like this. Beating someone to death with an ornament while their house filled with gas, there was no way that resembled an accident in anyone's book.

Still, it was too late to worry now – and I was out of options. Chas had given me a solid pummelling; I could hardly string two thoughts together. This was bad, but staying wouldn't make it better. I had to get out.

I don't know how I climbed that rope. The first time I tried, I could barely hang on; my fingers simply refused to work. Maybe the panic of that, the terrible prospect of being trapped in that hallway waiting for Chas to stir, or worse, of attempting to creep past him, gave me the strength I needed. Somehow, barely functioning muscles hauled me hand over hand, and once

I could use my feet as well, the going became easier.

But the ascent took everything I had – and even that was barely enough. I clawed my way into the opening, and in the roof space I flopped, not caring that I might put a knee or an elbow through the ceiling, oblivious to the weird reek of the insulation pressed against my face. The hours of fear, the adrenaline, and the pummelling I'd taken at Chas's hands – I'd never felt so weak and so helpless in my life. I was scarcely even conscious; my mind flickered like a faulty strip light.

I rolled onto my back. I couldn't tell if I was seriously hurt or just worn out. Chas had gone to town on me, but I'd taken beatings before. I tried to raise one hand and then the other, and though doing so was like lifting concrete, I found that I could. The periods of clarity were getting longer. Lying on my back hurt, so I rolled over again – and saw the hatch, with the clothesline dangling through it. Seized with sudden horror at the possibility that Chas might recover, might try and climb after me, I began to haul the rope up.

The effort went some way to bringing me round. And that made me realise – I could smell gas. I'd assumed it would take hours to permeate the house; perhaps, in reality, a few minutes would suffice. The odour was faint but unmistakable. And didn't gas rise? I was in the worst conceivable spot.

I struggled to my knees, more cautious this time. I slid the crude hatch into place, careful not to leave any gaps. Then I set to work on the rope, striving to pry it loose with numbed fingers. Now that this was happening, really happening, I couldn't leave any more evidence than I already had. But at first, freeing the line seemed impossible; the knot had contracted into a solid lump of fibre. I could still smell the gas. I tried to calm down, to actually think about what I was doing, to follow the entanglement – and at last it began to give. With a renewed effort, I managed to get the rope loose and bundled inside my pack.

By then, I was lightheaded again. I didn't know how much of that was the beating, how much the gas. I made a couple of steps, and my foot slid off a beam and nearly plunged through the floor beneath, so instead I dropped to my knees and crawled. Barely able to see, I navigated by touch. And when I found my own hatch, it was because I almost tumbled headlong into the opening.

I took a moment to catch my breath, to gather my bearings. Even telling up from down was no easy feat. Once I was confident I had my balance, I sat on the edge of the surround and slid through. For all my precautions, I still made a hash of it; there wasn't the strength left in my arms. I skidded off the stepladder, stumbled, and ended up in a heap on the floorboards.

I didn't care. I was in my own home. That was all that mattered.

Except that it wasn't. I couldn't rest, not with so much evidence left. What if the police came round tomorrow asking questions? Against my every impulse, I hauled myself to my feet and flicked the light on. Noticing the latex gloves I was still wearing, I peeled them off and dumped them in the bathroom bin. Then I spent five minutes screwing the loft panel back into place, though my head was spinning and through each second I was certain I'd go tumbling. When I'd done enough that the results might pass a cursory inspection, I flung the ladder and screwdriver and my rucksack into the spare room. Sorting that out, at least, could wait.

I staggered downstairs. My nerves were stretched to breaking point; the magnitude of what I'd done was sinking in. I was conscious that I needed to find my phone, though I couldn't say why. Maybe I could call someone. The police? No, not them. Perhaps Paul; maybe Paul would come and help me, would make everything somehow okay.

The room was dark. I'd forgotten to turn the light on. I bruised a shin against the settee and flopped onto it. I tried to get back up, discovered that I couldn't. I closed my eyes, just for a moment, longing to withdraw into nothingness – as if the ache that racked every inch of me, the fear and revulsion clinging to every memory, were intrusions I could hide from.

I must have passed out for a while. When I opened my eyes, they felt heavy and gummy. The light filtering from outside seemed to have subtly shifted. I lay staring into the gloom, willing myself to get up, no longer able to remember why I should.

As hard as I tried not to, I thought about Chas, lying on his floor, not moving – maybe never to move. I thought about his house filling with gas. I thought about what I'd done, how I now had to live with it somehow.

And then the world exploded.

CHAPTER FOURTEEN

The pain came long before consciousness did. For what seemed an age, I was dimly aware of it, and frustrated by my inability to relieve it. My head ached, my arms, my torso…one ankle was the worst. But mostly I felt as though the pain had been transmuted into some soft and clinging substance, like candyfloss, and I was wrapped deep within its folds. The sensation wasn't bad, merely constant, and only occasionally would a particular spike penetrate the murk.

Things went on that way for a long time. I had just enough awareness to be conscious that I was hurting, and the worse the hurt got — the sharper, the more protracted the spikes — the more aware I grew. Slowly, the cotton-wool sense faded. I wanted to hang onto it, but I couldn't; it was as if I was bobbing up helplessly from depthless dark water.

First to return was hearing. I could make out distant traffic noise and occasional, muffled footsteps and voices. The voices frightened me, because they reminded me of listening through the wall to Chas and his mates. But steadily I realised that these were different: calm and orderly for the most part, with none of the constant undertone of hostility I'd become accustomed to.

Next came touch. I couldn't feel much, though, except a muted impression of weight. Then, almost at the same time, smell and taste returned together. But all they had to offer was a slight chemical odour and flavour that hung on the edge of pleasant and stomach-turning.

I was awake. There was no use fighting it. I knew I was in a bed. But not my bed. This was too well made; that was the first clue. I could tell that the sheets had been starched. They were tucked tight around me, not loose and bunched as mine would have been.

There was one reason I could think of that I'd be in a well-made bed, in a room that smelled of cleaning products.

I got one eye open. That was difficult; they felt gluey and sore. Through the one eye, I saw that it was daytime. The next day? I couldn't judge. But the light was dreary, easing between slats in a half-open blind. The wall that light fell on was pale yellow, the sort of colour no one would ever choose for themselves. The blinds were a similar shade, and even the ceiling appeared faintly yellowed, as if the room had belonged to a heavy smoker for years.

At any rate, it didn't take much effort to deduce what I was looking at. I was in a hospital room. And there was no way that was good.

Nonetheless, I had no real desire to try and leave – though I knew that perhaps I should have. I didn't like the thought of what might have happened to put me there, and I didn't like not knowing. The last I remembered, I'd been curled on the settee, in bad shape but not *this* bad. Then – that catastrophic noise, louder and more awful than anything I'd heard, as if the world was made of paper and great hands were tearing it, scrunching it, preparing to throw it away forever.

Maybe I'd be all right to rest – just for a while. It occurred to me that this was the closest I'd come to peace in longer than I could recall. The pain was unpleasant but tolerable. I had a feeling that nothing was broken. However, the ache in my side was bad enough to make me suspect the possibility of a cracked rib, and I'd definitely twisted my ankle, probably as I tumbled from the attic. I supposed that at some point I'd been given painkillers, which now were wearing off.

That was okay. It was good just to be lying still; god, that was such a relief.

I should have known it couldn't last.

I'd been awake for about an hour – though perhaps 'awake' was too strong a word for my precise condition – when a nurse came in to check on me. He was black, in his late thirties or early forties, and gave the impression of having been on his feet for far too long already. Seeing my eyes open, he said, "Good afternoon."

How long had I been out for? "Good afternoon," I echoed.

"How's your pain?" he queried, with the same emphasis that most people would ask, *How're the wife and kids?*

"I'm...um, yeah, it's not brilliant."

He nodded. "We'll get you something for that." Then, with barely a break, "There's somebody waiting to talk to you. But Dr. Zia has said that she'd like to check you over again first."

Who could possibly want to talk to me? Nothing in his manner had given away whether it was a good someone or a bad someone, but given recent events, I was inclined to assume the latter. Trying to buy time, I asked, "What's wrong with me?"

"Bruises, mostly," he replied. "A portion of the bruising's on your ribs, which is why you're in so much pain. You're groggy because we had to sedate you when you arrived; you were very agitated." He looked as if he was about to say something else, reconsidered, and finally came out with, "You were lucky, Mr. Clay."

I didn't remember arriving, and I certainly didn't remember being agitated – though that wasn't hard to believe. So there wasn't any medical reason I should be avoiding conversation; would a crushed trachea really have been too much to hope for? Regardless, I dearly wanted an excuse to avoid this mysterious someone.

"Well," I mumbled, "if the doctor thinks it's okay for me to talk...."

The nurse nodded once more, perhaps catching my intimation. "I'll go and see if Dr. Zia is free."

*   *   *

For a brief spell I lay there expectantly, wondering what I might say to the doctor that would gain me a few more hours of peace. Then, when no one came, I decided that maybe I should try and sort myself out. Moving was no fun; I couldn't say how much of it was psychosomatic, but having been told I had bruised ribs had focused the pain into a tight ball there, and even the smallest twitch felt as though someone was kicking that ball with steel toe-capped boots. Still, with a huge effort I succeeded in manoeuvring myself enough that I could sit with a pillow wedged behind me.

I managed just in time. As I was catching my breath, waiting for the crackling heat in my ribs to subside, the door opened. When I saw who was there, it was all I could do not to throw up. In barely a moment, instinctive nausea was joined by alarm, and if I'd felt stronger, I might have tried to crawl out of the bed, to hide beneath it like some frightened kid. Then I took in what he was wearing – and then I had no idea what I was meant to think or feel.

Pierce was talking to someone out in the corridor, but I only heard his side of the conversation. "Yeah, all right," he said. "Yeah. You do that." His tone was firm to the point of aggressiveness; my guess was that he'd been arguing with the nurse or a doctor. Shoving the door closed behind him, he regarded me for the first time, took in my expression, and smirked: a big, shit-eating grin that showed nicotine-yellowed teeth the same colour as the walls. "Oh, right," he said. "The uniform."

I wanted to play it cool, I did. But Pierce was standing there in a police uniform, as if that was the most natural thing in the world. I opened my mouth, not having a clue what to say, and sure enough, no words came out.

"It's been a while since I got to wear it like this," he said, "but I figured I'd better just get it out there, so to speak. So as to clear up any misconceptions based on our previous meeting."

I shut my mouth. Then I decided that whatever damage I could do I'd already done; gaping at Pierce like a dying fish was hardly the way to impress him with how cool and collected I was. So I said, "I don't understand."

"Long story short: the last time we met, I was undercover. Slightly longer version: things were all a bit more complicated than that. To be clear, Mr. Clay, I'm letting you in on this because...well, because we're in a unique situation, us having met as we did. And when I talked the matter through with the higher-ups, we felt it was better to be straight with you, before any misunderstandings got made, and perhaps spread about to the wrong sorts of people. So here it is: there was some stuff we wanted that your neighbour, Chas Walker, knew – some proper nasty associations. And no one was confident we' could get an UC into his circle. I had mates who had mates, and frankly not the finest of reputations. It was still a proper gamble, though, I don't mind telling you."

"So – what?" I asked. "Chas knew you were a police officer?" That was hard to stomach, yet it made a degree of sense. Why else would Pierce be standing in front of me in uniform? And everything I'd seen of Chas had told me that, while he might have possessed a sort of wiliness, he wasn't exactly smart. The prospect of having a bent cop in his pocket, a low-level, pot-dealing thug like him – he'd have jumped at that like a puppy with a tennis ball. "I appreciate the honesty," I said. "You know, that you're trusting me with this."

"We are, Mr. Clay," Pierce agreed. "But principally I'm telling you to keep you from flipping out, and because there are going to be reporters trying to get in here with you who we'd obviously prefer not to hear a word of any of this. And, if I'm entirely truthful, because it doesn't matter anymore. Not since

Chas left his gas fire on half the night and then decided to flip a light switch and blow himself to kingdom come. That, frankly, is our investigation more or less shot. Those blokes he hung around with, they didn't know a thing; Chas was the one with the connections." He sighed theatrically. "Two years of work right down the drain."

My mind was absolutely numb. It was as if I was processing a dozen sensations all together and they were cancelling each other out. The best I could come up with was, "I'm…sorry to hear that."

Pierce nodded thoughtfully. "So I suppose that was news to you?"

He'd caught me perfectly off guard. All I accomplished was the opening bar of a choking sound.

Pierce laughed, with apparently genuine good humour. "Sorry, didn't phrase that very well. What I meant was, no one's been in to tell you what happened?"

"No one's told me anything," I agreed, pathetically grateful for so straightforward a question.

"It falls on me to give you the bad news, then."

Once again he'd lost me. "Well," I tried, "I'm sorry about Chas."

"Oh Christ! Not to impugn your good nature, Mr. Clay, but I'm sure you're glad to see the back of that prick. Excuse my French; too long hanging out with the wrong sort of people. No, I was talking about your house."

"My house?"

"That's to say, what's left of it. I hate to have to tell you, but an explosion like that…Chas's wasn't the only place that took a hit."

At first Pierce's implication didn't quite register. Then understanding came, in a flood of remembered images. There had been a gas explosion on the news a couple of months ago, caused by a leaking main. Clear in my mind's eye, I saw the aerial camera footage: a row of terraced houses and, at their midway point, a hole, as if a fist the size of a double-decker bus had punched through. One house had altogether vanished, and while a tail of debris stretched the length of the back garden and the one beyond, there still hadn't seemed to be enough wreckage to explain an entire building's absence – as though some of it must have dissolved into thin air. As for the houses to either side, they'd exhibited messy half-moon cavities, open wounds that revealed cracked beams, scorched plasterboard, and tenuous puzzle pieces of brickwork.

I thought of that being my own house: my scrappy, shitty little home, torn apart like that, as if by the hand of a malevolent god. And for a second I actually wanted to laugh. The instinct was so powerful that I almost did; but at the last I contorted my hysteria into a choking sound that might pass for some expression of distress.

"Yeah," Pierce said, with sympathy. "Thing is, those old houses, it doesn't take much. The fire brigade said that most of the damage was the roof coming down. Said you were lucky you got out in one piece; if you'd been upstairs, you most likely wouldn't have. Fall asleep with the telly on, did you? That probably saved your life."

"I don't believe it," I managed.

It was precisely the opposite of the truth. Yet to say what I'd be expected to say in such a situation, and even to sound sincere, was easy enough. My home was gone, and presumably my possessions too; my job as well, and Chas and the nightmare he'd entailed. Everything was gone – had been scrubbed out. And all I could feel, the only reaction I could find anywhere in myself, was relief.

"I've got to admit," Pierce said, "you're taking this better than I'd have predicted."

I froze.

"Maybe that's just me, though." Until then, Pierce had been staying to the other side of the room, languidly pacing between the end of the bed and the television set bolted high on the wall. Now, for the first time, he changed direction, sauntering towards the gap that separated the window from my bedside. "I suppose you're in shock. Hearing the news that your house is gone. That your neighbour's dead. I suppose anyone would be in shock after that."

He was close enough by then that I could smell the odour of old cigarette smoke rising off his uniform, along with a faint undertow of stale sweat. He was watching me steadily. I'd never heard anybody talk about shock with so little faith; he'd made it sound like ADHD and ME rolled into one.

And he had laid each word out as bait. All I had to do was say, *You're right, I think I'm in shock*, and the trap would spring shut. I didn't see how yet, let alone why, but I sensed the fact keenly. Perhaps it was only that Pierce had delivered his argument like an actor rehearsing a script, just waiting for the one possible response.

I didn't have time to analyse my predicament. All I knew was that I had to get off Pierce's script. "The truth is," I said, "I really didn't like that house. From the minute I moved in, it was one thing after another. God...I actually kind of *hated* the place. So maybe I'm in shock, I don't know, but all I can think is how glad I am that I don't have to worry anymore."

I felt I was walking out onto a precipice I couldn't see, with no idea of which step would carry me over the edge. Yet Pierce's eyes were on me, narrow and cold − expectant − and it seemed as though it was still my responsibility to fill the silence. "And if I'm honest," I said, "as much as I'd rather he were alive, I wasn't too fond of Chas either."

Pierce actually smiled at that. "He was a bit of a troublemaker, that one, wasn't he? Not the type you'd go borrowing a cup of sugar off."

Something in the way he said it was so deadpan that my own mouth tried to curl upward. Except that we were talking about the death of a human being, so of course I should be looking sad, not smiling. Incapable of either, I nodded dumbly and felt like an idiot.

"Only," Pierce said, "the morgue boys are having a bit of difficulty explaining all his injuries."

Oh god. Well, they would be, wouldn't they? I was willing to bet that a gas explosion could do ugly things to a human body, but they wouldn't be the same ugly things as being in a fistfight. "He must have...." I gulped, wishing my panicked brain would offer better words than the ones it had arrived at. "He must have been in quite a state."

Up until that moment, Pierce's manner had suggested that, even if we weren't on the same page, we were at least on approximately the same side. But there wasn't the faintest hint of that in his voice as he said, "That's your expert opinion, is it?"

"I mean," I babbled, "I'm not in good shape, and I was all the way next door, so...."

Pierce considered me as if I was a wasp trying to drown itself in his pint. "Now, Mr. Clay...a few cuts and bruises, that's better than being dead."

Then I really couldn't help but laugh: a pitiful, guilty-sounding *ha ha* that flopped out of my mouth and hung flailing in the air between us. And the only way forward was to pretend that Pierce had meant to be funny, though nothing in his expression backed that up, so I mumbled, "I suppose, if those are your choices."

Pierce let the silence gape – the silence that had so much more weight for my inappropriate laughter and my idiot remark. Then he said, "We'd like to know what went on in the hours before Mr. Walker's accident. And you've already told two police officers that you witnessed a lot of what he got up to. So it's a reasonable assumption that you might have heard something that night too. Heard something, or maybe seen something."

Reasonable assumption or not, I couldn't imagine a more

impossible question. I did my best to mentally relocate myself to my own home rather than Chas's foul, blood-spattered basement; to envisage myself sitting on the settee, having a normal evening, doing whatever normal people did in their living rooms. But the harder I attempted to picture the scene, the more memories of how I'd actually passed that time seeped in, and they were more vivid than anything I could hope to invent.

"I had the TV on most of the night," I said. I remembered Chas telling Dougie and Rick how he'd planned to occupy himself in their absence, and the distorted chatter and canned laughter that had filtered through to me in the cellar. "I'm fairly sure Chas had his TV on too. But, you know, I fell asleep quite early."

"So nothing out of the ordinary?"

"Out of the ordinary?" I parroted, as my mind replayed all the out-of-the-ordinary things that had happened in those few awful hours.

"I mean, people coming over. Shouting, arguing, sounds of a fight?"

"That would have been pretty ordinary," I pointed out.

I was pleased that something half-clever had finally come out of my mouth – which made me less prepared than ever for the look of raw contempt Pierce gave me. "Mr. Clay," he said, "if you're aware of pertinent details and you don't inform us, then I'm telling you, you're going to be in a world of trouble that has no—"

A knock from outside cut off his last word. Pierce eyed the door as though it were an adversary and he'd like to punch it – or perhaps only whoever was on its far side. I wanted urgently to say, *Come in*, but the syllables were glue clogging my throat. I stared mutely at Pierce, conscious that what happened next was entirely in his hands.

"Who is it?" he called. His attitude stated plainly that he wouldn't have cared if the Queen of England had come calling.

Rather than answer, the visitor chose to take Pierce's response as an invitation to enter. She was wearing formless grey linen trousers and a severe black blouse cut tightly around the throat. Nonetheless, I'd never been so happy to see anyone in my life – and I'd never found Yasmina more beautiful than in that moment.

For her part, Yasmina's eyes widened when she saw Pierce. To her credit, though, she took the revelation better than I had. "Constable Pierce," she said.

"Ms. Soroush," Pierce replied. "I'm afraid you'll have to wait outside for a few minutes. As you can see, I'm in the middle of asking Mr. Clay here some questions."

Everything he hadn't said was clear in his tone, like a giant neon sign that insisted in no uncertain terms, *Get out.* Yet Yasmina didn't budge, or so much as twitch a finger. "I don't think that Ollie is in any condition to be answering questions."

The look Pierce gave her summed up perfectly the extent to which he valued her opinion. "Mr. Clay's been coping just fine. In any case, Ms. Soroush, that's for the doctors to decide and not you."

"Then I'll get a doctor," Yasmina said. "And we can all discuss it." But still she didn't move an inch.

Seconds ticked by. Caught between the two of them, I felt I was watching a standoff, like something out of a black-and-white western. Whatever outcome I expected, it wasn't that Pierce would be the one to cave in. "Tell you what," he said, "why don't we let the patient decide. Do you reckon you can manage five more minutes, Mr. Clay?"

The threat was there in his voice: blatant, transparent. I was amazed that Yasmina appeared not to have registered it.

"This *has* been pretty tiring," I said. I sounded pathetic, but not in the way I'd intended; not as someone hospitalised by their lunatic neighbour blowing up their house should sound.

To my ears, mine was the sort of wretchedness you'd associate with a bad liar trying clumsily to cover his own arse.

Pierce contemplated me. His eyes seemed at once black and incandescent, like hot coals; it was all I could do to hold his gaze. "Then I'll come back tomorrow," he said, at last. "In the meantime, Ollie, maybe you can have a think. See what you remember." Those pitiless eyes bored into mine. "See if there's anything you'd like to tell me."

He stalked past Yasmina, missing her by a fraction of an inch, and slammed the door behind him with an impact that made the whole room vibrate. Yasmina stared after him, her expression enquiring eloquently, *What the hell was that about?*

Whereas the only thing I wanted to look at was Yasmina herself. It was so good to see her, and so unexpected. There were no end of questions I knew I should be asking – but all of them would have to wait.

"Yasmina," I said, "I need to get out of here. I need to get out of here right now."

CHAPTER FIFTEEN

"My god, Ollie," Yasmina said, "have you seen yourself? You're in no state to be going anywhere. Why don't you try and get some sleep, okay? I can stay for a while if you'd like. Sleep, and tomorrow we'll talk this all through properly."

She sat on the edge of the bed, so that her body was facing away from mine, and put a hand over my fingers, where they lay upon the sheets.

Even that small contact was enough to push me further towards panic. I wanted to withdraw my hand, but didn't. "Tomorrow might be too late," I said. Although I recognised how melodramatic and how paranoid I sounded, I felt in my heart that it was true.

Yasmina failed to quite hide her exasperation. "Too late for *what*?"

"I think Pierce knows—" I caught myself, so fast that I nearly bit my tongue.

"Knows what?"

"I mean…I think he thinks I did something. And I don't trust him. Doesn't it seem screwed up, him being a cop and coming here? Doesn't that seem awfully convenient?"

"I'm not sure that convenient is the word I'd use." Her brow furrowed. "But I don't like that he was here. I suppose he was working undercover in your neighbour's gang?"

"Something like that," I mumbled. "But, look, you don't understand." I realised how true that was. Of course she didn't; she had only a tiny percentage of the facts, and to sift through what I could or couldn't tell her would take longer than I was willing to spend. "Yasmina, a lot's happened since we last spoke. I have good reasons, very good reasons, not to trust Pierce. I need to get some space. I need to sort this all out in my head."

"If you're in trouble," Yasmina said, "then leaving is only going to make matters worse."

"It's not that I'm in trouble." I was surprised by how readily the lie came. But it was still the wrong answer; if I'd thought it through, I'd have tried to sound indignant.

"Whatever it is," she said, "you can't simply run away. You need a doctor. And if the police want to speak to you, you need to be where they can find you."

"I'm not running away," I told her. "I just want…god, one night, okay? One night, to get my head straight. I'll explain everything, and if you still think I'm doing the wrong thing, we can come back. I could even be here for when Pierce arrives. Can't I just have that?"

"It's not up to me," Yasmina said.

"At this moment it is. Look, I know things are…however they are between us. But I am so, so fucked right now, and maybe one night would—"

"Okay."

"What?"

She sighed. "Yes. One night. Okay. I understand that you need my help, Ollie. So I'm helping. Then, tomorrow – well, tomorrow we'll figure out tomorrow. All right?"

"All right," I agreed. Despite what I'd said, it was more of a result than I'd dared hope for.

"But you're going to need some clothes," she pointed out.

That hadn't occurred to me. In my plan, I would have stumbled through the hospital in my gown, flashing my bare buttocks at anyone who cared to look.

Yasmina smiled at my obvious confusion. "Don't worry," she said. "Give me half an hour. I saw a place on the street." She leaned in and kissed me on the forehead. Then, before I had time to wonder if I should be trying to read any significance into that, she was out the door.

*   *   *

Yasmina was gone more than half an hour, as it turned out. Long enough for me to begin to worry; long enough for fear to creep around the edges of my mind. What if she had been fobbing me off? She'd come to see me, maybe from a sense of guilt, and she'd barely had an opportunity to open her mouth before I'd started ranting like a conspiracy nut. Doubtless she was putting as much distance between us as she possibly could, while asking herself how she'd ever been so stupid as to get involved with someone like me.

Then there came a knock on the door, perhaps three-quarters of an hour after Yasmina had left, and I knew somehow that it was her.

She was carrying a cheap, semi-transparent plastic carrier bag, and I could see the outline of bundled clothes within. Catching me looking, she said, "I ought to warn you, they're horrible. And they might not fit that well. I couldn't remember what your waist size was."

I tried to grin through swollen-feeling muscles. "I'm sure people will be too busy staring at my messed-up face to worry about what I'm wearing."

Yasmina placed the bag on the end of the bed, cupped a palm around my jaw, and scrutinised me, eyes narrowed. "Actually," she said, "it doesn't look all that bad. I can't believe how lucky you were."

"Lucky?" I managed a pained chuckle. "Yeah, this is exactly

my definition of lucky. I'm so lucky that my neighbour blew up my house and almost killed me."

She leaned back. "But he didn't. And the hospital say that you're probably all right to discharge yourself."

"Wait, what?" No part of my tentative, desperate plan had involved telling the hospital staff I was leaving.

"Well, what they actually said was, they would strongly advise that you stay, because you've got bruised ribs and a sprained ankle, and there's a chance you have a mild concussion. But since none of that makes you a danger to anyone except yourself, they can't force you to stay if you're determined not to. Although they want you to sign a discharge form."

"Oh." I felt deflated. The one thing guaranteed to ruin a good escape attempt was someone holding the door open for you.

"Do you need help getting dressed?" Yasmina asked.

I wondered if there was any way to take that as a come-on, decided there wasn't, and said, "No, I think I can cope."

She slid the carrier bag over to me and went to stand by the window, gazing outward. More than anything that had happened since she'd arrived, that made me question why she was here, and what her presence meant for the status of our relationship. I wanted to say, *It's not like you've never seen me naked*, but her posture told me that I'd do better to keep my mouth shut.

I slid my legs out of bed, wincing at a dozen stabs and surges of pain, and tipped the bag out on the covers beside me. The clothes were genuinely rubbish. The jeans were a size too big, and Yasmina hadn't bought a belt. The sweatshirt looked like a knock-off of a knock-off of a designer label, and the shoes were plimsolls that resembled something the poorest kid in class would wear for P.E. But she had at least remembered underwear, which meant that as well as the jeans, sweater, and shoes, my entire worldly possessions also included five pairs of black socks and three pairs of Y-fronts. That was an oddly liberating notion – or else I really was in shock, and the impact just hadn't sunk in yet.

Dressing proved even harder than I'd expected; relationship quandaries aside, I found myself wishing I'd let Yasmina help me. In the process, I uncovered a dozen different bruises, most of them huge and purple-black, the worst being the patch that spread up my ribs and the stripe encircling my ankle, which was also startlingly swollen. But I got there in the end, and successfully propped myself on my feet. "Okay," I said. "How do I look?"

Yasmina turned around and appraised me. "Like a tramp who got run over."

I laughed. "Hey, you picked the outfit."

"Remind me never to shop for you again. I don't think I trust myself anymore."

I thought then how much I'd have liked to forget about Pierce, to forget about what the coming hours might bring, and just suggest that we go grab a drink or dinner. Even talking in a hospital room with Yasmina was vastly better than any instant of the last few days had been. Why had I wasted such quantities of energy on things that weren't her? This right here was what mattered to me, and why hadn't I put up more of a fight to protect it?

But now, doing that and defending myself from Pierce were one and the same thing. "I guess I'm ready," I said. "Let's get going, before they change their minds."

By the time I was through the door, I was limping on my right ankle – the one I'd come down on hard when I dropped from the attic. If walking wasn't much fun, however, the ankle did still bear my weight. I was glad of that, because it was sheer luck that no one had thought to wonder how

I'd received that particular injury, and I didn't want to draw attention to the subject.

We navigated a couple of identical-looking corridors that Yasmina seemed to know her way around, and then took the lift down. By the main reception desk, I was gritting my teeth against the discomfort – not only from my ankle, though that was worst, but from the sheer effort of making my battered body move.

There was a young woman at reception who appeared to be expecting us: she greeted Yasmina with weary resignation. I filled out the form she put in front of me, having barely glanced over it. I understood the gist: I was an idiot for leaving, and if I dropped dead the minute I exited the building, my demise was in no way on them. She gave me various warnings – don't drive, don't drink alcohol, if you feel nauseous or woozy get to an A & E as soon as possible – and scowled at me disapprovingly. I did my best to seem contrite. There was no getting past the fact that I wasn't being a model patient, but every passing moment made me more tense. What if Pierce should come back? What if he saw me here?

But Pierce didn't return, and we got out eventually. Yasmina had parked in the infirmary car park, no doubt at considerable expense. Somehow, I was almost as reassured to spot her green Mini sitting there as I'd been to see Yasmina herself; the little car was the final piece in making her presence real.

On her suggestion, I settled myself across the rear seats, where I could stretch out. As she waited to pull onto the main road, she looked back and asked, "Where are we going?"

I realised that, unknowingly, I'd already decided the answer to that question. "My mum's," I said.

Yasmina glanced at me again, missing a gap in the traffic.

"Is that a good idea? I mean, from what you've told me...."

I couldn't remember ever having told her anything about my mother. "What?"

"Ollie, seeing you in this state, I think she's going to find that distressing."

"Oh." She'd made a valid point. "It's okay," I said, "they're away on holiday."

"Then why go there?"

"Because the only places I can think of are your flat and my mum's, and of the two, maybe Pierce is less likely to guess this one."

"Are you serious?"

"Yes."

"If the police have more they need to ask you—"

"Not the police. Pierce."

"Is there a difference?"

"I don't know," I said. The conversation was exhausting me. Why would Yasmina imagine I had any answers? A couple of hours ago I'd been sedated, and even now there was a reasonable chance I was concussed.

Fortunately, at that moment another gap appeared, and Yasmina managed to pull out. It was early evening, and I assumed that we were catching the tail end of the after-work congestion. Normally I'd have hated all the stopping and starting, the crawling in traffic jams towards the verge of the city; I'd never been a patient passenger. But just then, it was okay. Being in a car with Yasmina, and being somewhere that wasn't my house or a hospital room, was thoroughly nice.

The silence lasted until we escaped the city for the motorway. There I gave Yasmina directions to my mum's house, which was out in a place called Linton-on-Ouse, the better part of an hour's drive away. I'd been enjoying the comfortable quiet between us, and was all ready to slip back into it. But before

I could, a question I'd been pondering without intending to ask bobbed into my mouth, almost unbidden.

"So why did you come to the hospital?"

As soon as the words were out, I appreciated how much they were the wrong thing to say. And though Yasmina didn't look round, I could tell I'd hurt her.

"I'm not a monster," she said.

"No, I don't mean...." I took a breath, began again. "What I meant was, how did you know I was there?"

"They had the radio on in the staffroom," Yasmina said. "They were discussing what had happened on the news. I came as soon as I heard your name." This time, she did glance back at me. "Ollie, just because I needed some space to think, that doesn't mean I don't care about you. I wasn't for one minute trying to hurt you."

"I understand that," I said. And while I hadn't until that instant, I did then. I could even see that, in her position, I might have done the same.

Yasmina didn't respond at first. As I was wondering how badly I'd offended her, she asked softly, "Was this my fault?"

She spoke so seriously that I felt I shouldn't rush an answer. Yet however much consideration I gave it, I came to the same one. "I guess maybe I'd have handled things a bit better if you'd been around. But no, of course it's not your fault. I'm just glad you're here now."

She kept her eyes on the road; but in the mirror, I saw her smile. For the first time, it occurred to me that perhaps this relationship might actually have meaning to Yasmina as well. Perhaps she'd missed me; perhaps she'd been glad of this excuse to end our enforced break. Though I could have been reading far too much into one small smile, it was an appealing thought at least.

Then I realised I was looking at something other than

Yasmina: something I'd been intermittently registering, but until that moment hadn't noticed consciously. I strived to piece together my distracted impressions from the last few minutes, to spy again what had jarred my attention. The mirror – it had been when I looked in the mirror, before I'd moved my head and the angle had shifted. I tried to reverse the motion, but all I could discern was traffic snaking into the distance, headlights infringing on the evening gloom.

The traffic. I'd been staring at the traffic – and now I understood why. "That car...."

"What?" Yasmina asked distractedly.

"That car, two behind us."

"What about it?"

I pointed at the rearview mirror. "See? The blue one. It's been behind us for...." Trying to figure out how long I'd been aware of the car, I found that the information was locked away too deeply in my subconscious. "It's been following us for a while," I said. "And I think I recognise it."

More precisely, I was suddenly sure that I'd seen the vehicle outside Chas's house. It was a dark blue Peugeot that had known better days, though not anytime in the last decade. Now that I was really looking, I even thought I could identify the person behind the wheel.

"Ollie," Yasmina said, "you're tired. You've had a shock, and I know talking to Pierce shook you up."

"Maybe I'm being paranoid," I agreed, managing to keep most of the mounting anxiety I felt out of my voice. "But maybe I've got good reason to be."

"Is there something you're not telling me?"

"A lot's happened in the last few days. So, yeah, there are plenty of things I'm not telling you. And I'll be glad to, if you want to hear them, seriously. But right at this minute, will you trust me a little?"

"I think I've trusted you a lot," she said. "Otherwise I wouldn't be here."

"I know. I appreciate that."

Yasmina's sigh powerfully conveyed what she thought of me — or perhaps of the state of my sanity — in that moment, but she began to reduce her speed. Sure enough, the blue Peugeot slowed too. Yasmina decelerated further, and the car between us was forced to overtake, meaning that the Peugeot was now directly behind.

I fought an urge to look round; seeing anything in the rearview mirror was frustratingly difficult, and I couldn't be absolutely positive that the driver was Dougie, as I'd convinced myself they might be. Then, as they were slackening their pace, attempting to widen the gap that separated us, Yasmina flung the Mini to the left. My heart bobbed into my mouth, until I saw that she was aiming for the hard shoulder. She clamped her foot onto the brake.

"Shit," I said. "That was awesome."

"Thank you." Yet Yasmina sounded shaken; perhaps she hadn't meant to stop quite that fast after all.

Ahead of us, I could see the blue Peugeot, getting farther away — but sluggishly, as though its driver wasn't certain of how to react. The car sped up, and — far quicker than it should have — slid into the overtaking lane and shot off.

"Well, that was strange," Yasmina conceded. She took a deep breath, and her tone was steadier when she said, "Are you going to tell me what this was about?"

A half-dozen lies flickered through my head, and none of them stood up to even the slightest scrutiny. Anyway, I had a suspicion that in this instance only the truth was going to cut it. "I think that might have been one of Chas's mates."

"Chas, your neighbour? Your dead neighbour?"

"Yes."

"Ollie, why on earth would one of his friends be following you?"

"I don't know," I told her. Which wasn't exactly a lie; having horrifying theories wasn't the same as knowing.

"We have a lot to talk about, don't we?" Yasmina said.

"We've a lot to talk about," I agreed.

"All right."

She rejoined the motorway. But for the next few minutes she kept to the slow lane, tucked in behind a lorry transporting dairy produce. Probably it had crossed her mind, as it had mine, that the driver of the blue Peugeot might have parked up somewhere ahead to wait for us.

However, that was either too smart a plan for them or else I really had been paranoid, because I didn't see the car again. We reached Linton-on-Ouse maybe half an hour later. The village was just as I remembered: about as nondescript and studiedly middle class as anywhere could hope to be. It had prospered thanks to the RAF base of the same name farther up the road, now used for pilot training and the reason my mum was there, since my stepdad Alan had been an instructor until his retirement the year before.

I went into the back garden, lifted the brick wedged in the gap between shed and fence, and there, nestled in the dirt, was the spare back-door key. I'd pointed out to my mum more than once how foolish leaving it there was, but she'd stubbornly refused to listen, and just then I was grateful.

Inside, the house was as impeccably tidy as ever. I found it hard to believe that my mum and stepdad were away; then again, believing that anyone actually lived there was equally as hard. The place was like a slightly too ostentatious show home, and as always, I felt as though I was causing a disturbance merely by entering. How much of this was my dad's influence, I wondered, not for the first time; was that period of chaos what had instilled in my mother this need to control every aspect of her environment? How many of the decisions we both made were still defined by those years of strife, before my father's first spell in prison had ruptured the family forever?

But morbid thoughts would have to wait, and so would anything else; I'd been dying for the loo for a good twenty minutes by then. I mumbled an explanation, slipped my rubbishy new shoes off to protect my mum's carpets, and hobbled upstairs.

Once the deed was done, I decided I wasn't quite ready to go back down and face Yasmina. I was afraid of the questions she was going to ask. Instead, I went into the room my stepdad called his office, which was largely dedicated to his great passion for World War Two aircraft: one wall was given over to books and DVDs, and there were models everywhere, smaller ones on the shelves and larger ones hiding the top of a long sideboard.

On the desk beneath the window was the laptop that Alan used mostly to write obscure articles on his subject of choice, which would sometimes appear in the clumsily produced magazines he'd occasionally tried to interest me in. I couldn't have cared less about World War Two aircraft, but I needed a diversion, and it struck me that a couple of days had passed since I'd bothered to look at my email. So I turned on my stepdad's laptop and logged in. A quick glance revealed a dense wall of junk, and I was preparing to delete the lot when one caught my eye.

It was a reply to an email I'd sent, and perhaps only stood out for that reason, and because the name attached was a person's rather than a company trying to sell me something. But it took me a moment more to remember how I knew that name, *Rebecca Ford*. I hesitated with my finger over the message, distantly recalling that it had once seemed important.

Then the memories flooded back. Rebecca Ford, the reporter who'd been investigating the rash of hate crimes and disappearances that, as of yesterday afternoon, I knew without doubt Chas had been a part of. Now Chas was dead in suspicious circumstances, one of his mates had turned out to be a cop, another might be tailing me – and finally Ford had seen fit to answer.

CHAPTER SIXTEEN

By the time I got back downstairs, Yasmina had the kettle boiling, and I recognised how urgently thirsty I was. Fortunately, there was some powdered milk in a cupboard, and though it made for tea that tasted like something from a church jamboree, I still felt better for a hot drink. We took our mugs through to the living room and sat at opposite ends of the plush settee, not looking at each other.

"This isn't how I expected to visit your parents' house," Yasmina said.

"I didn't realise you'd given it much thought," I told her. I'd intended it as a joke, but I immediately saw that the attempt had fallen flat.

"You know what I mean."

While I wasn't entirely sure I did, I understood better than to point that out. Instead, I tried to change the subject. "I'm really sorry I dragged you into this," I said.

"You didn't drag me into anything."

"No, but—"

"Ollie," Yasmina said, "so that we don't have to keep going over this, will you please accept that I came to the hospital because I was worried about you. And that I'm here now because I care about you. Can you do that?"

Could I? She'd said it so matter-of-factly, and still she wasn't looking at me. "I'll try."

"Okay. Thank you."

We lapsed back into silence. Obviously there were things

Yasmina needed to discuss, but my mind kept drifting to the email from Ford. After my run-in with Pierce, I felt keenly that I needed an ally, and perhaps it was fortuitous that Ford had picked this moment to get in touch. Only, of course, it wasn't; this was simply a reporter jumping on a story that they'd discovered had been sitting in their lap all along. Regardless, that didn't mean I couldn't work Ford's interest to my advantage. And as much as I knew that the right thing to do was to try and talk to Yasmina, maybe to reassure her, that possibility kept monopolising my attention.

"Look," I said, "I'm sorry to leave you on your own, but there's something I need to deal with."

Yasmina turned towards me then. "*What* do you need to deal with?" The curiosity in her voice was so frank as to border on suspicion.

I'd already resolved to let her in on the truth; it was sure to come out sooner or later anyway. "An email, from a reporter I got in touch with. Her name's Rebecca Ford. She was writing articles about some stuff that I think Chas might have been involved in."

But that was barely half an answer — or rather, one that raised a multitude of other issues I wasn't ready to get into. "Anyway," I continued, "I just feel like it might be good to have a friend in the media right now."

"I doubt," Yasmina said, with uncharacteristic hostility, "that this reporter wants to be friends."

"I know that. But it's bugging me, and I only need a few minutes. Then, I promise, we can talk things through."

I could see she was angry with me, in so much as Yasmina ever became angry. It made her face close up, hiding all trace of emotion. More, I could tell she was hurt, and that was the last thing I wanted. Yet, with my thoughts made increasingly listless by pain, I had no idea what I could do or say that would help.

"I checked the fridge and freezer," Yasmina told me, apropos of nothing. "There isn't much in there for dinner."

That wasn't a surprise. It would be just like my mum to have conscientiously run down their supplies in perfect co-ordination with the start of their holiday. "I think there's a shop in the village," I said. "But it's probably closed by now."

"We're not far from York, are we?" she asked. Not waiting for an answer, she decided, "Maybe I'll drive out that way."

"Are you sure you can be bothered? There's bound to be a takeaway nearby." But perhaps I wasn't the only one who needed some time alone. I could scarcely imagine how weird this whole situation must be for Yasmina, and so far I'd hardly been considerate of that fact.

I'd do better, I vowed; once she returned, I'd do better. But in the state I was in, it was going to have to be a case of managing one problem at a time.

*   *   *

Upstairs, I reread Ford's email. It said:

Dear Ollie, Sorry it's taken a few days to get back to you!!! Only just spotted your message. Condolences on the accident, hope that you're better soon. Also saw the news of your neighbour Chas Walker's death today. Would be interested to discuss it all with you, maybe even an interview, want to meet when you're out of hospital? Regards Rebecca.

It was certainly less literate than her newspaper articles, though given the standards of the *Evening Press* website, not by a huge margin. Obviously she'd thrown her reply together in a hurry. It was a safe bet she'd been ready to ignore me until she'd learned of Chas's untimely demise and my own close brush with death. Nevertheless, I wasn't about to hold that against her. All it meant was that, in Ford's eyes, I'd gone from being another crank to the star witness in a potentially long-running story.

Below the message was a signature block, with Ford's job title, links to the *Evening Press* website and her own, a Twitter handle of @newshound6060, and a mobile phone number. I contemplated calling her and then doubted myself; might I be better not to appear too eager? Instead, I wrote back:

Hi Rebecca, thanks for your reply. Actually already out of the hospital, just a few cuts and bruises! Would be glad to meet up and yes maybe give you an interview. But perhaps we could speak in the meantime? I have some questions I'm trying to get answers to.

I was about to give her my mobile number when I recalled that I'd left my phone in my house, and for all I knew it was in a thousand charred pieces. I settled for putting down my mum's landline. I considered waiting for a reply, but there didn't seem much point, and I was feeling thoroughly lousy by then; my bruises ached, especially my ankle, and a headache was readying to split my skull in two. I supposed I'd been running on adrenaline since my encounter with Pierce, and at long last it was wearing off. Without its sustenance, I felt like I'd been hit by a bus – which wasn't a million miles from the truth.

I turned the computer off and wandered into the bathroom, to hunt through the cabinet for painkillers. Sure enough, my mum had a varied stock of pharmaceuticals in there. I took two paracetamol, washed them down by gulping water from the tap, and slid the plastic sheet into the pocket of my new trousers, reasoning that I'd inevitably need them again before the night was out.

At that moment, the telephone rang, making me almost jump from my skin. Suddenly I was conscious that, once more, I was in someone else's home without their knowing. I was all ready to ignore the persistent ringing, until it occurred to me that there was a slender chance somebody might be calling from the hospital. I'd given Yasmina's mobile as a contact, but possibly they'd have had this number on record.

I hobbled into the bedroom, wincing every time I put weight on my hurt ankle, and grabbed the phone on the tenth ring. Realising belatedly that the call almost certainly *wouldn't* be for me and unsure if I'd want my mother to know I'd gone to her home without asking, I answered with a hesitant, "Yes?"

"Hello?" A woman's voice: mid to late twenties at a guess, and with a noticeable public-school accent. "Hello, can I speak to Oliver Clay?"

"Yes," I said, "speaking."

"Hello. Hi. This is Rebecca Ford."

Even though I'd emailed her with the number not five minutes before, that took me by surprise. "Oh," I said, "hi."

"Is this a good time?"

She was younger than I'd have guessed, and while she was trying to give an impression of professionalism, I wasn't certain it was much more than that. Either way, I had doubts over whether I was ready to trust her; perhaps I was only wary because she was being so brazen in her interest, having ignored me for so long when I wasn't a story. "Sure," I said, "I've a few minutes."

"Okay. Great. I'm glad you got my email. I take it you've been discharged from the hospital?"

Something in her tone hinted that she already knew the answer to her question. "To be honest," I said, "I decided to discharge myself. All I had was cuts and scrapes."

"You were lucky."

"So they tell me. But I've still got bruised ribs, a killer headache, and no home, so I'm not altogether convinced."

Ford laughed awkwardly, as though I'd made a joke that had

fallen flat. "Well, things could have been a lot worse."

"I suppose."

"I mean, your neighbour...."

I hesitated, caught abruptly by suspicion. "Yes."

"That must have come as a shock."

"Yeah. It was a shock all right."

"So now," Ford said, "you'll be able to get on with your book."

At first I had no idea what she was talking about. Then it came back: the absurd lie I'd invented all those days ago as an excuse to get in touch with her. I considered trying to bluff my way through, but with the painkillers doing little for my throbbing head, I was already past the point of ingenuity.

"Honestly," I said, "I'm not writing a book. There was some stuff I wanted to know, and I figured that would sound better than just asking."

"I'd rather guessed," Ford said. "You'd be researching the BFBA too seriously if you'd deliberately moved in next to one of their prominent members."

"You've got me. The truth is, I read your article and put two and two together. I'd seen some things, and—"

"What sorts of things?"

I was shocked by the speed of her reaction: it was like a hawk swooping for a mouse. "You know, looking back, nothing much. There was stuff going on in the area; a shop was firebombed. And I got the sense that my neighbour and his mates were up to no good."

Then I wondered why I was putting her off. Hadn't I contacted her in the first place to talk about precisely this? After all, she'd just confirmed the connection I'd made between Chas and the BFBA. Maybe it was time I started trusting someone.

"So with Charlie Walker gone, I suppose none of that matters," Ford said.

I recalled the blue Peugeot on the motorway. "I don't know...."

Ford's inquisitiveness was palpable. "Anything I might be able to help with?"

"No. I mean, I doubt it. Just something weird that happened." Thinking aloud, or perhaps not thinking at all, I added, "Maybe I should mention it to Pierce."

"Wait, you've spoken to Pierce? Anthony Pierce?"

"He never told me his first name."

"Tall, broad build, dark-haired? Broken nose? Late forties?" She rattled off the description as though she had every detail memorised.

"That sounds like him," I agreed.

"Look, this didn't come from me, but you might want to be careful around PC Pierce. That man doesn't have the best of reputations." Only, she said it in such a way as to imply that there was a hell of a lot more she *could* be saying.

"I am being careful around him," I told her. I was trying to think of a discreet way to ask what was so bad about Pierce's reputation when I heard the back door close. Yasmina had returned much earlier than I'd expected; presumably the village shop had still been open. "Sorry, I need to go," I said. "Could I call you tomorrow?"

"Of course," Ford said. "You've got my mobile number. If you'd like to meet up…."

"Well, I'm meant to be at the hospital to talk to Pierce, so I guess I should do that."

"In that case, like I said, be careful. Take a few minutes to read up on your rights. Remember, you don't have to answer any questions."

"Okay," I agreed. "I'll keep that in mind. Thanks. I'll be in touch."

And I hung up, without waiting for her to say goodbye.

*　　*　　*

When I went downstairs, Yasmina was emptying a carrier bag onto the worktop. She shooed me out of the kitchen, explaining, "I'm starving. Just let me get on, okay?"

So I watched television in the living room, my stomach rumbling as odours of cooking food drifted through the open door. Two advert breaks later and Yasmina called me back. She had laid the small kitchen table with two places; she'd made what looked to be spaghetti with meatballs, and two of my mum's best glasses were set out with a bottle of red wine. Somehow Yasmina had managed to clean up as she'd gone along, a trick I'd never mastered, and the kitchen was every bit as spotless as she'd found it.

"I thought we could both use a proper meal," she said.

"This looks amazing," I told her, and meant it. How long had it been since I'd last eaten? How much longer than that since I'd had real, home-cooked food? Actual injuries aside, I'd been treating myself atrociously for far too long.

Yasmina left me to devour my dinner for a while. In fairness, she'd have had difficulty stopping me; I hated to wolf the food she'd cooked, for a portion of my mind registered that it was delicious, but by then the hunger had taken over entirely, as though my body had slipped into some previously unknown repair mode and my brain was merely along for the ride. From the corner of my eye, I noticed distantly that Yasmina was only picking at her own food, and that her gaze was often on me.

Finally, as I was drawing near to finishing, she cleared her throat with a soft *hem* and said, "So, Ollie, you need to tell me everything that's been happening."

I hesitated, gulping down a last, half-chewed mouthful. "Everything?"

"Everything important. Whatever it takes to explain why you got so scared by Pierce coming to see you."

Well, I supposed it was time – or at least that I'd put this conversation off for as long as I possibly could. The food, too, had helped pick me up, as in no small measure had the wine. Altogether, I was as close to a suitable frame of mind as I'd been all day. I even had a sense of what I was going to say, and of how much I was willing to reveal.

"The thing is," I said, "that I'd done something wrong. What I mean is, something illegal; I don't know if it was exactly wrong. At any rate, when I did it, it felt like the only option I had left."

"Ollie," Yasmina said, with forced patience, "please just tell me whatever you think I need to know to understand."

One last time, I tried to weigh it all up: the risks of admitting the truth, what portions might be acceptable, how far I dared go. Struck by sudden doubt, I wondered if a lie might not be my best bet after all. But I instinctively felt that I'd already gone too far for that. Anyway, there was a part of me that wanted badly to share some of my harrowing secrets, and specifically to share them with the woman sitting before me.

"Chas," I said, "my neighbour...I'd been in his house. And I was scared that somehow Pierce had guessed that."

Yasmina put her knife and fork down with a clatter. "Oh my god." She gripped the edge of the table as though the room was starting to tip on its axis. "Ollie, tell me you didn't—"

"I didn't kill him."

It wasn't a lie. It wasn't. Maybe I'd set up some dominoes, but I hadn't been the one to tip them over. Had Chas had the gumption not to turn on an electric light when his whole house stank of gas, had he thought to open a window instead, he would still be alive now. And strangely, the fact that I'd said the words without a quaver in my voice made them seem truer in my head. Jesus, of course I hadn't killed him. I'd been crazy to imagine I might have, that I *could* have. Sitting there, with Yasmina opposite me and everything so normal, the possibility was inconceivable.

"But you were in his house."

"I got out. Then I don't know what happened."

"You *broke into* his house."

"I realise how it sounds."

"Ollie," she said, her voice strangled, "I'm not sure you do."

It hit me, as if I'd woken from a cosy dream into a terrible reality, that this was going badly – and that, if I didn't find a way to put the brake on, Yasmina's reaction might get a whole lot worse. "Look," I said, "I *do* know how it sounds. But you've got to understand, I thought something awful was happening. And I was right."

That caught her. "What do you mean?"

"You remember the youth worker who went missing a few days ago? It was in the news."

Yasmina considered. "I think so."

"Well, they had him. They'd been hiding him, down in Chas's cellar. Torturing him. It was…it was fucking awful. The state he was in. They'd had him walled up down there. Gagged. They'd beaten him."

My hands were shaking. I watched them with detached curiosity. It occurred to me, with that same sensation of remote interest, that I was suddenly very close to tears. I tried to bring myself under control.

"They…" I began, but I couldn't get any further, so instead I said it again, and one more time for luck. Each time sounded less like a word and more like I was choking.

Then, without my even noticing she'd moved, Yasmina was crouched beside me, her arms wrapped about my shoulders, her face nestled against my hair. I leaned into her, and with that I couldn't restrain myself anymore: sobs ripped through me, each one raking pain across my ribs. I didn't care. I'd been holding this in for so long and now it had to come out. It was trauma, it was the despair of the last days, it was the memory of that young man's battered face, all rolled together, and I could no more have resisted than I could have stood up in a hurricane.

Yet, for all its violence, my fit of emotion passed quickly. In a minute I was wiping a sleeve across my eyes. When Yasmina was sure I was calm, she ushered me to my feet and led me by the hand back into the living room, where we sat together on the settee.

"So you'd found out?" she asked me gently. "You were trying to help him? Why didn't you go to the police?"

Inside, I winced. Yasmina's version was so much more heroic than my reality had been. "No, I didn't know. I mean, I didn't know that was what it was. I just had this sense – this *conviction* – that they were up to something awful. And I'd tried the police, but they had nothing to go on. I thought, if I could find some evidence...."

"And that was why Pierce was talking to you? Because you'd told the police about what your neighbour had done to this man he'd kidnapped? But then surely—"

"I didn't call the police. Not after I saw them take the youth worker away. I didn't have my phone. I was going to, as soon as I got back into my house."

Could I genuinely have forgotten? I reminded myself that I'd taken a beating, that I'd been exhausted and probably deep in shock; it all seemed like so many empty excuses. When I retraced those last minutes, before unconsciousness had overwhelmed me, it was as though my memories were laced with swirls of black ink.

"But honestly," I said, "I'm pretty certain he must have been dead by then." And in my heart, I knew at least that was true.

Yasmina shuffled closer. She cupped her hand over mine, where it rested on my knee – yet when she spoke, there was a metal edge to her tone. "You should have told me all of this. Before you thought for a second about asking me to help you, to come here with you, you should have told me. I deserved to know."

I put my other hand on hers. "I should have. I haven't been thinking straight. I was scared, really scared. If the police find out what I did, it won't matter if I was wrong or right. The moment they decide I'm a suspect, there's no way anyone's going to be willing to hear the truth." Then a further argument came to me, one that was much more persuasive – that persuaded even me. "And I won't be able to do anything about it. Perhaps I'm the only one who knows what they were up to, Chas and those sick bastard friends of his. And Ford warned me not to trust Pierce. That he has a bad reputation. I need to figure out the right thing to do, or maybe no one will ever take this seriously."

Yasmina hesitated for a long while, our hands still folded together. Eventually, she said, "Tomorrow I want you to go back to the hospital and talk to Pierce. Not tell him everything, just talk to him. I think that this, today, was a mistake. And I don't want you to make the situation any worse."

I thought it through. "Yeah," I said, "okay."

"I'll take another day off work. I'll come with you."

"Thank you."

Yasmina leaned forward and kissed me on the cheek. "You're welcome."

★   ★   ★

We watched TV and finished up the last of the bottle of wine. There was a movie on that neither of us had seen, but I could hardly concentrate. Yasmina had cuddled up to me, and despite how much my body was hurting, despite the conversation we'd just had and the complications left in its wake, she was all I could think about. I was utterly shattered, yet her presence kept me at a distance from even the notion of sleep.

But the film came to an end, and the clock on the mantelpiece showed that it was nearly eleven. Yasmina was yawning, and I could feel myself drifting – as though, whatever my opinion on the matter, my mind was on the verge of shutting down. I carefully separated myself from her and stood up.

"There's only the one spare room," I said. "So I thought I'd make up my mum's bed and you can have that. I know it's a bit weird, but—"

"You don't have to," Yasmina told me.

"Well, look, I want you to be comfortable, and—"

Then, before I realised what was happening, her face was pressed to mine and her lips were against my lips. My senses were dizzyingly full of her. When I put my arms around her, she drew away as far as she could and watched me, so close that her face was merely an exciting blur of features.

"I did miss you," she said.

"Yeah?"

"Yes." She leaned back in, to kiss me lightly.

"And you're sure...?"

"Stop asking questions, Ollie."

So I stopped asking questions.

*　　*　　*

By the next morning, my whole body ached.

It wasn't the pleasant, post-coital fatigue I might have hoped for. All I'd managed once we got to bed was a little gentle cuddling, and I'd got the impression that had been fine with Yasmina, who had soon drifted off to sleep. I'd envied her that – increasingly so as the hours wore by. The pain had kept me awake through much of the night, despite more paracetamol. I could really have done with something stronger; I suspected my injuries warranted it, and that, if only I'd hung around the hospital, some serious medication wouldn't have been long in coming.

Still, I didn't want to move. It was good to have Yasmina beside me. The pressure of her body next to mine, and the way that she'd curled inside my arm, so that my palm was pressed against her belly, almost made the pain worthwhile.

And there remained, too, the awful sense that this might yet be taken from me. I didn't know what to make of last night. I didn't know what to make of this morning. Maybe it was pathetic, maybe I'd grown used to being paranoid, but I felt that whatever was between us could evaporate all too easily.

I was lying like that – fidgeting to find the position that hurt least, trying to enjoy Yasmina's closeness, tormenting myself with doubts – when I heard the car pull up outside. At first I didn't think anything of it. I couldn't even remember what the day was. A door slammed, and still the portion of my mind that was paying attention was quick to dismiss the intrusion; probably the noises were from across the street. Then came faint footsteps, and though it would have been easy to assume they were approaching a different house, somehow at that point they abruptly gained the whole of my attention – so that when the doorbell rang, the jangle locked my muscles rigid.

Yasmina, stirring beside me, mumbled, "Is that here?"

"I think so."

"Are you going to answer it?"

I was about to say that no, I wasn't. After all, this wasn't our house, and so there was no way anyone would be calling for us. But then the bell rang again: a long, discordant note, as if someone had held the button down hard.

I slid out of bed. "You stay here," I told her – and something of what I was feeling must have slipped into my voice, because she sat up, reflexively clutching the quilt against her chest in a way that at any other moment would have driven me crazy.

I hauled on my new jeans and sweater, leaving my feet bare. Before I'd reached the landing, the bell was ringing again, for even longer this time. I hobbled down the stairs as fast as my smarting ankle would allow. I could see a silhouette through the glass panel of the front door: large, stocky, definitely a man, and the aggressiveness of the pose, the unapologetic way in which they took up space, was enough to convince me they weren't here to read the electricity meter.

In fact, I think I knew who to expect even before I opened the door. I think a part of me had been anticipating him from the second I'd heard feet coming up the path.

Nevertheless, I did my best to appear surprised and to meet his gaze. "Good morning, Constable Pierce," I said.

CHAPTER SEVENTEEN

"Mind if I come in?" asked Pierce. He was in uniform, but still he managed to look relaxed, like he'd just rolled up at the home of an old friend and was checking in to say his hellos to the missus before we set out for the pub.

Pierce brushed past me, into the hallway, having not paused for an answer. I flinched at the line of black marks his shoes had left on my mum's carpet. He glanced around as though he owned the place, or at the least as if this was a slightly subpar hotel he was considering staying in.

"Let's go into the living room, shall we?" he suggested. "No, wait…why don't you get the kettle on first?"

The last thing I wanted with Pierce was any kind of confrontation. I did as I was told. "White, two sugars," he called from my mother's living room – and the strangeness of that detail threatened to wreck all my tenuous self-possession. How would she react if she knew there'd been a policeman in her home? What would she say if she knew *why* he was here?

I fussed over which of my mum's mugs to use for Pierce – nothing with flowers, nothing too chintzy – and settled eventually on one of my stepdad's, with a silhouette of a Lancaster bomber. Then I dithered further over whether to make myself a drink. I could feel nausea bubbling up from the base of my throat, and my headache was back in full force. I wished I'd taken some painkillers before I came downstairs; facing Pierce was going to be that bit harder given the state I was in. But the seconds were ticking by, and keeping him waiting would only make matters worse, too. I hurriedly made myself a coffee and carried both mugs through, barely managing not to spill them in my haste.

Pierce had chosen the armchair normally reserved for my stepdad. He was sitting with his legs sprawled apart, arms covering the rests. I placed the mugs on the glass coffee table, careful to use coasters, a habit driven into me by my mother that returned unbidden. Then I sat on the sofa, trying to look attentive and not sink into its plush depths.

Pierce took a sip from his tea, though it was still practically boiling. He made an exaggerated *Aaah* sound, smacked his lips, and said, "You make a decent cuppa, Mr. Clay." He set the mug back on the table, taking care to avoid the coaster I'd set under it. "So. I take it you didn't approve of the hospital food?"

My mind went to that old playground threat: *Want to end up eating hospital food?* "I never got to try it," I said, not quite grasping the thrust of his question until the words were out of my mouth.

"Oh no," Pierce said, "that's right. Because you're here and not there."

His tone was disdainful. I fought to keep calm. I'd done nothing wrong in leaving, or at least nothing against the law; I needed to believe that. "I decided to discharge myself," I said, as though that decision was precisely the most natural in the world.

Pierce considered me, letting the moment draw out. "I've got to say, Mr. Clay, some would think that looks suspicious."

I wasn't certain how much longer I could feign ignorance, but with nothing else up my sleeve, I decided to give it one more go. "I don't understand."

"What I mean is, walking out of the hospital when you're clearly in no fit state to, and especially when you've agreed to be there the next day to talk to a police officer…well, I'm not sure I can put it much more plainly. That. Looks. Suspicious."

I tried to work my face through startlement and then

comprehension, as if this were all news to me, though news that made perfect sense now that someone had taken the time to explain. "I freaked out, that's all. I'm sorry. But I'd found out that I'd lost my home, that my neighbour was dead. And I just needed to be away from there. I was going to go back today, so I don't know that it's *that* suspicious."

"Yet here you are," Pierce said, "getting all defensive."

I laughed; giggled really, pushing my performance another step towards self-parody. I coughed into my fist, using the gesture to cover a deep breath that I hoped might steady me. Pierce was on the warpath, that much was clear, and playing stupid was only giving him ammunition. "I suppose," I said, "that this brings back some bad memories. I had a phase, when I was a teenager. I got into a fair bit of trouble with the law. There was a year or two when I had more than my share of these conversations, sitting on my mum's couch talking to the police."

"Who'd have guessed it?" Pierce said. "Quiet bloke like you." He took a gulp of tea, and once again ignored the coaster in favour of the glass surface of the table, avoiding also the muddy halo he'd already made. "Nothing too serious, I trust?"

Well, I thought, *it wasn't murder*. But it could easily have been; a few more months and that was how my youthful misadventures might have ended. And for a moment I wondered if I'd been viewing my subsequent life all wrong. I'd been so sure that I'd dodged the bullet, that I'd set myself on a better course. What if all I'd done was delay the inevitable?

Then came another striking perception, even more out of the blue: what if I'd got it out of my system? Maybe these impulses had been festering in the dark of my subconscious, a morass of buried teenage afflictions and all their corresponding rage. Maybe a part of me, however small, had been contemplating murder for a long time. Now it was done – in the most indirect way possible, to somebody who was undeniably better off out of the world. So perhaps I'd killed, but I wasn't a killer, not really. And now that I knew what to look for in myself, nothing similar would ever happen again.

I remembered Pierce's question, and how long it had been sitting between us. "The usual teenage stuff," I said. "Drank too much. Did some drugs. Got into a lot of fights. In the end, my mum sorted me out." No need to mention that she'd done so by threatening to cut me off altogether, or how that promised betrayal had carved a rift in our relationship that had never quite healed.

"So you were a scrapper, were you?" Pierce waved a hand in the air, indicating the general region of my face. "That what's going on with all this then?"

He meant, of course, the blackening near my eye and the puffy patch of red and purple around my jaw, points where Chas's heavy fists had connected with my less resilient flesh.

I forced a laugh. "You know my house exploded, right?"

"I do indeed," Pierce concurred. "I also know what it looks like when someone's taken a few smacks to the head."

"To be honest," I said, improvising even as I spoke, "I did get into a bit of a tussle. But it was nothing to do with anything. I lost my job, I was walking home, and some blokes began giving me shit. They started it. But, yeah, I lost my temper. I took a hiding, though, so I suppose I got what I deserved."

Nothing in Pierce's expression said that he believed me even slightly. "That business with Dougie and Rick, who started that, then?"

"*They* did."

"Because if you'd been picking fights with Chas's mates, making a fuss about him to the police, and then he winds up dead in what we in the trade like to call 'suspicious circumstances'...."

"I don't know what you're implying," I said, despite the fact that it couldn't have been more obvious. "If you're accusing me of something—"

"Whoa there." Pierce held up a hand, palm flat. "No need for that sort of talk."

Once again, he recovered his mug and sipped from it, as though he and that cup of tea were the only things that mattered in the world. This time, however, he hung onto the mug and let the silence draw out. I knew what he was doing; it was the oldest trick in the book. He was giving me space to wind myself up, to ponder what was happening and how bad it could get.

Yet knowing I was being played didn't do me a great deal of good. There was already too much going around my head. More than anything, I wanted to ask Pierce how he'd found me. But to do so would be to play straight into his hands, and in any case, I could think of plenty of ways.

Anyway, the question of *how* wasn't really what was bothering me. What bothered me was that I was convinced we'd been tailed on the motorway last night, and this morning Pierce had turned up at my mum's doorstep. What if it *had* been Dougie behind the wheel of that blue Peugeot? Yesterday, Pierce had given the impression that his second existence as the bent copper who'd hung out with a few bad lads had ended the moment Chas's life had. But what if it hadn't? What if he'd kept some useful channels open?

"Now," Pierce said, "if it's all the same to you, that discussion we were going to have in your cosy little hospital room, we'll have it here instead."

In the back of my mind was the recognition that I had every right to tell Pierce no, to explain how I'd be glad to agree a time and date for an interview when I was feeling better. And I knew I wouldn't say either of those things, knew too that it was because Pierce understood how to push just the right buttons.

He wanted me off-balance, so I was off-balance. He wanted me scared, so I was scared.

"Sure," I agreed. I nearly added, *I've got nothing to hide*, even though it would have been the single most idiotic and suspicious-sounding thing I could possibly have said.

Pierce reached inside his jacket and drew out a small Dictaphone, an old-fashioned one of the kind that still used those miniature cassette tapes. He placed it on the table, neatly finding the centre of the coaster I'd set out for his mug, and said, "I hope you don't mind if I record our conversation?"

Here was my last chance, and we both knew it. "No," I said, "go ahead."

Pierce pressed a switch on the side of the device. I expected him to open with the usual formalities, or at the very least to state our names. Rather, he said, "Do you have any reason to think that Charles Walker's death might not have been an accident?"

Unprepared, I mumbled, "Um, no. No reason."

"Are you aware of anyone who might have wished Mr. Walker harm?"

"I mean, there probably were people. But no, not personally."

"What sort of people?"

"The sorts he hung out with."

"Who were?"

"Rough people. People who did drugs. Who liked to start fights."

"You knew Mr. Walker's friends then?"

"I didn't know them. I'd seen them around. I got beaten up by two of them."

"Were you ever inside Charles Walker's home?"

"Of course not."

"Why 'of course not'? You were neighbours, weren't you?"

"We weren't friendly."

"And why do you think that was?"

"Because," I said, letting a portion of the frustration I felt into my voice, "he was an antisocial arsehole who was hell to live next door to."

"So you didn't like Mr. Walker?"

"No, I didn't like him."

"Were you ever engaged in a physical altercation with Mr. Walker?"

"No, I wasn't. I'd barely even spoken to him."

"Yet you were in an altercation with two of his associates?"

"As I said, they beat me up. They attacked me in the street and they threatened my girlfriend."

"But you didn't press charges?"

"I discussed the incident with two police officers and decided not to take it any further."

"Did you have any notion that Charles Walker might have been participating in criminal activities?"

My mind was beginning to whirl. I'd been told once that half lies were more convincing than full-blown ones, but concocting a decent half lie took time that Pierce wasn't allowing me. "There was a corner shop down the road that got firebombed. I thought maybe he was involved."

"Why did you think that?"

"Because he seemed the kind of person who'd do it."

"Which means?"

"He seemed like a racist thug."

I thought that roused the slightest smile on Pierce's granite features. "Did you ever overhear any of Mr. Walker's conversations?"

"It was hard not to overhear things."

"What kind of things?"

I checked myself. "Just…drunken banter. Shouting. Swearing."

"Did anything you heard make you suspicious?"

"Not really."

"Not really?"

"Well, he was always drunk or stoned, and there was banging and shouting all the time, so yes, I was suspicious."

"What did you suspect?"

"That he dealt drugs. That he was violent. That he enjoyed hurting people."

"What sort of people?"

"Innocent people."

"Innocent people like yourself?"

"No. Like—" I came close to saying, *That poor fucking youth worker*, so close that my lips formed around the shape of the words. "People he didn't like the look of."

"Did Chas ever mention a farm?"

Pierce said it with such calm, such matter-of-factness. I could control what came out of my mouth, but I couldn't stop my face – and I knew it had betrayed me. "A farm?" I repeated. "No, I don't think so."

"Would you remember if he had?"

"Yes," I said, "I think I'd remember a detail like that."

Pierce reached to retrieve the Dictaphone, clicked it off, and returned the device to his pocket. "And that," he said, "concludes the official portion of our interview."

Something in the way he spoke that word, *official,* made my blood run cold. Rationally, I was certain that Pierce had been grasping; he couldn't possibly know what had happened between me and Chas. He was the proverbial broken clock, and chance had made him adequately right to put the wind up me. Yet even if all he had were suppositions, wasn't it bad enough that they were running so near to the truth? And why had he mentioned the farm? More importantly, what had it meant, that flicker distorting his face when my instant of hesitation had revealed my lie?

The clack of china against glass drew my attention back to

Pierce. He was making a noisy show of finishing his tea. As he drained the dregs, he screwed up his face to indicate that the drink had grown cold while I'd been suffering beneath his interrogation. I half expected him to spit the last mouthful out onto the carpet. Instead, he swallowed, with obvious distaste. The look he gave me was one of unmitigated loathing, as though I'd brought him here and made him barrage me with endless questions and failed to keep his beverage suitably heated out of stubbornness or spite.

"Is anyone else in the house with you, Ollie?" Pierce asked.

As he'd intended, the query caught me off guard. But perhaps I was getting more used to lying to him by then, because my voice was steady as I said, "No, I'm here alone."

"Oh?" Pierce raised an eyebrow in puzzlement. "Is that right? Only, before I came, I made some enquiries regarding a Miss Yasmina Soroush. And I was told she hadn't gone into work this morning."

Glancing at the clock on the mantelpiece, I was shocked to see that it was nearly ten o'clock; late enough for Yasmina's absence to have been noticed at the school. I hoped I hadn't got her into too much trouble.

"And," Pierce continued, "I'm fairly confident that's her car out there on the drive."

Shit…I hadn't thought of that. The falsehood I'd been preparing died in my mouth. "She went for a walk," I said. "Looking for a shop to get some bits for breakfast. I don't know how long she's going to be."

"Well," Pierce said, "don't be offended if I say I don't believe you. Thing with being a copper is, if you believed every single word anyone told you, you'd have an awfully quiet life, but you wouldn't get a fuck of a lot done."

"I've no reason to lie."

Pierce looked amused. "I've never met anyone who had no reason to lie."

"I mean, about that. About Yasmina."

"Oh, I can think of reasons. Maybe you're being a gentleman, Ollie. Maybe you're trying to protect her."

I almost asked, *Do I need to protect her?* But I already knew the answer, even before Pierce got to his feet.

"I'm going to take a gander upstairs," he said breezily. "If you've no objections, of course."

I thought frantically. The possibility of him finding Yasmina, perhaps even still in bed, filled me with unreasoning horror. "This is my mum's house," I said. "She's away on holiday and I haven't told her I'm here yet. So, no, I'd rather you didn't go upstairs." I was pushing my luck, maybe beyond its breaking point, but nevertheless I added, "Unless, that is, you've got a search warrant."

"Is that what we've come to?" Pierce tutted disappointedly. "You know who talk about search warrants, Ollie? Same people who don't like to answer questions. Guilty people. People with dodgy shit they'd like to hide."

"And," I said, "people who've done nothing wrong."

"Not in my experience – and it's safe to say I've had more of it than you. Also, I seem to recall you telling me that you've done plenty wrong in your time."

I desperately tried to remember what I'd said to that effect, and saw straight away that I was only letting Pierce pull my strings. "Look," I told him, "I'm through co-operating. All right? You turn up here, at my mother's home, and—"

"Do I need to handcuff you, Ollie?"

The remark was so abrupt, so out of nowhere. And the threat was so explicit: to make me powerless, more even than I felt I was already. "Are you arresting me?" I asked, making a tremendous effort to keep my voice from trembling.

"Don't need to arrest you to handcuff you," Pierce said. "Oh, there might be some debate afterwards. But frankly, what with you having a concussion and what with you running away from hospital, I don't know that you'd be considered much of a reliable witness. So how's about I do the question-asking, and you stick to the answers?"

"No," I said. "You don't need to handcuff me."

"My old man," Pierce began thoughtfully, as though I'd never spoken, "he knew plenty of tricks with a pair of handcuffs. Those old cuffs were heavy. Put them on in a certain way and you could break a man's ulna."

He tapped the side of one forearm to illustrate.

"Some bloke's giving you bother? Snap the cuffs on, just *so*, and you snap his wrist while you're at it."

Pierce's introspection deepened; his eyes glazed.

"He used to tell me about this one time when he didn't quite get it spot-on. Somehow managed to drive the arm of the cuff right through between the bones."

Pierce held his wrist up again, sleeve rolled down, so that I could clearly see how such a thing might happen.

"Screamed his head off, that bloke did, the way my dad told the story. Well, you can imagine. Resisting arrest, they'd call it. Anything where the suspect needed a little extra attention, that was what it got filed under. Someone hits their head too hard on the pavement, gets bounced around a bit much when they go into the van, looks as if they've had a shoeing. Someone gets a broken wrist bone. Resisting arrest."

Pierce grinned. "Course, you can't do things like that these days."

I got to my feet. Whatever moral I'd been meant to infer from Pierce's tale, all I'd actually taken away was that under no circumstances could I let him be alone with Yasmina. "I'll come with you," I said.

Pierce's grin widened. "Make sure the dodgy copper doesn't have off with mummy's silverware, is that it?"

I was done with trying to keep on his good side; it was increasingly obvious that he didn't have one. "Maybe."

"You don't need to worry about that," he said. "I've got bigger fish to fry."

He led the way through to the hall, moving with an easy swagger that potently reminded me of the sorts I'd hung around with in the bad old days. Pierce had that same manner, though with him it was more subtle; not the promise of violence that my teenage cronies had strived to maintain but only a subtle implication.

At the bottom of the stairs, he hesitated, like a game dog pausing to scent the air. Was there some way to distract him? To divert him long enough for Yasmina to escape? Because I was sure now that I'd been right about Pierce. He wasn't just here as a policeman asking questions; there was more going on. He'd taken a risk in explicitly threatening me, and at this very moment he was actively breaking the law.

That recognition hit me fully as he started up the stairs: Pierce was not here as a copper. He was no less a trespasser in my mother's home than I'd been in Chas's. Even if he arrested me, I'd have solid grounds for a complaint, and no lack of evidence to back it up. Whatever uniform he might be wearing, that fact made him dangerous.

I realised I'd been closing on him as we climbed the stairs. My body had made a decision that my mind hadn't yet caught up with, had begun readying for a confrontation it had accepted as inevitable.

I didn't want to fight Pierce. I was already in more than enough trouble. Even if I did, I was far from certain I could handle him; he might be older than me, but he was bigger too, and he wasn't nursing bruised ribs or a sprained ankle. As he neared the landing, I slowed, letting the gap between us stretch.

A good job, really – because otherwise he would have taken me with him.

It happened fast. Yasmina had been hiding in the bathroom. I discovered this in the moment that Pierce did, the moment she appeared before him. There was something in her hand; it looked like a table lamp. She brought it round in a rising sweep that ended at Pierce's chin. Pierce took a step back — onto nothing. As his foot probed for a stair that wasn't there, he toppled. I had an instant in which to dodge aside, to crush myself against the banister.

Then Pierce was tumbling past me, all flailing arms and legs — until he reached the bottom, head first, with a revolting crunch.

CHAPTER EIGHTEEN

There was a second when I was certain Yasmina had killed him, a second in which my mind played through in fast motion a future where I had another death on my conscience.

Then Pierce moaned, and clutched at his head with one hand. With the other, he tried to haul himself up by grasping the banister. Apparently lacking the strength, he succeeded only in flopping onto his front. There was blood; I could see it smeared upon the skirting board. It seemed to be coming from his forehead. Pierce groaned again, and the noise sounded very much like the word *fuck*.

As he'd shifted, I'd noticed something, and before I could think it through, I'd made my decision. Stumbling down the stairs, I pulled the handcuffs free from his belt, to snap them around his right wrist and – with a sharp yank to bridge the distance between – his left. By the time he thought to struggle, I was done. I retreated out of reach and stood there, breath coming in rapid bursts, inspecting my handiwork.

"You prick," Pierce managed.

He was stretched out on his front like a basking seal, arms immobilised behind him. The position looked incredibly uncomfortable. I decided I much preferred him that way.

I turned my attention to Yasmina. She was still holding the weapon she'd used: one of my mum's bedside lamps, with the shade and bulb removed. A crack ran down its side and large shards had broken inward, giving the impression of an egg about to hatch. Yasmina was dressed and even had her coat on.

She'd been observing Pierce blankly; now her eyes fell on me, and she stirred.

"He's all right?" she asked.

"He'll live," I agreed.

Yasmina hurried down to join me, watching Pierce all the while and taking particular care as she passed him. At the front door, she paused and said, "Ollie, let's go."

"Wait," I said, "just wait. Aren't there things we need? What are we going to do for money?"

"I've got money," Yasmina said, exasperated. "Please. Let's get out of here."

I knew she was right, yet a doubt was nagging at me. I tried to retrace my thoughts. They'd snagged on something Pierce had said, something that had seemed important. The farm, that was it – he had asked me about a farm. And of course Chas had referred to a farm too, and I'd barely given his words a moment's consideration since. But he'd listed directions, hadn't he? If I could remember them, perhaps I could find the place; if I could find it, then maybe I'd finally have some hard evidence that would make all of this go away.

I darted past Pierce, half expecting him to try and trip me, feeling almost disappointed when he only glared at me sourly. In my stepdad's study, I grabbed his laptop, yanked the plug from the wall, and coiled the power cable around my arm. As I dashed back down the stairs and saw the look Yasmina was giving me, I gasped, "I'll explain later, okay?"

This time, though, Pierce was ready for me. When I slipped past him, he growled, "You're dead, Ollie."

I should have ignored him. But there was such authority in his voice that to do so would have been nigh impossible; he spat those words like they were prophecy.

"Today," he said. "Tomorrow. You might even last three days. But you, your girlfriend here – you've just killed yourselves. Do you understand me?"

For an instant I experienced the most overpowering urge: to go into the kitchen and find my mother's largest, sharpest knife and come back and plunge the blade up to its handle into Pierce's chest. I saw and felt myself doing it, as though I was remembering an event that had already happened. Then the impulse passed, with a shudder that trickled down my spine like iced water.

"Ignore him," Yasmina said. She pushed through the front door, and seconds later I heard her car starting.

"Good luck getting out of those handcuffs," I told Pierce, turning to follow her.

"Whoa. Whoa! Think a minute."

In a flash, his entire manner had changed. Once again he was the jovial, charming Pierce, the one for whom everything was a joke.

"Take the cuffs off," he said. "Let's sit down and talk, the three of us, like grown-ups."

He shuffled about at the base of the stairs, until he'd levered himself into a sitting position. Then he fixed his gaze on me.

"It's your only choice. If you don't, this ends badly. Badly for you and worse for your girlfriend. Calm down, Ollie. Take responsibility. If you walk out that door, there isn't going to be another chance."

He sounded so sure. It wasn't even a threat, simply a statement of fact, as though he'd be equally as helpless to avoid this outcome hurtling towards us as I would. In my mind's eye, I pictured one of those frantic mine-cart chases from the cartoons, and the point when they reach the inevitable fork: one way safety, one way certain death, and too much momentum to slow down, let alone to stop. Yeah, Pierce had called it right. Our cart was out of control, and we were speeding into the void.

"If you ever threaten Yasmina again," I said, "then, police officer or not, I will break your fucking neck."

And I walked out the door.

*   *   *

"You know, you could have killed him."

"Maybe." Now that Yasmina had calmed down, she didn't sound very convinced.

We were driving north, towards Darlington — towards nowhere in particular. Those were the first words we'd spoken to each other in the twenty minutes since we'd left the house.

"Why did you do it?" I asked. "I mean, I'm not saying it was the wrong thing...."

"I was listening from the stairs," Yasmina said. "Ollie, I told you: before we came here, my mother and I, we had our problems. Have you heard of the *Lebas Shakhsi*?"

"No."

"Or Evin. Evin Prison?"

"I haven't," I admitted ashamedly. I knew next to nothing about Iran or Yasmina's past there, and it occurred to me that part of the reason I didn't know was that I hadn't wanted to.

"Evin," Yasmina said, "is the prison where my older brother died in custody. They said he had a heart condition. The truth is that he died under torture. A friend with an uncle who was a guard there told us."

"I'm so sorry," I replied. The words seemed entirely useless in the face of such ugliness and tragedy.

"It was a long time ago. In another life. You think you'll never learn to live with something like that, but you do. The point is, I've seen bad men. I've heard how they talk. I know the sort of threats they make and how they make them. And Pierce was ready to hurt you."

I considered. "Yeah," I agreed. Had a part of my brain not been reliving teenage traumas, I'd have seen the reality more clearly at the time — and now I recognised that Pierce had made use of that fact. Likely he'd known about my youthful record after all. At any rate, he'd gone far beyond the bounds of reasonable police questioning. Even the recording he'd made would be inadmissible, and he must have been aware of that. He'd been playing with me, manipulating me. But to what purpose? And was this really all about Chas?

"We need to stop somewhere," I said.

Yasmina glanced at me. "Why? I'm not sure it's a good idea."

"Because there are things I have to figure out." I patted the laptop, where it rested on my knees. "And...." I only realised I was going to say the words as they were coming out of my mouth: "I haven't told you the whole truth, and I need you to know."

*   *   *

Yasmina found us a service station. She filled the tank, and as I sat there, I wondered what she was planning. Was she anticipating a high-speed chase across the country? Then again, perhaps she was just being practical; she seemed so much better at keeping her head than I could ever be.

There was a fast-food restaurant past the filling station. I barely noticed which particular chain it belonged to. Although I hadn't had breakfast, the prospect of greasy processed crap didn't appeal even slightly. At least the place was all but empty, and at least it had Wi-Fi. I chose us a booth well away from the counter, while Yasmina bought us two coffees in cardboard cups. She sat down opposite, pushed one of the cups towards me, and said, "I think we have to phone the police."

"Maybe," I agreed.

"I don't see a choice. Pierce threatened you. He was trespassing; he had no search warrant. You'd asked him to leave and he refused."

"Yeah."

"It's not even our word against his, Ollie. He had no warrant. You hadn't been charged with anything."

"No, you're right."

Yasmina sighed, evidently frustrated by my inadequate answers.

I looked away, out of the window, at the barren expanse of the car park. "It's not just Pierce," I said.

"Then what is it?"

"What I told you yesterday. I was honest about all of it, except for one thing. I didn't kill Chas, but...." Confessing the truth was harder than I'd expected, as though the sounds were hunks of gristle I was trying to hack up. "I did make it happen." I'd stall again if I paused, so I forced myself not to. "I left the gas fire on. I meant to do it. I saw what he'd done to that boy, and I hated him. I knew he deserved to die."

I didn't dare to observe Yasmina's reaction. Putting what I'd done into words had brought those deeds home in a way that nothing had until then, had made them real and concrete, and they had sounded so much worse than I'd ever imagined they could.

Yasmina wasn't saying anything. I'd hoped she'd say something. I didn't want to have to bear the weight of the conversation anymore; I felt as if I'd hollowed myself out. Reluctantly, I tore my attention from the car park and its reassuring lack of character or humanity.

Yasmina was watching me. Her gaze was like a beam that I found myself entering. Her eyes were dark pits in the pale surface of her skin.

"I'm sorry I lied to you," I said. "But I'm not sorry I did it. He was a monster. The world's better off."

"You...." She fought with herself; I could see the struggle playing out. Tiny muscle movements convulsed her mouth, as though words were constantly forming and dissolving. Then in a rush came a flood of syllables: "You do not get to decide that!"

Abruptly she was rising to her feet. As she stood, her coat clipped her coffee cup, sending its contents gushing over the lacquered tabletop. Even as I reached to grab the cup, desperate to stop boiling liquid interacting in unpleasant ways with my stepdad's computer, she was already heading for the door. By the time I had the situation under control, Yasmina was gone.

I sat there, numbed. Would she go to the police? Likely she would. And who could blame her? Maybe it was even for the best. I'd exhausted the last of my options, and I had nowhere left to run to. At the least, I'd be going down for assaulting a police officer; at worst, I'd be facing murder charges. Prison seemed like a fate I'd been trying to change for years, and now that it was finally inescapable, I was very nearly relieved.

Still, I might as well make use of whatever time I had. I got up, took some napkins from the counter, ignored a look from the girl standing behind it that enquired without much interest what I'd done to piss off my girlfriend so badly, and returned to mop the puddle of coffee, which by then was dripping onto the plastic-tiled floor.

That done, I set up the laptop and connected to the burger restaurant's Wi-Fi. I opened Google Maps and zoomed until I was looking at the area around Leeds. What had Chas said? But my recollections were a blur; listening to his instructions had been the last thing on my mind. I scrutinised the routes out of the city, hoping to jog my memory. There were limited options, and hadn't he given a road number? The A660 maybe? The A61? Then my eyes snared on a name, and a piece clicked into place. *Take the 65 past Kirkstall,* that's what he'd said.

All right. I had a starting point. And from the way they'd talked, the farm couldn't be too far away. Now my memories of the conversation were swimming into focus. I remembered Chas insisting on something, an important detail he'd made Dougie repeat. But why? To differentiate between two similar place names, that had been it.

While Yorkshire wasn't exactly short of similarly named places, especially if you factored in the smaller villages, there were only so many options out in that direction. Knowing what I was looking for, I saw it immediately: over to the north-west of Leeds was a village named Burley in Wharfedale, and not far off was another called Burley Woodhead. With that, the entire memory came back. *Woodhead, not Wharfedale*, that was what Chas had said.

So all I had to do was find a farm – probably a derelict one – near Burley Woodhead. That shouldn't be too difficult. How I'd make use of the knowledge was another question, but it was one I had no intention of dealing with just then. Especially since, with Yasmina gone, I had no means to get there, not even money for bus fare.

I wondered if there was someone else who might help me. Paul would surely have picked me up, but I didn't like the idea of dragging him into my problems, or for that matter of trying to explain them. Next I considered Thornton, a possibility I quickly moved on from; there was no good way of telling her that my girlfriend had smashed a table lamp over her colleague's head, or that I'd left him handcuffed in my mother's home. What about Rebecca Ford, then? Hadn't she proposed us meeting up? If I couldn't phone her, I could at least email her and hope she spotted the message quickly. However, when I went into my webmail, there was already a reply waiting from her. It read: *Hi Ollie, tried to call but no answer, give me a ring when you have a minute, Rebecca.*

I briefly pondered what I wanted to say – or rather, how much faith I was willing to place in her. In the end, the fact that she'd warned me off Pierce was what made my decision.

I wrote: *Hi Rebecca, sorry I missed your call, had to make a move. Had a run-in with Pierce. Should have listened to your warning! Maybe we could discuss?*

Recalling my lack of a phone, I contemplated getting the number of the payphone outside, until I remembered how my stepdad Skyped regularly with his half-sister in New Zealand. I checked, and the app was there; not only that but it had retained Alan's log-in details, and there were even a few pounds of credit on his account, should I need them. I added the relevant details to my email and clicked *Send*.

Mere seconds had passed before a call came through. I clicked to accept it.

"Hello, Ollie," Ford said. "Good to finally meet you face to face."

Ford was much as I'd pictured her: perhaps twenty-five, certainly not thirty, pretty in a moneyed way, her blond hair cut neatly to just past her ears, with a calculated compromise between business-like and attractive that her makeup echoed. Nothing in that face gave me the slightest clue as to whether I could trust her, and I sensed that I could spend hours around her and still be none the wiser.

"Hi," I said. "Thanks for getting back to me so quickly."

"Are you kidding? A 'run-in' with Pierce? I could hardly let that one sit."

"I'd like to know what you know about him."

"And I'd like to know what 'run-in' means."

Clearly Ford didn't intend to make this easy. "He came to my mother's house and threatened me."

"That sounds about right."

"So my girlfriend broke a lamp in his face and knocked him down the stairs. Then I cuffed him with his own handcuffs."

It was almost all worthwhile to see Ford's self-control crack so entirely. "Holy shit."

"Yeah. Holy shit."

"Listen, I can help you. Will you talk to me before you go to the police?"

"I don't know if I'm going to the police," I said. "Or, I am – soon. Obviously. Just, not straight away. Look, do you remember that young guy who went missing a few days back? The youth worker?"

"Of course. I wrote the article."

"I think Charlie Walker had a hand in his disappearance. I mean, I don't think. I have evidence. And there's a farm, not far from here. I'm pretty sure that's where they took him to."

Even on the grainy video, I could see how Ford's eyes had lit at what I'd told her. "Where is it?"

"First, tell me what you know about Pierce."

She sighed, a petulant, little-girl sigh that seemed at odds with what I'd thus far seen of her character. "I don't *know* anything."

"Then tell me what you think you know."

"There's not much." She hesitated, accepting perhaps that I wasn't likely to be fobbed off with half an answer. "Well, there's his dad, that's one thing. He was a notorious arsehole. Those tales you hear of cops in the Seventies and Eighties…the racism, beating suspects, corruption, falsifying evidence…he was so deep into all of that that it was practically common knowledge. But for whatever reason, they never pinned anything on him. He retired early, and that was the end of the matter."

"Pierce told me something along those lines," I said. "About the stuff his dad got up to."

"Seriously?"

"Yeah." I shuddered at the memory. "A little horror story involving handcuffs."

"Hell. You weren't joking when you said he threatened you, were you?"

"No," I said, "I wasn't."

"Anyway, Pierce Junior had already joined up by the time his daddy left under a black cloud. And for a while it looked as if he was following in his father's footsteps. There were some ugly rumours. Then, before it could all blow up, he seemed to settle down. That was a few years ago now."

"And that's it?" I asked. "That's everything?"

"That's everything."

"So you didn't know about Pierce being undercover with the BFBA?"

Ford didn't even try to hide her surprise. "You're joking."

"I'm not. He was friendly with Chas Walker, or pretending to be, depending on who and what you believe." I realised then how convenient it would have been for someone like Pierce to get a foot in the door with an organisation like the BFBA; if he really was dirty, wouldn't that be the perfect environment for him? "Do you think—"

"So where's this farm?" Ford interrupted.

I'd got all I was going to get out of her, and I didn't see how it could hurt for her to know. "Near a village called Burley Woodhead. I'm not exactly sure where yet."

"And where are you?"

I gave her a description of the service stop.

"Oh," she said, "I live in Harrogate. And I'm working from home today. I can be with you in half an hour."

"I don't know if that's such a good idea."

"Well," Ford said, "I'd like to spend my day productively. I could always just put in a call to the police instead."

Perhaps I should have been angry, but having never much trusted her, I had difficulty persuading myself that I was being betrayed. "Fine," I said. "But hurry, all right? I've got no money, and I'm already bored of sitting in this shitty fast-food restaurant."

And I cancelled the call before she could reply.

Once again, almost without noticing and certainly without meaning to, I'd taken a step that couldn't be reversed. So Ford and I were partners? At least for as long as I was useful to her career, which gave me the rest of the day at most. In fact, if she had any sense at all, she would tip the police off now to avoid facing repercussions down the line. Then I thought that maybe I should phone the police myself, this very minute; that, at any rate, was a call I could make with no money.

Except that I wanted to see this through. Talking to Ford had brought everything back – the atrocities I'd witnessed in Chas's cellar, my fear of Pierce, all the seething rage of the last few days – and finally there was an end of sorts in sight. That the police wouldn't listen to a word I said was a given; once I was in their custody, any hope of getting to the truth would be gone. So handing myself in could wait – and probably there was no way that waiting could make the situation worse.

With half an hour to waste, I occupied myself by googling the Britain for British Army. Nothing I found made for pleasant reading. Unlike so many far-right organisations, they appeared to have no political agenda – or none beyond 'Everyone who's different from us can get the hell out of our country'. Although, judging by the quantity of attacks, property damage, and general havoc they'd been linked to in recent years, you had to wonder if even that was truly a priority. After all, if they ever achieved their goal and claimed the nation for whatever choice few they considered British, they'd only have to find someone else to vilify and torment.

In short, the BFBA was everything Chas had represented; they were Chas writ large. And I swore to myself that, if I somehow got through the next days with my freedom intact, I'd do all that I possibly could to screw with them.

A shadow fell across the table. I expected Ford, until it struck me that she couldn't have arrived so quickly. When I glanced round, Yasmina was standing there.

I stared at her, mouth open, knowing I looked idiotic but too startled for any other reaction. Eventually I said, "I thought you'd gone," and recognised immediately what a stupid, futile thing it was to say.

"I've been walking up and down." She slipped into the seat opposite. "Trying to clear my head."

"Did it work?"

"No," she said, "not really."

"But you came back."

The look Yasmina gave me made me wince. "You shouldn't read too much into that. You're not off the hook, Ollie."

"I'm not asking to be off the hook. I know what I did was screwed up."

"I don't understand you," she continued, as if I hadn't said anything. "I don't understand how you could do the things you've done."

"Neither do I. It's like—"

Yasmina held up a hand. "No. I don't want to hear you explain. I don't want you to try and convince me that what you did is somehow okay. We're not having that conversation."

I could hardly blame her; it wasn't a discussion I'd much desire to have either. I could make all the excuses I liked, but in the end, the truth was that I'd done what I'd done to Chas because I chose to. Maybe it really was better if I didn't examine too closely the insights that gave into my psyche.

"So what happens now?" I asked.

"We'll go to the police," Yasmina said.

"And tell them what? That I killed Chas?"

"I'm not going to tell them anything except what happened this morning. What you do is up to you."

"No," I said, "I can't."

Yasmina actually appeared surprised, as though her proposal was the only possible solution and it hadn't occurred to her that I might think otherwise.

"The youth worker," I said. "The man they'd beaten half to

death and bricked up in a fucking wall. When they took him out, they mentioned a farm. Well, I'm fairly certain I've worked out where it is. Perhaps there's a chance he's still alive. If not, perhaps there's evidence."

"Even more reason to call the police."

"And then what? Pierce knows something about the farm. Those cuffs won't have slowed him down for long; it will be his word against ours. And his word will put us both in jail long before anyone decides to wonder if conceivably we were telling the truth."

Yasmina considered. Her brow furrowed, as though the thoughts moving behind it were tumultuous as waves. "Maybe you're right."

"I don't want you involved in this, any more than you want to be involved. And I won't blame you if you never speak to me after today. But please, would you drop me off there? If I could find something, then at least when I go to the police I won't be empty-handed."

Her expression was inscrutable. I had no idea which way she'd go until she said, "All right. I'll help you. Just for today."

"Thank you."

I felt there was more I should say, but Yasmina was already on her feet and heading towards the door. As I was preparing to follow, I remembered Ford, and the fact that she was on her way to pick me up. I thought about suggesting we wait and that the three of us travel together; a reporter might be useful to have around. On the other hand, that would mean giving Yasmina time to change her mind, and I still had my doubts regarding Ford. So instead I said, "Just a moment," and fired off a brief email:

Rebecca, sorry, change of plans. Don't come to service station, I won't be there. Will be in touch soon, Ollie.

It wouldn't fill her with good feeling towards me, but it might keep her off my back for a couple of hours, long enough for me to figure out if she was more ally than threat.

I closed the laptop and hurried to join Yasmina, who was waiting by the door. "You're sure about this?" I asked, as she led the way across the car park.

She didn't answer, and I concluded that it was a question I'd do better not to ask twice.

* * *

The drive out to Burley Woodhead took an hour or so. I passed the time searching Google Maps on Yasmina's phone, trying to track down a precise location. There were a couple of possibilities, but after a few minutes I was leaning towards one: a place called Broadbank Farm. Even in a satellite image it looked like a dump, a handful of decrepit buildings huddled in the midst of some uncultivated fields. Of course, maybe my assumptions were wrong; for all I knew, the boss that Chas had referred to was a world-class agriculturalist. Still, I felt the odds were good for Broadbank.

So I read out further instructions as we drew near to Burley Woodhead. They led us off the main road and down one lane and another, until a gated dirt track peeled away on the left and the directions declared that we'd arrived at our destination.

Yasmina pulled up on the verge, and I got out to check the gate. It was secured with a rusty chain. The padlock, too, was coppery with rust. Nevertheless, it was large and sturdy, and I saw that someone had taken care to keep the mechanism itself in working order. There was no sign, nothing to indicate we were in the right place; but though the track ran between fields and was lined with close-packed foliage, I could just discern the rise of buildings in the near distance.

Hearing Yasmina's door open, I glanced back and said, "No, you stay here."

Her expression made it clear that I was in no position to be telling her what to do.

"Probably there's nobody about," I said. "But if there is, we might need to leave in a rush. I'd rather you were ready."

"Then I should go," Yasmina said. "You're in no state to be playing detective."

"I'm not in any state to be driving a car either," I pointed out.

She sighed. "I don't like this."

"Turn around," I said, "and park a little up the road. If you hear anyone coming, get out of here. Go call the police." Thinking rapidly, I added, "There's a PC Thornton based out of Leeds; she gave me some advice. She was trying to help me." But Thornton's business card was somewhere in whatever remained of my house. "I'm sure that if you phone up and ask, they'll put you through to her."

"Don't be long," Yasmina said. There was genuine concern in her voice, far more than I felt I deserved after everything that had happened. "Half an hour, all right? No more."

"Yasmina...." I knew I shouldn't say it, but I also knew that I had to, in case another opportunity never came. "I love you."

She smiled – sadly, I thought. "Just be careful, okay?"

Then she had reached to close the passenger door behind me and was reversing onto the road. A moment later and the car was gone from sight.

I stood there staring, thinking how easy it would be to abandon all this and go after her. But the decision was made – perhaps had been made for me – and there was no going back. Returning my attention to the gate, I remembered I still had the painkillers I'd taken from my mother's medicine cabinet in my pocket. That was good news, because my headache had returned, my ankle was troubling me, and a dozen other sore spots vied for attention. I popped two tablets, gulped them down dry. Then I clambered over the gate and stared up the overgrown track, past a band of low treetops to the juts of buildings barely visible beyond.

This, assuming I had the right location, was where Chas had sent Rick and Dougie with the kidnapped youth worker. Pierce, too, seemed to consider it important. In short, this was a place that meant a lot to some truly bad people – and a molten feeling in my gut told me that it would take more than a couple of painkillers to prepare me for whatever I would find there.

CHAPTER NINETEEN

The track was churned and potholed, and my ankle was still uncomfortable to walk on. Reaching the farm proper took me a good ten minutes. The scruffy trees and thick hedgerow of hawthorn, bramble, and dog rose grew densest around its edge, forming a natural barrier that hid the buildings almost entirely from view until the last moment.

There was a second gate on the periphery, set into a wire fence, the posts of which had been dragged askew by the surrounding foliage. This gate was unlocked, but its hinges were stubborn, and the angle of the fence meant that I had to lift it to drag it open.

The yard beyond was an expanse of cracked concrete, some of the fissures so severe that weeds had poked through the gaps. There were three buildings, set irregularly upon each of its other sides. To my left, the farmhouse itself was in the best repair, though that was strictly relative: tiles were missing from the roof, the guttering was cracked, and every window had been boarded up.

The other two structures were both barns of sorts. The first, directly ahead, was a characterless construction of mottled breezeblock and rusting corrugated iron, single storey but much wider than the farmhouse. It was fronted with two sliding doors of heavy metal, both secured with padlocks. The last building, to my right, was set back some way from the yard, behind a swath of nettles and high grass, and was clearly the oldest of the three. Once it had been stables, and a deadly looking external staircase led up to a windowless second floor. More recently it had been sealed up, and presumably was now derelict or else used as a store.

At any rate, there were no signs of life. That was a relief, but also made me wonder. Had I come to the right place? Was there even such a thing as a right place? For all I knew, 'the farm' was a code name, maybe criminal slang I was unfamiliar with. There was every likelihood that this entire expedition was a waste of time, and that, by coming here instead of handing myself in to the police, I'd thrown away my last chance of salvaging this mess.

Then again, as I dragged the gate closed behind me, I discovered that someone had visited recently after all; the yard was coated with a thick patina of dirt and, in it, tyre tracks were faintly visible. When I hobbled to examine the lock on the farmhouse door, I could see that, as with the one on the first gate, its mechanism was shiny and clean. That still didn't necessarily mean anything, but somehow it was enough to make my pulse quicken. Suddenly I felt exposed.

There was no obvious way into any of the buildings, and probably no way at all that wouldn't involve property damage. So I kept moving, past the farmhouse and along the leftmost edge of the modern barn. An unsurfaced path ran there, and in the muddier patches I could make out the imprints of feet. When I crouched to study them closely, the marks didn't look like they'd been made by boots or Wellingtons, such as a farmer might wear; the soles had been almost flat. And maybe I was reading too much into them, but it occurred to me that they were deeper than the tracks I was leaving, as though whoever had last passed this way had been carrying some heavy burden.

Standing, I crinkled my nose. There had been a noticeable stench in the air from the moment I'd joined the path, but only then did it begin to separate from the general odours of mouldering hay, rotting wood, and prevailing damp and mould.

While none of them were pleasant, this was something else altogether, like an open sewer laced with toxic chemicals, and I could taste it on the roof of my mouth.

The smell brought back vivid memories. When I'd been a kid – before my dad was hauled away for good, before everything finally fell apart – I'd played at an old, semi-abandoned farm a lot like this one. As such, a part of me knew what to expect, even as I drew near.

Past the barn, the path meandered on through a fringe of bushes and occasional trees. It was dark under there, and the stench was overpowering. I paused at the edge of the band of foliage, beside a stooped elder. Ahead was another concreted area, and towards its far side, before a verge led down to unkempt fields, there sat a squat brick structure roofed with sheet metal. Within was a hollow the size of a small swimming pool – though if you tried to swim in this one, you'd last all of about five seconds.

The stink aside, which this close was appalling, the slurry pit looked dangerous. It had only a low wall around its rear two sides, and all that cordoned the edges facing me were drooping lengths of chain strung from a post in the nearest corner. Beyond, the surface appeared deceptively solid, like levelled earth. Yet I knew that anything dumped on that thin crust would be sucked into the depths below and soon consumed. Just as I knew – if I hadn't already – that I wasn't going to find the youth worker alive. He was gone, long gone. And something about that isolated spot, so well suited to the vanishing of evidence made of fragile meat and bone, made me certain he hadn't been the first.

I briefly contemplated investigating further. But what did I expect to find? No, all I could do was somehow convince the police to dredge that putrid mire, and hope that it hadn't altogether done its work.

I turned back. My head was spinning, and not only with the awful reek of shit and poison. The disgust and horror I'd felt when they'd dragged that poor bastard out of the hole they'd been keeping him in had returned in full force. I'd barely had a moment since to consider his subsequent fate, but now it was all I could think about. That man was dead, and for no other reason than that he'd fallen foul of a bunch of hate-filled, sociopathic arseholes.

Trying to explain to Yasmina, I'd felt bad for what I'd done to Chas. Now my sole regret was that I hadn't invented a way to get the whole damned lot of them. Well, maybe I still could: if I was right — and I knew I was — then at the least they'd be facing manslaughter charges.

Once again, I found myself in need of evidence. And that, I decided, as I retraced my steps to the farmyard, meant seeing what was inside those three buildings. But where to start? All three were sealed up tight; if only I'd thought to buy some tools on the way here. There was no chance I'd be getting through the metal shutters of the main barn, that was for sure. And time was against me; I'd probably already used up half the thirty minutes I'd agreed with Yasmina.

I decided to have a closer look at the farmhouse. There was definitely no way I'd be entering by the front door — which, on re-examination, offered yet more proof in favour of my suspicions, as though the paintwork was cracked and faded, the lock was newer and disproportionately sturdy.

I continued past the front of the house and turned the far corner. There was only one window on that side, high up on the first floor. I kept going, paddling through thigh-high grass. Around the second corner, the foliage grew practically against the wall; trees scraped their branches across the brickwork, the tallest clutching for the guttering.

As I squeezed between the back wall and the encroaching

bushes, an option at last presented itself. There were three windows, as well as a rear door. The windows had been boarded over, yet I noticed almost straight away that the boards had merely been nailed into the ancient frames. I made an inspection of the nearest. If I'd had any tool, even a screwdriver, I'd have pried the planks off easily; with my bare hands the attempt would be hopeless. I pressed on, wading through nettles and bramble, trying to ignore how scratched and stung I'd already got. The second window was no better. But the third, the one closest to the door…a tendril of branch had wound beneath the lowest board and begun to tease it loose. I dug my fingers under and hauled with all my strength.

The plank gave. Within a minute I had it completely off. The next two were even easier. The boards were good, the nails too, but the frame they'd been driven into was more than half rotten. Even better, the glass it had once held had been broken long ago. I removed a shoe, slid it over my hand, and bashed away a few stray shards. Then I pulled my shoe back on and leaned into the gap I'd made.

The only source of light was the window I was blocking with my body. I could see, barely, that what I was looking at had been a kitchen. Now, it was filthy and squalid – though not from disuse. There were stained gaps where furnishings had stood, but a battered refrigerator remained in one corner, an oven sat opposite, and everywhere there was rubbish, in bags or scattered upon the counters and floor. Much of the garbage was old and mouldering; the smell alone gave that away. However, one stack of takeout pizza boxes looked fresher, enough to suggest the room had been used recently – and certainly since the house had been boarded up.

Fortunately, the patch of floor directly under me was relatively clear. Flopping forward, I managed with some effort to haul myself through. The floor was greasy and foul, and I hopped quickly to my feet. There were two ways out of the kitchen, their doors stripped to leave empty frames. The one to my right led into what had probably been a dining room and was now entirely empty. The other, ahead and to the left, opened onto a passage that appeared to run the length of that side of the house.

I chose the dining room, and since there was nothing to see, kept going. Another doorway at the end – this one with an actual door – led into a larger space. Like the dining room, it was mostly empty, but as with the kitchen, there were signs of recent use. Most of those were in the form of empty beer cans and bottles, which brought back jagged memories of my time in Chas's house. But there were a few cardboard boxes stacked in one corner, and when I opened the top one, I was vaguely surprised to find piles of cheaply photocopied leaflets, from three or four different militant hate groups. Checking another box, I discovered stickers with slogans like 'IMMIGRANTS OUT' and 'BRITAIN FOR THE BRITISH'.

If it wasn't the proof I needed, it at least left no doubt that I had the right place. Clearly the BFBA had been meeting here in this rundown old house, and that was enough to tie the farm to Chas and his mates. At any rate, I was out of time, and the last thing I wanted was to worry Yasmina more than I already had.

Still, I couldn't leave without a quick look at the upstairs. As I'd expected, the second door off the living room led into the hallway I'd spied from the kitchen. The stairs there were rotted and in multiple spots broken, and the banister was cracked; I climbed with care. On the first floor were a bathroom – one glance confirmed what my nose had told me, that a lack of working plumbing hadn't stopped anyone from making use of the brimming toilet – and three further rooms that I assumed had once been bedrooms. One contained grubby sleeping bags and a portable gas stove. The others were empty. None showed any evidence that the youth worker, or anyone else for that matter, had been forcibly confined there.

Perhaps that only meant he'd been killed in one of the other two buildings. But there was no way I was getting into either of them, and even if there was, I already felt I'd pushed my luck to its limits.

I was back at the top of the stairs when I learned how wrong I'd been. I hadn't pushed my luck; I'd broken it. For a moment I thought the distant rumble of an engine belonged to Yasmina's car – but it was approaching the farm, and that meant whoever was driving had got past that first, locked gate. I froze. It wasn't so much that someone was coming and the immediate threat they might pose, more the rush of recollections the sound brought. In that instant, I was in Chas's cellar once again, listening to his car pull up in the street outside – and knowing I was trapped.

But this wasn't Chas's cellar. I *wasn't* trapped. All I had to do was hurry.

Easier said than done, I realised, as a broken stair halfway down the flight almost sent me tumbling. I caught the banister in time, and though it complained, it slowed me. Staggering the last few steps, I stopped myself by crashing hands-first against the front door. Beyond it, I could hear the engine grumbling into silence. The car had parked in the yard.

I cursed myself. *Don't panic*, I insisted; all I had to do was make it out, to get into that dense hedgerow behind the house, and I'd be safe. This time I took the other exit, down the corridor that led to the kitchen.

Partway along, I remembered I'd left the boxes open, their contents obviously rifled through. Again I had to remind myself that I wasn't sneaking around my now-dead neighbour's house; it didn't matter if I was found out. Except, mightn't they hide the evidence before I could persuade the police to come here?

I dashed back to the main room via the hall. I was already starting to stumble; all this activity was putting too much strain on my ankle, and each ragged breath felt as if someone was trying to tug my ribs out through my side. I could hear muffled voices: two of them, impossible to distinguish. Then, to my horror, came the sound of a door opening – but it was too faint to be the farmhouse, so it must have been the old stables.

Barely knowing what I was doing, I rearranged the contents of the two boxes I'd searched and pressed the lids closed. Perhaps my effort would pass a casual inspection. I lurched into the dining room and on to the kitchen. The gap in the window looked so much smaller than when I'd climbed in. I had petrifying visions of getting stuck, of being found like that, and for a moment wondered if I might not be better off hiding upstairs. But no, that was foolish; in any case, Yasmina would be worried sick by now.

So I shoved my head and shoulders into the space between the windowsill and the remaining planks. There was no way this wasn't going to hurt; under me was a tangle of nettles and thick cords of bramble. From somewhere behind me, I heard a thunderous rattle. They must have opened one of the shutters that secured the main barn. That meant they were checking each building in turn – and *that* meant this one would be next.

I clapped a hand to either side of the window and squirmed. The only way I was getting out was to fall. There was a branch within reach, so I grasped it and hauled. Splintered wood scraped my torso. I released the branch and my hands jolted against the ground; thorns gashed my palms. Then my body was following, and I did what I could to protect my head as I rolled into the undergrowth.

I'd made far too much noise. But it was a sound I definitely hadn't caused that paralysed me: that of the house's front door being opened. I'd had hopes of jamming the torn-off planks back in place. That ominous creak dashed them all. My one option was to get out of there, as quickly and quietly as I could.

I'd hoped, also, that I might clamber deeper into the bushes and escape on the other side. But close up, I saw how unfeasible that would be. They were too dense, and even if I managed to thrash my way through, I was sure to be heard.

Towards the corner, though, a crooked tree had carved a narrow opening in the foliage. At a crouch, I crept along the rear of the house, flinching at every brush of leaves and every snapping twig. I could no longer hear what was happening from the front, or if whoever had been there was now inside. The spot I'd been aiming for was barely a metre away, and I could see a route through, patches of dirt and sky visible beyond the encroaching green. I pushed to my feet, stole a glance around the corner—

And found myself staring straight at Pierce.

He grinned. "Hello, Mr. Clay."

He raised his hands, so that I couldn't possibly miss the shotgun he was holding.

"You know," Pierce said, "I thought I might find you here. Predictable as you are bloody stupid." He lowered the gun – just long enough to hammer his left fist into my jaw. "Stupid, and incapable of minding your own fucking business."

I fell on hands and knees; then Pierce's meaty paw was dragging me back to my feet.

"That's for that bollocks with the handcuffs."

He spun me past him, shoved me hard, and when I tottered to a halt, pushed me again. Realising he'd only keep doing it, I stumbled on ahead of him, towards the front of the house. There, parked in the yard, was the blue Peugeot that had pursued Yasmina and me after we'd left the hospital. And there in the doorway of the farmhouse stood Dougie, mouth agape.

"What did I tell you?" Pierce addressed him. "Seek and ye shall find."

Without thinking, I'd hesitated on the edge of the concrete. Pierce gave me another shove, this time in the direction of the old stables.

"People know I'm here," I said.

"You say that," Pierce observed, "like it's a reason not to kill you."

I understood then, with sudden, fearsome clarity, that there was no chance I was talking my way out of this. If Pierce was indifferent to the risk of being exposed, what other defence did I have?

"Lead the way, Dougie," Pierce called, and Dougie jogged past us, to climb the stairs leading to the first floor of the stables. The door, I saw, was already open – and something about the sight of that warped opening unsettled me deeply. For an instant I considered making a dash for it, before I remembered my hurt ankle and Pierce's shotgun trained at my back.

I was careful on the stairs, which were broken and slick with moss. Dougie waited at the top, where the final step was wider, and grinned at me as I went past. I stepped into deep gloom. The room above the barn was a single long space, and there was very little in there: only, at the far end, a solitary wooden chair, which might once have belonged to the farmhouse. Around it, on the bare boards, were splashes of black that I knew in better light would have appeared red.

"Why don't you take a seat, Ollie?" Pierce suggested from close behind me. There was mockery in his voice.

I walked as far as the chair, but I didn't sit. Instead, I decided to hazard turning to face him. Pierce was still near the doorway, not even bothering to hold the gun on me. "It was you," I said, "wasn't it? Running all this."

Pierce looked at Dougie. "Wait outside. Stay out of sight and keep your eyes open." When he seemed about to protest, Pierce repeated, "Dougie. Wait. The fuck. Outside."

Dougie didn't try to argue twice. He trudged out, head hanging, and vanished from the abrasive rectangle of daylight. Pierce reached to slam the door shut. Then he crossed the distance between us, without haste.

"Course it was bloody me. Do you think any of these knuckle draggers would have had the wherewithal? That sad prick Chas? When I found him, all he was good for was starting fights and dealing a bit of pot, and he wasn't much cop at that."

Pierce stopped before me, put his free hand against my chest, and pushed. The pressure was slow but inexorable. I had no choice except to slide into the chair, which shuddered under my weight.

"Didn't I tell you," Pierce said, "to sit down?"

He walked around me. Again, for an instant, I felt a compulsion to try and run. Then Pierce had hold of my left arm. Conscious of cold encircling my wrist, I heard a distinct *click* and another – as Pierce snapped his handcuffs closed.

"There," he said. "How do you like it? Good job I'd brought Dougie along, wasn't it? Or I'd have wasted the day sitting in your mum's fucking hallway."

I heard the creak of decrepit floorboards, and he was in front of me once more. He leaned forward, bringing his face quite near to mine. His breath smelled like a Sunday roast left out too long. "So did you kill him? Chas, I mean. I can't imagine for a fucking second how you would have; then again, I've got a good copper's nose, and you have definitely been up to *something*."

"I didn't kill anybody," I said. "I haven't done anything."

"You're a guilty little shit," Pierce told me, conversationally. "My nose doesn't lie." He poked the barrel of the shotgun against my cheek – not in a threatening way, but as a child might prod at an adult with a favourite toy. "If nothing else, you're guilty of bollocksing up a perfectly bloody brilliant arrangement."

Pierce glanced around, as though expecting to see a second chair for himself, and looked disgruntled when he didn't find one.

"Couldn't have worked out more nicely. I have Chas and his monkeys at my beck and call, and I don't even have to lie about being a copper. I've got the force watching my back, and all I need to do is feed them a few crumbs...cut off the odd low-hanging fruit. Which works out nicely too, as it turns out, because there's always some wanker fishing for trouble or not toeing the party line."

Again he jabbed experimentally at my cheek with the barrel of the gun, as if he were trying to line up a perfect angle he could see clearly in his head.

"We found your girlfriend's car. But she's not in it. That, in case you were wondering, is the only thing keeping you alive. Not for long, mind you, so don't go getting any ideas. I've got Rick and a couple of his mates on the way, and as soon as the gang's all here, we'll wrap this shite up once and for good."

"She'll be long gone," I said. "Gone to get help. I told her to phone the police."

"Oh. Right." Pierce shrugged. "Fuck it then. I may as well kill you now."

Part of me wanted frantically to beg. I'd always imagined that in such a situation I'd be able to keep it together somehow, and another portion of my mind was genuinely astonished at how potent the impulse was. No matter how I tried to argue otherwise, I felt certain that, if I could only plead hard enough, I could save myself.

"Look," I said, "you don't *have* to kill me. You're right; I've made a real mess of things. But all I want is for this to go away. I don't know anything. I never did. All I want is my life back."

Pierce considered me thoughtfully – the way a scientist might regard some specimen smeared across a microscope slide. "Well, that's not going to happen. What're you going to do? Go home? Your house is a bloody crater." He chuckled. "You know what, other than that shit with the handcuffs, I really don't have much against you. I mean, that and your dodgy taste in the ladies, but I'm sure that's just a bit of youthful twatishness. Still, I'd sooner it hadn't come to this. If I'm honest, Ollie, I'd rather be working with a nice smart lad like you than these witless tossers." His eyes narrowed; they flickered between me and the gun in his hands. "But you fucking liberal types, you wouldn't know your enemy if they were kicking you in the balls and nicking your wallet while they did it."

Seeing the expression in his gaze, the rawness and the depth of his mania, I abruptly found that some of my fear had evaporated. "I know my enemy," I said.

Pierce laughed. "What, me? Mate, the only reason I'm your problem is because you *made* me your problem. What was your beef with Chas anyway? Was all this because Dougie and Rick gave you bother that time in the street? You need a thicker fucking skin, you really do." He smirked. "Of course, right now you could have the hide of a bloody rhino and it wouldn't do you a bit of good."

He stooped to lay the gun down on the grimy floorboards, and for an irrational instant I felt the beginning of hope – until Pierce reached into a pocket and pulled out a short knife, not unlike the one I'd found in Chas's shoebox. He tested the blade with his finger, or perhaps only pretended to, and pulled a face, as though he'd cut himself.

"You know, Ollie, my old dad hated the blacks. Then eventually he decided that maybe Pakis were the problem. But basically he just liked putting the boot in, any chance he got. When you get down to brass tacks, it's all shite, isn't it? Truth is that sticking it to some pillock is a thrill like no other; the old man never taught me much, but he taught me that. And while I'm sure cutting you open isn't going to be quite so fun as hacking up some whining darkie, I plan to have a field day once we turn up your cunt of a girlfriend."

Strangely, where I'd felt no need to defend my own character from Pierce, that mention of Yasmina brought an uncontrollable surge of anger – and not for the traditional motives either, not from chivalry or any such rubbish. No, it was that Yasmina was a genuinely nice person, and a piece of shit like Pierce had no right to speak ill of her, just as a piece of shit like me had had no right to drag her into my problems. And I was about to say something, something that probably would get me hit or much worse – when there came a knock from outside the door.

Pierce snorted peevishly, as if he'd been told to stop playing and come get his dinner. He hesitated a moment, and then marched to the door and flung it open. "*What?*"

Dougie, framed in the doorway, looked defensive. "There's a woman."

"The girlfriend," Pierce affirmed, with mocking patience. "Just grab her."

"I know what the girlfriend looks like," Dougie replied, sounding faintly hurt. "*Another* one."

For the first time, Pierce actually appeared to be paying him attention. "You what?"

"I was watching from the house. She was sniffing about the big shed. Then she kept going, towards the pit. She didn't see me."

Pierce turned to me – and there was darkness in his eyes. "Who is she?"

I thought quickly. "Her name's Rebecca Ford," I mumbled. "She's just some reporter who—"

"A reporter?" Pierce exploded. "Are you fucking kidding me? For someone with not one clue what's going on, you've managed to bring down a real shit-storm, haven't you?"

"She doesn't know anything," I said. "She's looking for me. When she can't find me, she'll go."

But Pierce wasn't listening. He was stomping back and forth, his fists clenched; even from a distance, I could see the knuckles turning white. "This won't do," he said. "This won't bloody do."

Finally he came to rest before me, huffed a deep breath,

and coshed me across the side of the head with the flat of his hand, hard enough to topple both me and the chair and send me crashing to the floorboards.

"All right," Pierce said. "I'll take care of this. You keep an eye on that prick."

He snatched up the shotgun, clumped through the doorway, and was gone.

Dougie watched for a moment, presumably following Pierce's progress down the stairs and around the corner of the building. Then he walked over to me and casually booted me in the stomach. The kick hurt all the more because I couldn't flinch away, and because I hadn't been expecting it. I tensed, certain he'd do the same again, but he didn't. Instead, he wandered back towards the middle of the room, whistling tunelessly.

Somehow, that kick brought my circumstances home in a way that Pierce's intimidation had failed to do. It made plain my utter helplessness. And hadn't that been the theme of the last few weeks? Events had slid further and further from my control, every problem and threat spiralling to nightmare proportions. Now it had all come to a head, and I was going to die. As soon as Pierce returned, or as soon as Dougie got bored and decided to really put the boot in, I was done for.

I tried to move my arms. Pierce had run the cuffs around a slat in the back of the chair, and it occurred to me that maybe the fall would have done enough damage that I could break free. But antique as it was, the chair had held together; I couldn't shift my hands at all. I should be attempting to save Ford, and I wasn't even going to be able to help myself.

Tup.

The noise had come from somewhere outside — small, yet clear in the silence. Straining to see Dougie, I could tell that he had heard it too.

Tup. Tup.

Two flat, uneven notes, like raindrops falling on a slate roof. Dougie looked perturbed, as though the noise were deliberately trying to aggravate him. He scowled, plodded over to the doorway, and stuck his head out. When a glance in the direction of the farmhouse apparently revealed nothing, he took another step, onto the narrow protrusion at the summit of the stairs.

From the steps below, at full tilt, Yasmina hurled herself at him.

She hit his back with her shoulder and the top of her head, and there was nothing considered or graceful about the attack, only desperation. But on the tiny platform, that was enough. Dougie had no hope of keeping his balance, and – as he staggered out of view – no hope of controlling his tumble towards the ground. From the sound of it, he landed hard.

Yasmina stood there, watching him intently. Her breath was coming in rapid spasms. When she turned to me, there was something fierce and animal in her expression; it frightened me almost more than Pierce had.

Then some of the wildness in her eyes died, and she seemed to see me, properly, for the first time.

"Get up," she said, "we have to go."

CHAPTER TWENTY

I was about to point out that the reason I was lying on the floor was precisely that I *couldn't* get up – but by then Yasmina had recognised my predicament. She strode past me, took a moment to inspect the chair and the way it was interacting with my battered body, and slammed a foot down on its frame.

The impact didn't do much beside drive the chair's back against my spine. "Ow!" I yelped.

"Sorry." She didn't sound it; rather, she sounded on the very edge of panic. Perhaps she adjusted her approach, though: the second time she dashed her heel down didn't hurt so badly, and I heard a distinct cracking. The third time the crack was clearer, while her fourth attempt brought a messy, wrenching crunch. I could tell by feel alone that the chair had finally succumbed.

"Hold on," Yasmina said.

She spent a few seconds yanking at the disintegrating frame. I realised my hands were free – excepting the fact that they were still cuffed to each other. I rolled into a sitting position, and from there it was possible to tuck my wrists under my bottom and slip my legs through the circle of my arms, so that at least the handcuffs were in front of me rather than behind.

"Please, Ollie, we have to hurry."

"How did you—"

"There's no time!"

I heaved myself to my feet. Seeing the shattered heap that had been the chair, I reached to grab one broken leg, though I had no idea what I imagined I could accomplish against a shotgun.

Yasmina, who'd crossed back to the doorway, was staring down at the yard. Joining her, I saw Dougie. He was curled foetal, clutching one arm with the other, his face crumpled with pain.

Yasmina hastened down the steps, and I followed more carefully. My whole body hurt – from the blows, from cramp, from all the old bruises yet to heal. In the yard, Yasmina paused. She was staying well clear of Dougie, who squinted at her with agonised loathing.

I moved to join her, and she shivered slightly at my nearness. "There was a woman," she said. "Pierce went after her."

"Her name's Ford," I explained. "She's the reporter I told you about. Look, you get somewhere safe, call the police, and—"

"I've *already* called the police. I spoke to Thornton, like you said. But there's no way they can get anyone here in time."

"Then you head back to the car, and I'll try and stop Pierce."

"Ollie!" There was fury in Yasmina's eyes. "Look at yourself! You can barely walk. You go, and—"

The gunshot cut her off. I'd only ever heard gunshots on TV; this one was so much louder than I'd have expected, and its echoes rolled from the walls.

"Oh god," Yasmina whispered.

I had a flash of that face I'd seen, Ford's face, distorted by the burger joint's lousy Wi-Fi, and then of what a shotgun blast would do to those features. The vision was vivid enough that I had to reach for the lichen-encrusted stone of the stables to steady myself. "I need to know," I muttered through clenched teeth.

When I looked at Yasmina, she seemed calmer – almost resigned. She took a couple of steps towards the perimeter of trees and bushes that ringed the farm buildings. On this side, the foliage was farther back, and the rear of the stables met first with a broad strip of tall grass disrupted by sprawling mounds of bramble. I could see the trace of a path through the grass.

I was ready to follow her. But the sight of Dougie, curled

on the concrete, arrested me. He was still watching Yasmina. He didn't look as if he'd be warning Pierce; I could tell just by its angle that his arm was nastily broken. Nonetheless, I didn't like the risk. Before I could second-guess myself, and before Yasmina could possibly intervene, I limped over and swung my chair leg as hard as I could into his face.

The blow was a messy one, limited by the handcuffs, but it did the trick. Dougie's nose had practically exploded; blood had spattered in gouts across his lips and chin. He was breathing in ragged gasps and no longer looking at Yasmina, or at anything much. I thought about hitting him again, and then maybe again. I remembered what his boot had felt like impacting with my stomach. I restrained myself – and wondered to what extent that was because I knew Yasmina was watching.

"Keep your trap shut," I told Dougie, "or I'll kill you." I was distantly surprised by how sincere I sounded.

When I turned back, Yasmina was wading through the belt of grass. I hurried, as well as I could, to catch up. By the time I reached her, she was crouching to pry a low branch aside. She'd found a tunnel in the undergrowth, much like the one I'd been aiming for behind the farmhouse; she must have arrived this way, having approached across the fields.

Navigating the channel amid the bushes on hands and knees played havoc with my bruised muscles, but in seconds we were through. Just as beyond the slurry pit, there was nothing to be seen except another field left fallow, and past that, another straggling hedgerow. Or rather, this must be the same field and the same hedgerow, viewed from a different perspective; we'd come out farther around the ring of foliage that encompassed the farm, and the slurry pit lay somewhere to our left.

Together, keeping to the verge, Yasmina and I set out in that direction. All my instincts were protesting. There was simply no sense in what we were doing. Ford was surely dead, and we were heading towards, not away from, the man who'd gunned her down in cold blood.

Then I saw her. The sight of Ford alive brought a shudder of relief that rocked my whole body – until I comprehended what was happening. She was perhaps a third of the way across the field. But she was moving slowly, like an exhausted swimmer crawling through turbulent waters – and the reason was the shotgun pellets that had left a bloody half circle on her clothing, from her left hip down to her calf. Pierce couldn't have done more than wing her, yet the result was still an ugly mess. It was a miracle she was walking at all, if that crouched stagger could be called walking. Probably only adrenaline was keeping her upright.

Yasmina and I stayed close to the bushes. As Pierce came into view, I think I knew what to expect. He was standing nonchalantly beside the clumsy structure built around the slurry pit. The smell, noxious even from where I was, didn't appear to bother him. Though he had the shotgun trained loosely on Ford, nor did he seem particularly concerned by her progress. No wonder, for she was getting slower and slower – and as I watched, she went down on all fours. She kept on crawling, but fitfully. The whole left leg of her jeans and much of her shirt were now stained black.

I knew perfectly what was going to happen. In that moment I felt I understood Pierce, at least fractionally. It meant something to him that Ford should believe she had a chance. I had no doubt she wasn't the first to have crawled for her life across that field. She wouldn't make it halfway. She couldn't. And when at last she had nothing left, she would know that her own weakness had killed her in the end.

I understood, too, that Pierce was genuinely insane. He'd built up this little empire of hate, torture, and murder, and here he was, fiddling like Nero as it burned down around him.

All right, he didn't know the police were on their way; but he couldn't imagine he could murder a reporter, who'd likely have told people where she was going, and get away with it. No, whatever vestige of sanity had let Pierce keep his extracurricular activities hidden for so long was vanished now, and if I waited for the police, Ford would be dead.

We were close by then – approaching Pierce from behind and to his right. It was relatively easy to move soundlessly on the soft earth of the field; even if it hadn't been, Pierce seemed too hypnotised by Ford's feeble crawling to ever notice us. So I began to jog. I had no idea what I thought I could achieve. All that needed to happen was for Pierce to glance my way and I'd be finished. Yet I ran on, to the best of my ability, across the rutted ground.

The stink of the slurry pit climbed up my nostrils and clawed at my brain. The pain from my ribs and ankle was giddying; halfway to Pierce I was already slowing. Still he didn't look my way. He had tensed; he had the shotgun raised. At any second he'd start towards Ford, to haul her back or perhaps to empty both barrels into her head – and I wouldn't have the strength to follow.

So I threw everything I had left at my aching calves. I was maybe five metres from him when Pierce finally sensed my presence and began to turn. As his face entered my view, as panic jolted me like a blow, I almost tripped. At the last instant, I managed to turn a stumble into a swing, putting all my weight behind the chair leg. The shaft fell diagonally upon the point where Pierce's neck and shoulder met, with a resounding thump – and snapped clean in two.

Pierce fell against the chains, which billowed behind him. The stink from the pool was overwhelming. I dropped my remaining half of chair leg and grasped him with both hands, not even certain of what I meant to do. Clutching a scrap of jacket, knotting fingers in his hair, I clung on and pushed.

From the corner of my eye, I could see that Pierce had caught hold of the chain. But anchoring himself was having the opposite effect to what he'd intended; since the chain was sagging, all he was doing was pulling it down farther. I pushed harder. Pierce's upper body began to tip. If he'd released the gun, he could easily have fought me off; with neither hand free, he was virtually helpless. All of a sudden, the distribution of his weight shifted. Abruptly top-heavy, with his head and shoulders well past the border of the pit, he rolled backward. I let go before he could haul me after him and instead grabbed at his legs, giving the last shove he needed to go tumbling into that vile morass.

I'd thought – I'd hoped – that might be the end of him. But Pierce still had one hand on the lower of the sagging chains; somehow he'd clung on. That kept his head out of the filth, though the smell must have been beyond belief. I'd read a news story once about a kid who'd drowned in a slurry pit, and it had sounded like the worst death imaginable. Right now, the fumes in there, that indescribable mix of chemical and biological waste, would be working to corrode Pierce from the inside out.

It seemed a fitting way for him to go, amid whatever remained of the others he'd dumped into that rancid mire. Yet I couldn't quite convince myself that anyone, no matter what they'd done, deserved to die in so horrifying a fashion. Part of me wanted to help him. Another part wanted to kick at his hand, to watch him sink. With neither portion coming out on top, I stood there, frozen by indecision, and contemplated his struggle.

Pierce screamed something – or tried to. The simple act of opening his mouth nearly did for him. I saw his eyes bulge, as those appalling fumes strangled him from within. Then he began to scrabble more frenziedly, practically thrashing, and for an instant I was sure that all he'd accomplish would be to lose what fragile grip he had.

There was an ear-splitting crack. I reeled back, not

understanding at first what had happened. I hadn't realised Pierce had kept hold of the shotgun; even if I had, it wouldn't have occurred to me that anybody could be so malicious as to try and take someone else's life rather than saving their own. Then again, perhaps to Pierce's mind he *was* saving himself. For now that I was well away, he'd hooked the arm with the shotgun over the chain and was putting all his energy into hauling himself up. Already he had one leg up onto the pool's surround; it could only be a matter of moments before he freed himself entirely.

I thought about rushing him. More than fear prevented me. Whatever Pierce's crimes, I had enough blood on my own hands – and this time, too, I'd have a witness. But where *was* Yasmina? Glancing past Pierce, I saw that, while I'd been wrestling with him, she had run to help Ford. Yasmina had hooked one arm under the other woman's shoulders and was half leading, half carrying her towards the distant field edge.

At that, I felt a strange surge of satisfaction. If Yasmina got away, and Ford with her, then maybe everything was okay. All I had to do was keep Pierce occupied until the police arrived. How difficult could that be?

Pierce fired again. The blast was like a hard slap to my face. Though rationally I knew that he'd missed me, that he'd emptied both barrels and that probably he could barely see for the filth he was drenched in, I felt as if the shot had knocked me spinning. I staggered towards the bushes, furious at myself for neglecting my chance and not drowning the bastard in shit when I'd had the opportunity.

By the time I reached the trees, I knew what a mistake I'd made. All the knocks I'd taken over the last few days were screaming at me, and my ankle was a ball of pain barely willing to take my weight. Even with what he'd just endured, I hadn't a hope against Pierce – and now that he was on my tail, the noble sacrifice of leading him away from Yasmina and Ford had lost its appeal.

I made it to the barn, and there at least I had a solid surface to lean on. Though I could hear Pierce crashing through thick grass, I didn't dare look back. I faltered on, past the corner. I was certain I'd see Dougie on his feet and waiting for me, but he remained curled on the concrete, and the sound of my approach wasn't enough to make him stir.

Where to run to? Every place seemed impossibly far. I wouldn't make it across the yard, let alone to the gate. The house, then – the house was nearest. But as I pushed free of the barn, even those few metres looked like a mile. I knew Pierce must be close and gaining. I knew he'd be reloading, and that I made for an easy target. And with nothing to bear my weight, my ankle was drilling pain up through my calf into my thigh.

I got to the house and grasped its crumbling brickwork gratefully. But I could feel Pierce's proximity, as if he were some huge animal and his breath was searing my neck. Clutching at the doorframe, I tipped myself inside. In the hallway, the choices bewildered me: two doorways and then the staircase, rising like a mountainside. From outside I could still hear Pierce; his footsteps were stumbling, his breathing was laced with an asthmatic whine. In moments he'd be on me. I had to decide where I was going.

Or maybe I didn't. The pain was what settled it; the prospect of climbing stairs or hurrying along a corridor rooted me to the spot. Instead, I floundered around the door and crammed myself into the gap behind. I had no plan. I was barely thinking. Perhaps I was just yielding to a childish impulse to hide, and a childish conviction that out of sight I would be invisible.

I smelled Pierce before I saw him. The stink of the slurry pit roved ahead of him like a poison gas cloud; even at a distance it was ghastly. But his stench was the warning I needed, and somehow it told me what I had to do. I flung all my bulk at the door. The wood was solid, despite its appearance, and I had desperation on my side. The slamming edge cracked into Pierce, then dragged and pinned him. He roared as his right arm wedged in the gap.

Except I'd hurt myself as much as I had him; my own left arm was numbed. I backed off, meaning to slam the door again, but Pierce seized that opening to kick towards me, and I stumbled. Freed, he dragged himself all the way into the room. *This is it*, a sliver of my brain assured me with awful calm – until I saw that his hands were empty. His arm was hanging loosely, and he'd dropped the gun. I assumed he'd go back for it, but he didn't seem to have noticed.

I made a snap decision. Perhaps I was just following another primitive instinct, an urge for higher ground; at any rate, I dashed for the stairs. I managed five or six before my ankle gave out and dropped me hard, which in turn sent agony through my numbed arm. I slid against the wall, dragged myself away, and by then Pierce was after me: a creature barely human, dripping foulness, his bared teeth the sole whiteness in a face black with filth.

Frantic, encumbered by the handcuffs, I began to climb. Pierce was faster. His furious scrabbling devoured three stairs for my every one, and before I was halfway to the summit, his fingers were grasping my ankle. I lurched to my feet, hoping for the burst of speed I needed – and my heel drove through the step.

I'd forgotten how rotted the staircase was. So, apparently, had Pierce; the snapshot I saw of his face as I tumbled towards him showed nothing but surprise. He grunted with frustration as he grabbed for the banister, missed, and lost his balance. Then we were both plummeting, Pierce's sewage odour flooding my nostrils.

Though we could only have fallen a dozen steps, it seemed like far more. Each jarring of bruised ribs or numbed arm threatened to tear me from consciousness, until, by the time we stopped moving, I imagined I was beneath a vast, grey fog. The pain was catastrophic. I could feel it crushing me, striving to drag me through the floor and suck me into some nightmare hell. Then I discovered that at least part of the weight was real – as, on top of me, Pierce shifted feebly. Murmuring a word that might have been *fucker*, he attempted again to lever himself free. As he pushed upon my shoulder, I gasped and rolled aside.

The fog was beginning to clear. I saw that there was blood everywhere: smeared across the steps beside my head and striped across the floor and the peeling wallpaper. Abruptly I understood that it wasn't blood at all but the foulness coming off Pierce – and with that revelation, everything seemed suddenly unreal. Was this what came out of the bastard when you cut him? Did the man bleed slime? At that moment, I believed it.

I tried to stand; the ambition proved more than I was capable of. But I did succeed in pushing my back up against the banister post. Pierce, too, was trying to rise on bowed legs. There was perhaps a metre between us. It was nowhere near enough, not to save me – for Pierce's hand was buried in his jacket pocket, and when his fingers returned to view, they were wrapped around the hilt of his knife.

I saw what was about to happen. I practically felt it. And that presentiment reached through the mist that wrapped me, and past the pain, and somehow got me to my feet. Partly leaping, mostly falling, I flung myself onto Pierce's arm.

Lucky for me that it was the one I'd trapped in the door, otherwise all I'd have done would be to hurl myself within reach of his blade. As it was, I heard the knife skitter across the floorboards. My relief lasted barely an instant. Pierce moved fast. He thrust his brow forward in a clumsy head-butt, and while I hardly felt the impact, it tore away what semblance of balance I had. I went over on my back, and Pierce came with me.

His heaviness was incredible. The stench of him was stomach-churning. Both kept me immobilised, the stairs digging into my spine. His face was close to mine, his mouth open, and slaver foamed on his yellowed teeth. Even without his calves upon my thighs and his hands gripping my arms, the fear alone would have held me tight. Pierce petrified me. He didn't look like anything I could stop or defend myself against. He was a monster, and he had me, and now he was going to tear me apart.

Only, that wasn't what was on his mind – not yet. "You killed him," Pierce hissed, showering me with spittle and worse. "Chas. You killed him. Didn't you, you fuck?"

We were past the point of lies. "Yeah," I muttered. "I killed him."

"You must have really hated his guts. To let your own house get totalled, just to take him out." But perhaps he read the truth from my expression, for I could see his dawning understanding. "Oh my fucking god! You didn't even realise, did you? What did you suppose was going to happen? Didn't you ever stop to wonder why nobody sticks their heads in bloody gas ovens anymore?" He chuckled. "And to think I had you pegged as some sort of an intellectual." Then all the humour drained from his face, leaving nothing whatsoever in its place. "He was an arsehole, Chas was," Pierce said, enunciating with care, "but he was my mate."

I could see that he expected a reply. "He deserved it," I got out.

"You stupid bastard." Pierce's mouth turned up into a rictus grin. "We *all* deserve it." He spoke the words as though they were a philosophy of life, which maybe they were. "You," he said, "you fucking deserve it."

For an instant, he released me – but only so that he could rebalance his great weight and wrap his fists around my throat. His hands were huge. I felt as if they were covering the whole of my neck and jaw. The shit-stink of them crawled into my nose, making me want to gag – except that I couldn't, because I couldn't breathe.

That, more than fear of dying, was what made me fight: not the knowledge that I was suffocating but that I wanted so badly to be away from Pierce's appalling fetor. The horror was like an electric charge. He had me pinned securely, yet somehow I found a way to buck and twist. That we lay against the angle of the stairs gave me the slightest advantage. But I wasn't thinking that, or anything. My resistance was unconscious, and fiercer than any emotion I'd known. I simply couldn't bear to inhale more of the reek rising from the fingers that encircled my throat.

Still, Pierce's strength was inhuman. His hands were a band of steel. I felt as though my head was bloating, a blister about to burst. My struggling was getting weaker.

Maybe someone would come, I told myself. Yasmina had rescued me once. The police were on their way. Maybe somebody would arrive and save me, and so I'd be okay to give in.

But I recognised the lie for what it was. No one was coming, not this time. It was just Pierce and me – until the end.

I scraped at his head with both hands. I got a brief grip on his ear; I pulled and scratched. I grasped a clump of sewage-slimed hair and wrenched sideways, as if I could tear his head clean off if only I tried. None of it worked, and the world was turning red and black, as though filling to the brim with blood and shadows. Desperate, I balled my fists and drove for the side of his head.

Thanks to the cuffs, all I managed was to clip his nose. But Pierce flinched back with a grunt, and somehow that was enough to gain me the leverage I needed. I tumbled us sideways, and his head cracked against – then halfway through – the rotted banisters. As the pressure slackened on my throat, I did my best to pull away. I didn't get far before Pierce grabbed for me again. Once more, the two of us rolled.

This time, however, I came out on top. Pierce was barely resisting. His forehead was bleeding, where the splintered banisters must have grazed it. He was blinking dazedly — but he would soon recover. And I was utterly spent. Even staying upright, straddling his chest, was too much. Dizziness was battering at me, and when one violent wave nearly toppled me, I threw out my hands to catch myself.

My fingers brushed something cold. Metal. At first I could make no sense of it. Then I remembered the knife — Pierce's knife — and a cool thrill went through me, ending in my heart. Exploring with my fingertips until I was touching pliant plastic, I clutched the hilt and raised the knife towards me.

Pierce saw it as I did. His gaze locked upon the blade and remained there. I was too weak to keep my hands steady, so the sliver of metal bobbed and weaved between us. Pierce watched its progress, and I did as well. Now that I had the weapon, I had no idea what to do with it.

Dimly I could hear the pulse of distant sirens. I could tell Pierce had heard too, from the way he was trying hard to smile. He opened his mouth and a rattling came out, as if he was full of old clockwork and it had all come loose. But he was only clearing his throat, and his voice was the same as ever when he spoke: firm and scornful. "You'll have to kill me. You know that, right?"

He thought I wouldn't understand. He wanted badly to explain. For a moment, he held my eyes — then his flickered like an old bulb and their light went out.

"I do," I whispered.

I released the knife. I left it where it was, wedged up to the guard between two of Pierce's ribs. There was already a lot of blood coming out of him, and I didn't want to be near that spreading pool of red. I wasn't thinking clearly, but I knew without doubt that it would be foul and poisonous. Pushing myself up, I managed two steps before my strength gave out. I fell to my knees; suddenly unable to tell up from down, I pitched forward.

I'd made it half out of the doorway, which was more than I'd dared hope for. I could see Pierce's shotgun, not far off. If only he'd gone back to get it, I would be the one bleeding out on that dirty floor. Then again, what pleasure would a gun hold for him? Pierce liked to work in close.

Had liked, a small voice corrected.

A noise, rising and falling like a tide, plucked at my brain. The sirens were near. For Pierce? For me? I didn't know or care. My part was done; let them pick up the pieces. Pierce was their problem now, and so was I.

The darkness was coming in torrents, promising a way out from the pain, the guilt, the fear. It wanted to draw me under. All I had to do, all I'd ever had to do, was let go.

So, for the second time in as many minutes, I let go.

EPILOGUE

"Here's to Ollie and Yasmina."

Paul chinks his outstretched glass against his girlfriend Lucy's, then goes around the rest of us: Aaron and his new 'business friend' from London, Camille, and Yasmina and me. It's the first time I've seen Aaron since the night of our disastrous expedition to the Hare and Hounds, and he looks happier than I've known him to be in a long while. Whatever the precise relationship that *business friend* stands for, it's obviously doing him good.

"Thanks, everyone," I say. "It's really great to see you guys. And to meet you, Camille" – as Lucy I've met a couple of times before now, when Paul insisted on visiting me in the hospital. She's nice, down-to-earth, and witty, and her patience with Paul is remarkable. She genuinely seems to care about him, and maybe that's why they've endured so much longer than any of Paul's past couplings.

As though catching my train of thought, Lucy smiles at me. "Paul was telling me you're going back to teaching?"

"Actually," I reveal, "I started a week ago. Yasmina managed to find me a place at her school."

I suspect the decision had more to do with emotional blackmail on Yasmina's part than with my CV, because they certainly hadn't given much sense that they wanted me there. But I don't care, and I'm not intending to blow it; I'm even kind of excited. It's a good school, and while there are always going to be troublemakers, I'm confident I'll never have to deal with another Liam Sutcliffe.

I spend five minutes answering Lucy's polite queries regarding my first week, and though she's discreet about it, I can tell how big an effort she's making. Yasmina puts in the occasional interjection, while Aaron and Camille keep quiet and huddle close together, exactly like two young lovers.

I find myself wondering why I've put this off for as long as I have; why, despite endless texts and phone calls from Paul over the last month, I kept finding excuses. I remember the reasons I gave myself: that I still felt too breakable, that maybe Yasmina and I were too fragile to risk in even the smallest social gathering, that someone might ask the wrong question and I'd end up in the cold sweats of a full-blown panic attack, as I had so often in recent weeks.

It was all bullshit. I see that now. These people are my friends, or friends-to-be; just being in their company feels like a weight lifting. And I recognise the same in Yasmina's face: a relief from the claustrophobia that's been our life through these last weeks.

Paul throws back the final mouthful in his glass, contemplates the empty bottles in the middle of the table, and gets to his feet. "Time to restock," he declares.

"Could you check the oven while you're in there?" Lucy asks.

"Course I can," Paul says. "Why don't you come and give me a hand, Ollie?" he adds significantly.

I've been expecting this. Under the shallow surface, I know Paul is someone who cares deeply about his friends, and that he worries about them; that he's been worrying about me. If he needs to get that out of his system, I can hardly begrudge him.

I follow him to the kitchen and watch as he opens the oven and inspects its contents with a critical eye. "Lucy seems really nice," I tell him.

"Lucy," Paul replies with gravitas, "is all sorts of bloody marvellous." He straightens, takes a bottle down from the wine rack, considers, and withdraws a second. I don't recall Paul even owning a wine rack before, let alone having any idea of what to put in it. "And you, mate. Your Yasmina." He draws closer, as though sharing a secret. "She's a good find, that one.

Sticking with you through all this, a lot of women wouldn't have done that."

I barely catch the flicker of self-correction as he replaces *birds* with *women*; Lucy truly is having a positive influence on him. "I know," I say. "Seriously, I know."

And I do. I hadn't believed for a moment that our nascent relationship could possibly weather the storm I'd put it through. At first I'd been certain Yasmina didn't either. She had come to see me because she couldn't bring herself to walk away from a man in hospital with internal bleeding, concussion, and more scrapes and contusions than anyone could be bothered to count. Even after they let me out, when I went to stay with my mother (who'd barely got back into the country – explaining what had happened in her house had been one of the most difficult conversations of my life), I had no doubt that a sense of duty rather than any lasting affection kept Yasmina returning to try and cheer me up each day. Duty, and perhaps something worse as well: a recollection of shared trauma, a pull that drew her practically against her will, like a dog gnawing at an open sore.

Viewed that way, there had been one other link in the brittle chain that held us during those first days – one more fellow survivor. For entirely different reasons, I think we'd both felt a responsibility to Ford, who we'd begun checking in on together almost as soon as I was able. Despite my final run-in with Pierce, Ford had surely come even closer to death than I had; by the time the ambulance crew had reached her, and for all Yasmina's efforts, she'd lost a great deal of blood. But she'd pulled through, and there was no question that she'd got the story she was after. Now there was already talk of a book deal, which both Yasmina and I had had to make abundantly clear we wanted no part of.

Paul is busy uncorking one of the bottles. The other he shoves towards me. "Carry that, will you? I don't think one's going to cut it."

I know what he wants to ask me, what he's wanted to ask ever since we arrived. I decide that it's time to put him out of his misery – and maybe myself too. "So," I say, "the police gave me the all-clear."

He glances up, and I see that I've surprised him. Probably he'd thought the subject was taboo, even between old friends. "Yeah? Shit. That's brilliant news."

"Something to celebrate," I suggest, holding up my unopened wine bottle.

"Seems as though there's a lot to celebrate," Paul says. He's still working at his bottle with the corkscrew and exaggerated clumsiness, like a caveman who's just discovered the sharpened rock.

I can't help but watch his struggle with cruel amusement. "I guess you're right," I agree.

Thornton was the one who let me know there wouldn't be any charges, or any further questioning. We had spoken a couple of times, and I got the impression that she'd been fighting my corner. Maybe she felt bad about what had happened; maybe she thought she might have averted it if she'd played things differently. I'd almost told her that, as far as I was concerned, she'd already done more for me than she should have, but there had never been a suitable moment.

By then, I'd long since realised something else, as well – something I definitely couldn't tell Thornton. Whatever she'd done on my behalf, it was Pierce who had saved me from the police.

In the days after his death, a story had developed, without much input from me. Chas's demise had fitted neatly into that narrative, even with little in the way of actual evidence. Faced with two generations of murderous psychopaths in their ranks, the last thing the police had wanted was loose ends. If that meant tying off every thread as quickly and conveniently as possible, then nobody seemed to care much; certainly not the press, who were too busy having a field day, and too drunk with the fact that one of their own had got tangled up in the web of vile crimes and newsworthy evil that Pierce had spun.

Once they had my version of events – or the bits, at least, that related to Pierce – they had rapidly lost interest in me. And Pierce was the gift that kept on giving; the more the media dug, the more that was learned about his past and his family, the clearer it became that the happenings of recent months were far from an aberration. Pierce had been a mad dog all along, like his father before him, and he had hidden in plain sight. Who could blame me for his death, by a wound inflicted with what was beyond doubt his own knife, in a manner that could easily be read as an accident, after a confrontation that had almost cost me my life?

No one could blame me, that was who.

There's a muted pop at my elbow: Paul has finally managed to get the cork out of his bottle, though in multiple pieces, to judge by the debris scattered upon the kitchen counter. He regards the corkscrew with loathing, inspects within the bottle for any remaining fragments, and announces, "Right, job done. Let's get back to it."

I want to follow, but my feet choose not to comply. "I just need a minute."

Paul hesitates in the doorway. His posture radiates worry, yet his tone is light as he asks, "Something on your mind?"

"Yeah. But it's okay. Honestly, I just need a minute."

"Okay. Sure, mate. I'll say you're taking a piss." And he shoves through the door, closing it behind him.

For a moment I stare after him, trying to find a way out from under the pressure of my thoughts. *Something on my mind.* That's the truth, all right. Something I've told none of them; something I can never tell, that I've carried with me ever since that day, that will stay when the last scar has faded.

Most of the aftereffects are already abating. The panic attacks are growing scarcer. Probably I'll never feel safe alone on a street at night, and probably it will be months before the final dull ache fades from my ribs and my ankle. But those are repercussions I can live with, and that I know time will take the edge off.

No, what haunts me is what I observed in Pierce's eyes as the blade went in, more potent even than the abrupt appreciation that he was about to die.

The understanding – not only of what was happening to him, but of me. The kinship. The familiarity.

He saw in me what, for the first time, I saw clearly in myself. That, as I pushed the cold steel into his flesh – and even through my own pain and fear – I was glad. He recognised the sheer, anesthetising joy I felt to be ending his existence. And he approved.

It bothers me. What bothers me most is how little it *really* bothers me. I've killed two men, and with so much time passed, I'm beginning to wonder if my conscience is ever planning to kick in.

Not a day goes by when I don't tell myself I should leave Yasmina; that I should walk away, in case the thing in me that killed two people and forgets to feel guilty should find a reason to claw its way out again. I should go, because that's what a better man would do.

It's not the man I am. I may not have earned a second chance, I may not deserve the new life I have, but it's mine now. I will fight to keep it.

With that realisation, suddenly my feet are willing to move. I tighten my grip on the bottle I've been holding all the while, open the door, walk unhurriedly through the living room, and by the time I reach the dining room there's a smile on my lips that feels real enough to fool almost anyone. Expectant faces greet me as I take my seat. There's worry on Yasmina's, and if I try, it's not hard to read that as affection. So that's what I do.

Paul is looking at me, though, with faint but undeniable concern. "Are you all right, mate?"

"I'm fine," I tell him.

And I am.

FLAME TREE PRESS
FICTION WITHOUT FRONTIERS
Award-Winning Authors & Original Voices

Flame Tree Press is the trade fiction imprint of Flame Tree Publishing, focusing on excellent writing in horror and the supernatural, crime and mystery, science fiction and fantasy. Our aim is to explore beyond the boundaries of the everyday, with tales from both award-winners and original voices.

•

Other titles available include:

Thirteen Days by Sunset Beach by Ramsey Campbell
Think Yourself Lucky by Ramsey Campbell
The House by the Cemetery by John Everson
The Toy Thief by D.W. Gillespie
The Siren and the Spectre by Jonathan Janz
The Sorrows by Jonathan Janz
Kosmos by Adrian Laing
The Sky Woman by J.D. Moyer
Creature by Hunter Shea
Ten Thousand Thunders by Brian Trent
Night Shift by Robin Triggs
The Mouth of the Dark by Tim Waggoner

•

Join our mailing list for free short stories, new release details, news about our authors and special promotions:

flametreepress.com